INDENTURED LOVE

by

Irene O'Brien

WHISKEY CREEK PRESS
www.whiskeycreekpress.com

Published by
WHISKEY CREEK PRESS

Whiskey Creek Press
PO Box 51052
Casper, WY 82605-1052
www.whiskeycreekpress.com

Copyright © 2007 by *Irene O'Brien*

Names, characters and incidents depicted in this book are products of the author's imagination or are used fictitiously. Any resemblance to actual events, locales, organizations, or persons, living or dead, is entirely coincidental and beyond the intent of the author or the publisher.

No part of this book may be reproduced or transmitted in any form or by any means, electronic or mechanical, including photocopying, recording, or by any information storage and retrieval system, without permission in writing from the publisher.

ISBN 978-1-59374-934-7

Credits
Cover Artist: Jinger Heaston
Editor: Melanie Billings

Printed in the United States of America

Other Books by Author Available at Whiskey Creek Press:
   www.whiskeycreekpress.com

The Bandit's Lady

Dedication

Indentured Love is dedicated to you, the reader who loves not only romance but the fascinating appeal of times past. I also dedicate this book to all the people at Whiskey Creek Press who made its publication possible.

Prologue

April, 1773

"Man overboard!!"

The water-soaked, dripping-wet man was being hauled to the deck by a rope when Captain Zachary Fitzsimmons arrived. "Who are *you*?" he asked.

Shivering and confused, the man said, "I don't know who I am. Where am I? I have no memory. When I came to, I was in the icy water swimming toward shore." He put his hands on either side of his temples. "My head hurts; I must have hit it when I fell."

"Or jumped. Excuse me, Captain. This man is Bryant Taylor. We boarded the *Desiree* in Dublin, and traveled with it to Liverpool, where we took on more passengers. He's a pest. He has followed me on my nightly walks on the deck and quizzed me about my life. He is to be put on the auction block and sold as an indentured servant for four years."

"And who are you?" the captain asked.

"I, sir, am Shamus O'Toole. I came to the Virginia Colony to run my late Uncle Thomas O'Toole's tobacco plantation." His Irish brogue was thick, his voice coarse.

"It's glad I am to meet you, Shamus O'Toole. I will introduce you to your nearest neighbor , Patrick Maguire, who is waiting for the auction to begin."

Abruptly, Captain Zachary turned his attention back to Bryant. "And what were your crimes? Were you a thief, a murderer; did you come to the colonies to find freedom?"

"I don't know, sir..."

Shamus interrupted coldly, "It's perfectly clear, sir. He was trying to escape indenture. He's obviously bad, and pretending not to remember can be a ruse to cover up his many violations."

They had arrived at the dock. The Captain dismissed Bryant to the coastal guards who had captured him. "Tie his hands and take him to the block," he ordered.

Chapter 1

Excitement tingled deep inside Maureen Maguire as she stood at the dock beside her papa and watched the dockhands moor the ships and unload the cargo. Her eyes fastened on a waif of a girl about her same age. The raw fear in the young immigrant's ebony eyes, the wild black hair and a reed-like beauty captured Maureen's full attention.

"Papa, that's her," she said, pointing toward the auction block. "You and Mother want a companion for me. Please, please let it be that poor trembling girl."

Patrick Maguire looked down at his gentle, serenely wise, and beautiful sixteen-year-old daughter. The wind gently fluffed her soft golden-red curls. Steady green eyes implored him.

"Hurry, Papa, before it's too late. She will be snatched away quickly for although she is timid, she is healthy. If you don't save her, she will be enslaved."

"Stay here then child," Patrick said. "I shall return after the business is taken care of."

Maureen had cajoled her papa into bringing her along on the spring buying trip at the Williamsburg port on Virginia's York River. Each year, as quickly as possible after the tobacco was planted, Patrick came here to find strong young bondsmen to work the plantation. All able-bodied slaves, male and female, were put to work in the tobacco fields. If he found five healthy new slaves, he declared it "a fine trip."

Adult slaves were worth thirty to forty pounds, but it took a long time before they could be trained to farm work. During the first two years, many died at the hands of lurking Indians and from fevers and disease.

The early morning fog had lifted. Sunshine dazzled the white-blue sky and sparkled on the bay waters. The waterfront teemed with activity. Ship captains leapt ashore to enjoy the hospitality of the planters and to amuse them with news and stories about lands across the seas. Sailors and ship boys clustered together to spin yarns of life at sea—of pirates, of sea serpents large enough to sink a ship, of whales, of sharks waiting for a man to fall overboard, and of ships becalmed or tossed by tempests.

Captain Zachary Fitzsimmons, of the *Desiree*, had docked his schooner an hour earlier. He had arrived from Liverpool, by way of Dublin, with men and women who were willing and more to be indentured for their passage to the new world. Maureen was so engrossed with the scene at hand, she scarcely noticed when her papa returned with the girl, who stood trembling behind him. Captain Zachary was introducing an attractive stranger.

"This, my friends, is your new neighbor, Shamus O'Toole. He is heir to his late Uncle Thomas O'Toole's plantation. Seeing as how there is only a limping child and an aged grandmother living on the place at present, Mr. O'Toole, late of Galway County, Ireland, will live among you."

Maureen let out her breath. She stared at the tall, beautifully proportioned body. He was strong boned and rakishly good looking and, she decided, had the most classical features. His full lips blended into a strong chin. She watched his fine, curly, collar-length golden hair swirl around his face from the gentle breeze. Mellow blue eyes. *The color of robin's eggs*, she thought as he glanced engagingly at her and grinned. Shamus O'Toole was handsomely attired in a white linen shirt and broadcloth knee breeches. A scarlet velvet vest peeked out from the dark blue square-cut coat that matched the trousers. Maureen felt his potent magnetism wrap around her. *He possesses a secretive humor around the mouth and eyes, this gorgeous man, this Shamus O'Toole who is our neighbor,* she thought.

Shamus acknowledged the introductions with a dignified dominance, then looked directly into the crowd and quickly moved slightly aside. Maureen sighed as she watched him disappear with trunks in tow by a Negro slave. *I'll relish getting to know him better when the time comes.*

But her full attention was quickly fixed again on the platform. African slaves and the white indentured men and women paraded across the auction block. Captain Zachary called out their names, until the one who had been captured by the coastal guard stood soaking wet and shivering before them. That one's story had made the rounds by the sailors anxious to entertain by being the first in its telling.

The captain said, "This be a bound man who often walked the decks like he was royalty. He's a liar, at least, and none knows what more. The criminal was offered passage and freedom for indenture and then tried to escape by jumping ship. We hauled him out of the icy river water. He claims he doesn't remember a thing about himself, but Mr. O'Toole has given us his name. We checked it on the books and all seems to be in good order. This be Bryant Taylor. He be bad, but he be strong. Make your offer."

Thoughts fled through Bryant's mind. *I wonder what I look like. There must be a glass somewhere about.* But the Captain was glowering at him. Completely out of the air and not knowing why, Bryant Taylor stood tall and regal and corrected the Captain in a well-educated and articulate, authoritative voice; his Irish brogue was hardly noticeable. "I am Bryant *Rory* Taylor."

His deep and husky tone made the gooseflesh rise up Maureen's arms, and sent a ripple of awareness through her. *This one has more golden hair than Shamus O'Toole; and more startling blue eyes, cornflower blue,* she thought, *hidden under thick yellow brows.* Bryant's hawk-like features were arresting and elegant, though he wore threadbare baggy breeches and a cheap travel-stained shirt; he was scruffy. Hands tied in front, he managed to brush back a shock of hair that the water had plastered down before the wind had obviously whipped it out of place. Bryant Rory Taylor just stood there, silent in the hush.

Maureen felt a bursting of magic bubbles in her head and she realized with numb astonishment her body was whirling with feelings she had never known before. She stared across at him, her heart pounding. He looked up and their eyes met. She barely controlled a gasp of surprise. His eyes were charged with a fierce sparkle. She watched the play of emotions on his face, and could feel the light of desire illuminate his eyes, and caress her.

As a terrifying awareness washed over her, Maureen was shocked at an electrifying depth of emotion that sent her pulses spinning. She felt warmth spreading through her limbs. Her senses twisted with a golden wave of passion. She closed her eyes. Her emotions seemed out of control and her mind reeled with confusion. She could not stop thinking about the strong craving within her and knew with certainty that although she would never see him again, she would not soon forget a single detail of Bryant Rory Taylor's face and his bronzed and beautiful body.

Maureen's papa shattered the spell. He leaned toward her, but spoke more to himself. "That man looks strong and healthy. He spoke intelligently. I need to indoctrinate a new overseer to replace Jeb who needs to take it easier at his age and can move to the stables he loves. I'll bet we can use Bryant Taylor well at Tucker Plantation."

"But Papa," Maureen cried out. "He doesn't even remember who he is. He may be dangerous."

Ignoring her outburst, Patrick said. "When I finish purchasing my choices, we shall leave for home."

Opening her eyes, Maureen hurtled back to earth as reality struck and she turned to the girl who would be her friend. "Tell me your name."

Apprehension siphoned the blood from the Irish girl's face, but she spoke quietly with the soft brogue of Ireland, "I be Sabrina O'Connor."

"And how old are you, Sabrina O'Connor."

"I be sixteen come July."

"We'll be the same age; my birthday was last month, in March. You don't have to be afraid. Papa bought your indenture; you don't have to pay him back. He bought you to be my companion. My sister died when I was six-years old; my baby brothers died a year later. I get lonely; you will be my sister."

Sabrina's deep shy eyes studied her with curious intensity. She managed a tremulous smile.

"There now, that's better," Maureen said. "You'll love Mother and you will be at home with us in no time. Do you ride?"

Sabrina shook her head in dismay. "Me mum and me pa be poor, and there be seven little ones. I be the oldest. Now I'm gone, me sister Alina be takin' care of the little ones. There be three brothers and two sisters. Pa rides an old nag to work in the potato fields, the cattle fields and around Dublin, findin' work where he can. Ma keeps house for a rich ma'am and she does some sewin' for the town ladies."

* * * *

The following day at home when they reached the huts, Patrick said to his daughter and Sabrina, "Wait for me here while I take the new hands to their quarters. Then we'll go together to find your mother."

Maureen watched them walk away. She went over their names. Joshua and Sarah were black, man and wife; Moses, Toto and Yon would go to the fields. Bryant *Rory* Taylor, the indentured criminal, followed silently behind, his tall carriage towering above the rest.

Before he turned the corner, he looked back at Maureen. His extraordinary blue eyes blazed with intelligence and independence of spirit, although the expression in them seemed to be confused, and pleaded for friendship. Maureen felt a strange, cold excitement fill her whole being. A brief shiver rippled through her and she felt her pulse beat in her throat. She wondered where her papa would place Bryant in the scheme of Tucker Plantation, and she thought of another golden blond, blue-eyed man, Shamus, the new master of O'Toole Plantation.

Both parties, Patrick Maguire's and Shamus', had stayed the previous night at the Hunter Inn on the edge of Williamsburg. Except for the timid and nervous Sabrina who had already been pressed into the roll of Maureen's companion, the slaves and indentured immigrants slept in separate quarters near the barns. Patrick and his circle of longtime friends had invited Shamus to dine with them.

"I shall court you, my dear," Shamus had whispered to her while the others discussed again the Boston Massacre and the climbing import duties.

The pleasant, secret sound of the fragrant pine log crackling and burning on the hearth behind them seemed to close them in together. Maureen was fully aware of the possessive touch of Shamus' thigh brushing against hers.

"Papa will surely protest," she said gently, "for I am much too young for courting." But her face had burned and flushed as memories of another golden-haired, blue-eyed man came to her unbidden.

"*Papa* need not know for now. I shall court him as well," he said, only half in jest.

He's witty and clever, Maureen thought now. *I shall savor getting better acquainted with him if Papa allows it.*

* * * *

Kathleen Maguire stood waiting on the front porch when the three travelers rounded the corner of the house. She was smiling and radiant as her husband picked her up and swung her around. Maureen gave her mother a happy hug, then stood back and watched Kathleen welcome the shy and frightened Sabrina. Kathleen put her arms around Sabrina and held her close until Sabrina's lips softened and curved up in a sweet gentle smile.

In the weeks that followed, Maureen watched Sabrina and her mother form a bond unlike she and Kathleen had ever known. Admiring the two of them together, she thought, *Now, I can follow Papa to the fields, and without a head full of guilt, for Mother has Sabrina.*

Maureen loved Kathleen quite as much as she loved her papa, but she could not enjoy learning to be mistress of Tucker Plantation. Without envy or bitterness, Maureen acknowledged her mother's perfection. Kathleen did all the chores, from supervising the setting of the turkeys to fighting a pestilence. There was nothing that was not her work, except for the housekeeping and cooking provided by Selma and Emmie, and her personal needs taken care of by Minnie.

Kathleen was mistress, manager, doctor, nurse, counselor, teacher, and slave. She was an expert seamstress and had long since mastered the jenny spinner. Maureen, on the other hand, hated the recurrent hum of spinning wheels.

"They sound," she told Sabrina in a persistent tone, "like the drone of some great insect, as bad as the bees you and Mother tend. I get hot and faint confined in cabin rooms where the turbine spinners spin their fleecy rolls from the clacking looms. Making homespun for the plantation is dull and tedious work."

But Sabrina disagreed, and followed Kathleen everywhere.

And Maureen was free to love the land with Patrick.

From early spring, the time the seeds were sown in beds, until the leaves were cured in late summer, Patrick and Maureen watched over the tobacco fields with eager care. They scrutinized with anxious, matching green eyes the storm clouds of midsummer, for a hailstorm could ruin the crop in a matter of minutes. They helped the slaves remove the grass and weeds with a hoe. By hand, they helped to pick off caterpillars and other worms that threatened to riddle the broad green leaves. They breathed easier when at last the ripe leaves, just turning a pale yellow-green, were plucked, tied into hands and slowly dried on sticks suspended in the tobacco barns.

One glorious fall evening after dinner, and the chores finished, Patrick called Maureen into his office. As she entered the room, his eyes looked fully into hers and his smile was full of warmth for his daughter as he motioned her to a chair. Lighting his favorite pipe, Patrick said, "I need you to learn how to keep the books," he said, "and Bryant will be coming to sit with us in a few minutes. You have perhaps seen me training him to take over the job of overseeing the plantation. You will be working together quite a lot."

"Papa, I have seen you training Bryant, and I am appalled." She felt as hollow as her voice sounded. With a shiver of vivid recollection, the image of Bryant focused in her mind and burned with the memory of their last meeting across the row of tobacco they were working together. His muscular arms were wedged into a tight gray shirt. It was easy to recapture his gentility. He had a natural charm and the way he moved carried its own excitement. Only once when he winked and seemed to look at her sensuously did she feel the flush rising in her cheeks with a pang of passion, and felt the innocent fabric of her being torn apart.

"We still don't know what crimes brought him to be indentured. He looks at me, watches me sharply and assesses me. I'm afraid of him—there are too many unanswered questions."

"Nonsense, my girl. He is very bright and very capable. He's trying to recall who he is. He remembers only the name 'Rory' and doesn't know why."

The light knock at the door interrupted their conversation. "Come in, Bryant," Patrick said. "I want you and my daughter to get better acquainted. Maureen will be learning to keep the books. You two will be working closely together."

Maureen sat stiffly in the comfortable straight-backed cane chair facing him, but not looking directly at him as Bryant moved into the room. He moved confidently, calmly, and sat down in a chair facing Patrick, but his startling blue eyes clung to Maureen's.

Green eyes. *Green, like polished jade,* he thought, until she lifted her head and shot him a withering glance. His eyes searched her face, seeming to reach into her thoughts, as he reached up to brush back that thatch of errant golden hair away from his forehead.

A spurt of hungry desire spiraled through Maureen, but she caught herself as Patrick began to speak. "We must begin planning for the sale of last year's tobacco crop, and decide how to improve production next year. The first acreage past the slave quarters is wearing out; we've farmed it four years and that seems to be the limit. We've used it up, but we can plant a small part of it in corn and the rest in wheat, to market. There's land for sale south of us, quite a large chunk. Shamus doesn't seem interested in it, so I'm going to look into expanding."

Another knock on the door was abrupt, and harsh. As it opened, Shamus said, "I will announce myself, Selma. You may go back to the kitchen or whatever it is you were doing."

Selma shrugged her shoulders at Patrick and disappeared. Maureen did a long slow slide with her sharp green eyes. Shamus was dressed in a dapper putty gray cape-coat with matching silk breeches ending at the knee, and silk stockings. His shirt was powder blue, exactly the color of his faded dust blue eyes. He swept the group with a piercing glance, and amusement lurked when he saw Bryant. "You may go, too, Bryant. What I have to discuss with Patrick is private."

Bryant's eyebrows shot up in surprise, but Patrick was quicker. "Wait, Bryant," he said.

Chapter 2

Patrick settled his elbows on the desk and steepled his fingers. Then came a well-measured response. Fixing the same bold green eyes as his daughter's on Shamus, he began calmly. "What we are doing here may interest you greatly. Bryant is my new overseer; he will be supervising our interests. There's available land along the south of my land and your land. I understand you're not interested, but we need additional land for a number of reasons. The tobacco tax is getting steeper each year. Until the colonies break away from British control…"

In a sudden outburst of emotion, Shamus looked at Patrick with wide, almost alarmed eyes, and interrupted, "I can't believe what I'm hearing. Britain is like a parent. We should be thankful for British protection."

"May I have permission to speak my views, Mr. Maguire?" Bryant asked respectfully.

But Shamus cut in again. "What do you know? You don't even know your own name or where you came from."

Patrick ignored him. "Of course, you may express your opinion, Bryant."

Maureen watched Bryant take charge with quiet assurance. He looked like he had an indefinable feeling of rightness. "I may not know who I am or where I came from," he said, "but I read every issue of the Virginia Gazette. I'm sure as I'm sitting here that I came to the colonies to be free. Although the Brits protected the colonies in the beginning, they soon became a nuisance. They ruled early on that British ships should carry colonial goods to their home country, which cut out our foreign competition. Today, the British and Parliament are treating us like a possession. They're taxing us to death, for their own gain. We must not let it go on. I'm sure before it's over, we'll have to fight for our rights"

Shamus leaned forward and lowered his voice. His voice was courteous. "While I can't agree with you and won't fight against the mother country, I have to respect your views, and apologize to you, Patrick. I came here on an entirely different matter."

His gaze took in Maureen. His burning eyes held her still. An electrifying shudder reverberated through her. The magnitude of his smile spread through her. Featherlike laugh-lines crinkled around his eyes, which returned to Patrick. "This night I have treated you badly. I barged into the middle of your meeting and made a pest of myself. If you will forgive me, I'll take my leave and return when you have time to see me."

Patrick relit and took a long draw on his pipe. He said, "It seems our business can be put to the side for another time. You may be excused Bryant. Maureen, see Bryant out the back door."

As they closed the door behind them, Bryant laced his fingers through hers. Maureen took a quick breath of utter astonishment and tried to let loose of his hand, but Bryant held tight. He looked down longingly. "I've wanted to touch you since the first time I saw you from the auction block."

Maureen burst out, shocked, "How *dare* you? You are indentured to Papa. You don't know who you are or what crimes you may have committed or what else you've done!"

Her reaction seemed to amuse him. His eyes held a lazy laughter. "You're right, of course. I don't know, but I get flashes of memory or rather knowledge about myself. I've got pieces. I know I'm educated. I read papers from wherever I came. I knew much about the unrest of the American colonies and now your father lets me read the Gazette when he finishes with it. I know how to play chess. I saw your father's chessboard and he invited me to play a game with him tomorrow night. Please trust me until the pieces of the puzzle of me falls into place."

His deep-timbered voice was low and seductive. The look on his face mingled eagerness and tenderness. He quirked his eyebrow questioningly.

Maureen pulled her hand away and flung out her hands in simple despair. Her voice was shakier than she would have liked. "Shamus will court me. He said he would ask Papa for permission. He's our kind of people."

Bryant shook his head vehemently. He stood there tall and angry. His voice was quiet, yet held an undertone of cold contempt as he whipped out the words impatiently. "Shamus O'Toole is *not* your kind of people. He's arrogant and rude, and obnoxious." He glowered at her and turned away.

Maureen opened the back door motioning for him to leave. As he walked past her, Bryant leaned down and gently kissed the tip of her nose. She felt his lips touch her like a whisper before his face went suddenly grim. He walked out into the quiet of the night shadows. Far away an owl filled the night with questions—who, who, who? The stone center of Maureen's heart crumpled. She felt suddenly weak and vulnerable in the face of his anger.

Later, she lay in bed puzzling over Bryant. What if he *were* good? What if she had been wrong about him and he was from an educated and fine family? Her thoughts probed and poked, keeping sleep at arm's length until, finally, she fell fitfully into a restless sleep with Bryant's deep blue eyes caressing her gently.

* * * *

The following morning, although she felt lifeless and not hungry, Maureen passed by the sideboard selecting her breakfast. Seeing the dining table set only for two she thought, *Mother and Sabrina have already eaten and are most probably tending the bees or at the spinning wheel.* She smiled a singularly sweet smile. *My companion has truly become a valuable helper for Mother.*

Selma stood at her side as she sat down. "Would you be having eggs, Miss?"

"Not today, thank you. The porridge is enough."

"You need to eat hardy Miss Maureen. You be wasting away."

"Papa and I have a light load today, Selma. I'll not be needing more food. Oh, there you are Papa," Maureen said. She smiled wanly and looked up into his eyes.

"You look tired, my dear. What's bothering you Maureen?"

"It's Bryant, Papa. He's going to take advantage of you somehow. I feel it."

"I'm sure not. He's a steady worker. I've asked him to

join us, but before he comes, I have news for you. Shamus has asked permission to court you. It's full time you got out with young people and had a little fun. Before we know it, you'll be coming out and looking to find a suitor. Shamus will be the first, and, though I don't look forward to you leaving your mother and me, it's the way of life."

Maureen's thoughts turned to Shamus. The man was tall and straight, devilishly handsome. When he had looked at her the evening before, his mouth quirked with humor, and something more. Was it a gleam of hope, a ripple of excitement, or just sheer, dazzling determination?

But her thoughts moved on to Bryant. He towered over Shamus by a full three inches. His movements were swift, and full of grace and virility. She remembered his parting kiss. She touched the tip of her nose and wrinkled it self-consciously. An uneasy energy tingled inside her when she remembered how his cornflower blue eyes had held her entranced with an unspoken caress.

Sabrina joined them. Her smile spread and sparkled through her jet black eyes. "Your mother told me to take a few hours of leisure this morning before we get to the bees—said she was going to spend some time with the slave families; she loves her weekly visits with the mamas and the babies. The children love her, too; she reads or tells them stories.

Both men came through the door.

"Bryant, good morning," Patrick said, "help yourself to the buffet. Selma will have Emmie fix your eggs to your liking. Shamus, will you join us?

He sat down, but said, "No thanks, Patrick. I had my fill with Grandmama Abigail and Cousin Amanda. I've come to spirit Maureen away. The mists are rising and day has dawned brightly. It's too sunny a day for work." He turned then to Maureen. His eyes scanned her from the tip of her golden-red ringlets and the escaping wisps of hair that fell around her face to the beige dress held fast around her small rounded breasts and flowing elegantly downward to her tiny waist and slim hips.

"Would you join me, Maureen, for a ride along the river?"

Glancing at the saddened look in Bryant's eyes when they met hers, she said, "I'm sorry, Shamus. Papa and I have work this day."

Patrick put the matter aside with sudden good humor. "Oh, my dear, go along with you. The books will wait. Bryant and I will get started loading last year's cured tobacco to take to the ship and make room for the new."

A sharp knock at the back door brought Selma scurrying through the dinning room to the kitchen to answer. A moment later, Captain Zachary entered the room. Bryant and Patrick stood. Patrick put out his hand, and asked, "To what do we attribute the pleasure of your visit, Captain."

Captain Zachary stood at the doorway with nonchalant grace, taking in the whole scene before him. He looked very powerful, his chest broad and muscular. His hard-working hands were long-fingered and strong. There was a look of inherent strength in his face and his eyes were black. His hair was coal black and silky straight, tapering neatly to his collar. Manly wisps of dark hair curled against the v of his open shirt.

Maureen watched the quick look that passed between Sabrina and Captain Zachary. He was around twenty-years-old, she guessed. His father, Alfonzo Fitzsimmons, had died a couple of years before, and his father's first mate had stayed on to finish training Zachary to command the *Desiree* in place of Captain Alfonzo. Her papa sorely missed his friend Alfonzo, but at the same time sincerely enjoyed Zachary's admirable fortitude.

Now, Zachary said, "Well, I see, Patrick, you are surrounded by good company. Good morning Miss Maureen, Shamus, Bryant *Rory* Taylor, and Sabrina, as I recall." He turned back to his host. "But it is you, Patrick, that I have come to see. Is there someplace we can talk?"

"Certainly, Captain. Come to my office," he said, then turned to the others. "Maureen, enjoy your ride with Shamus, and Bryant, you go see to the hands and the loading of the tobacco. We'll take it to market in the morning."

Patrick led the way to his office, and with a nod toward a comfortable chair, seated himself behind the desk and filled his pipe. "Would you care for a cigar?" he asked.

"No, thanks, Patrick. I'll have my pipe."

"How can I help, you, Captain?"

"My business is short. I know you are a busy man. I noticed when I was here six months ago that you picked the best of the slaves on the auction block. I've made some discreet inquiries and I find you are sided with the American Colonies, so I'll get to the point. I have decided to take tobacco directly to a private dock, to the owner of which I have an agreement."

"You mean smuggle your return cargo?"

"The larger part of it, yes. The rest will go directly to London, so there will be no repercussions or questions about whether the *Desiree* is on the side of the Brits or the colonies. Your hogsheads of tobacco can be loaded directly from your own dockside onto the *Desiree* and will, if you agree, be tax-free both when loaded and again when delivered in England.

"The risks?" Patrick asked.

The Captain's eyes sparkled with the love of combat. He grinned a lopsided grin. "Don't fret yourself. Just leave the details to me."

* * * *

"I'll change to my riding habit, Shamus." Maureen said. Then turning to Bryant, said, "Bryant, would you mind asking Jeb to saddle Little Princess on your way to the big barn? I'll help in the drying barn when I get back." Maureen felt her cheeks grow warm when Bryant's eyes met hers disparagingly.

"Of course, Miss Maureen."

His extraordinary blue eyes prolonged the moment before he turned away.

Two hours later Shamus pulled Black Warrior up and beckoned Maureen to pull Little Princess up beside him. They sat quietly at the fork of the James and Pamunkey Rivers and felt the lazy breeze as it came off the water. The sun cast a shower of gold over the ever-shifting panorama. The couple had talked little on their ride along the beautiful quiet road that started out from Williamsburg. Under the arch of the colorful dogwood trees, they were surrounded by the rest of the fall-brilliant colors of reds, rusts, yellows and oranges.

Shamus reached out and caught Maureen's hand in his. "Come, let's walk."

He watched Maureen gracefully dismount her cherished filly. He noticed Maureen's bright copper curls flash gold in the sunlight. Windblown, the golden mist encircled her heart-shaped face, tumbled carelessly down her back, and enhanced her forest green riding habit. Shamus' arm encircled her tiny waist as they began to walk. "You are beautiful, Maureen. You can't know how privileged I am to have lucked out as neighbor to you."

"Grandfather Tucker and your Grandfather O'Toole were very good friends. They once hoped my mother and your uncle would fall in love and marry, but it wasn't to be."

"Couldn't the Grandparents have insisted they marry? It would have joined the plantations."

Maureen spoke with light disbelief. "How silly," she said, "you don't *make* people marry anymore like they did in the old country. This is the free America Colonies. Besides, Grandfather Tucker was very happy when Papa courted Mother and was willing to take over the plantation. It left Grandfather free to go back to teach literature at the William & Mary College, which was his first love."

Amusement flickered in eyes that met hers. "That's fine with me. Then we'll just have to see to the marriage and merge the plantations." The last was spoken with cool authority.

Maureen stepped out of his encircling arm. "We'll see," she responded matter-of-factly.

Shamus' voice hardened and his tone was coolly disapproving when he spoke again. "I see the way Bryant Taylor looks at you, but he's a lowly indentured servant. Probably a murderer. You will not work near him as long as I am courting you. And, when we're married, you will not go near the tobacco; I don't know what your 'papa' is thinking. You should be with your mother, learning to run the household, and how to be a gracious hostess—and a lady."

Maureen stared at him and then burst out laughing. "My, aren't you the gentleman suitor. And I guess Papa will decide whom I work with, or not."

Shamus hesitated, measuring her for a moment. For an instant a wistfulness stole into his expression. "Okay, my dear, I was out of line; way ahead of my dreams." His tight expression relaxed into a smile. "Today, Grandmama is sending an invitation to your mother for a dinner party to help me meet people. How about if we start over?"

He radiated a vitality that drew her like a magnet. She was by no means blind to his attraction. Even as she tried to keep her heart cold and still, her pulse began to beat erratically. He picked her up and swung her around excitedly. "It's going to be perfect."

Maureen was caught up in his enthusiasm. She felt an unwelcome surge of pleasure.

* * * *

Confusion gripped Maureen as she walked into the big barn an hour later. Bryant came toward her. He was so very good-looking and she reacted so strongly to him; her heart danced with excitement. She wondered how she could react to two men with the same shiver of wanting that ran through her now. She started to move toward him, barely able to repress her passion. Bryant's compelling eyes riveted her to the spot. "Did you have a good ride, Miss Maureen?"

"Yes, thank you, Bryant. While the men remove the bales, I'll work with Papa to help get the hands of tobacco ready to age."

"Your papa is still with the captain; they're bringing the *Desiree* up to the dock so the hands can load it. I'll be working with you." His steady gaze, soft as a caress, traveled over her face and searched her eyes, then moved slowly over her body.

Maureen didn't miss his obvious examination and approval. She was almost embarrassed at how happy that made her and an unwelcome blush crept into her cheeks. But the silence became comfortable as they began to work, and, finally, their conversation of books and music and interesting connotations of words matched the easy rhythm of their pace as they completed their tasks.

When Maureen would leave, Bryant leaned forward and lowered his voice. He spoke without a hint of bitterness or boastfulness. "Your papa trusts me, Maureen. I will learn my story in time. I have only to wait four years for the end of my indenture." He pushed stray tendrils of hair away from her cheek and caressed her cheek. Smiling sadly, he added in a lower, huskier tone, "Wait for me, Maureen. Trust me."

"We'll see," she said as casually as she had said those same words to Shamus a couple of hours before. Then she turned toward home. Looking back, Maureen allowed her subconscious thoughts to surface. She knew he was kinder than he dared let anyone know, or maybe dared to know himself.

Chapter 3

Walking toward the front of the house, Maureen once again felt a thrill of wonder. She stopped to admire the three-story dark red brick home that she loved. The front steps led up to a terrace running across the front of the house. The striking feature was the impressive doorframe of white marble. Maureen tarried and mentally skipped through the inside of the plantation mansion.

The ground floor had four spacious rooms: the long and wide living room across the front of the house was complete with a smaller reception room. In the hallway rose a curving flight of stairs that ran gracefully to the second floor. On the right of the hallway was Patrick's library, den and office, behind which was the kitchen. On the left side of the dwelling and hallway was the vast, welcoming dining room.

Two chimneys, one at each end of the house warmed four rooms: Papa's den; Mother and Papa's bedroom immediately above; the dining room; and Maureen's room above that. Mother had allowed a bed to be moved into Maureen's room so that the girls could be together.

The four tiny bedrooms at the back gave space for the house servants, and the third floor attic above was used for storage.

Maureen sighed contentedly. As the only surviving child, she had been so lonely before Sabrina, but now although they separated during the day, they giggled and played silly games at bedtime. "Who are you going to marry?" Sabrina would ask.

"The man in the moon," Maureen would say. "And who are you going to marry?"

"Humpty Dumpty. I can't get to the moon," Sabrina would answer.

"I can. I'll ride with Sally the cow; she jumped over the moon, but what if Humpty Dumpty has a great fall?"

"Then Old King Cole will get my call."

Maureen felt ridiculously happy, fully alive. Tonight she would talk seriously to Sabrina about the two men in her life, before they talked about parties and what they would wear to Grandmama O'Toole's dinner party.

* * * *

True to Shamus' prediction, Abigail O'Toole invited the Maguires, and included Grandfather James Tucker, a self-made mouse of a man, to a handsome dinner party to introduce Shamus to their neighbors. Also invited were families from miles around. The guests included the Nelsons, the Carters, the Smiths, the Custises and the Harrisons who brought their young people. And, true to her spirit, Abigail had invited Sabrina. When they arrived, Abigail, resplendent in a voluminous strawberry-red silk dress, sat comfortably in her favorite earth-brown leather chair, an old dog crouched at her feet. Patrick and Kathleen greeted Abigail and introduced Sabrina who shyly responded and then reached down to pet the dog. "Her name is Joy," Abigail said.

"Such a beautiful Lab," Sabrina said, "I had one at home. Her name be Susie; I miss her."

Tears glittered in Sabrina's deep black eyes. Abigail patted Sabrina's shoulder. "Come see Joy whenever you're lonely," she said.

Maureen reached down and kissed Abigail on the cheek. "I'll bring her myself, Grandmama O'Toole. She works too hard. She loves learning from Mother."

"As you do not." Abigail's smile turned to a chuckle. "You're the son your papa never had. Go on, you two; join the other young people. Enjoy."

It was James Tucker's turn to greet Abigail. Looking stunning in a shirt of white linen with lace ruffles on the bosom and at the wrists; scarlet velvet knee britches with matching coat and silk stockings, James bowed low over Abigail. He said in her ear, "May I escort you to dinner, my dear?"

She grinned mischievously, "Don't you always?"

* * * *

Friends since childhood, Maureen and Amanda O'Toole, who had been crippled with one short leg since birth, embraced each other fondly. Shamus, looking handsome in white shirt, blue silk breeches and matching vest and stockings, approached the girls.

Ignoring Amanda and Sabrina, he threw his arm around Maureen's waist. "Come on, let's get seated."

"Shamus, wait. Grandmama Abigail has not yet announced dinner."

Shamus frowned and his lips twisted into a cynical smile. "I am the plantation owner. I can do what I want."

Maureen showed her disbelief in the tone of her voice.

"For heaven's sake, Shamus. Where did *you* come from? Your mother surely taught you better manners. Grandmama O'Toole is your hostess; she will announce dinner when it's ready. Go enjoy the rest of your guests."

Once all were seated on benches at the sides and ends of the large oak table, Maureen looked around the room. Cedar logs, laid directly on the square stones that formed the surface of the hearth, blazed in the huge fireplace, giving forth an odor reminiscent of a forest in summertime. All around the dark-paneled room, as there were around the living room, sconces for candles were set in the walls. Fresh candles had been used for this party.

Dinner proceeded amiably. The courses were timely and smoothly served: turtle soup, roast goose stuffed with boiled peanuts and wild turkey meat pies, sweet potatoes, corn and carrots. The desserts were stewed fruit mixed with sweetened cream and an apple pie.

Comfortably full and satisfied, Maureen observed the candles under their pink shades, which lit the table with a soft glow and left the rest of the room in a shadowy twilight of the silver sconces.

"Maureen, I'm talking to you."

"Sorry, Shamus, I was admiring your Grandmama's silver sconces; they're unique."

"I was just telling this group that I heard about the disaster. They're calling it the Boston Tea Party. It happened two days ago. It's a disgrace. How can people treat the mother country with such lack of respect? The nerve! To boycott British goods is disloyalty. They repealed the Townshend Acts. What more do you people want?"

All the guests became silent.

"Yes," Patrick said, "we all read about it yesterday in the Virginia Gazette. Don't you take the paper?"

"I've better things to do with my time. Why would I sit around and read some silly old paper?"

"We all came here to be free. Parliament retained the Tea Act and we, the colonists, are protesting. If you kept up with the news, you would realize the tax on tea is an attempt to rescue the British East India Company from bankruptcy. We are refusing to buy the English tea and have decided not to permit British ships to unload it. We may have to fight for our independence. Kathleen's father, James, whom you met tonight, is a delegate to the House of Burgesses. Likewise, Abigail's other guests, Mr. Nelson, Mr. Carter, Mr. Custis and Mr. Harrison and myself are all active in various activities to preserve the rights of the colonists. You might consider studying up so you can better support your grandmother."

When he spoke again, Shamus' voice grated harshly. "I think you are all out of line. I stand by my own beliefs." His words were sarcastic and loaded with ridicule.

He turned to Maureen. When he spoke again his voice was warm. "Maybe you can help me learn. Let's go get a breath of fresh air, my dear."

She said in a voice that seemed to come from a long way off, "Not tonight, Shamus. I will go home with my family."

Shamus turned then and stormed out of the room.

The guests began to leave, quietly consoling Abigail. Maureen leaned over and kissed her once more on her wrinkled cheek. "Don't fret, Grandmama O'Toole. I'll help Shamus learn the importance of our freedom.

Abigail squeezed her hand. "Thank you, my dear, I am sure it will all work out."

Indentured Love

* * * *

While Patrick, Maureen, and Bryant were eating breakfast the following morning, a familiar knock came at the back door. Selma slipped past them to answer.

Shamus entered the dinning room. Ignoring Bryant, he took in Maureen's cream-beige dress and golden-red hair piled up on top of her head and tied with a rust-colored ribbon from which streamers flowed down her back. Wisps of hair sprung out from the ribbon and framed her face. *She's unaware of the captivating picture she makes,* Shamus thought as he leaned forward and touched her hand. "I owe you an apology, Maureen. I acted horribly last night."

Turning quickly to Patrick, he continued, "And you, sir. I was so completely not myself. Can you forgive me?"

"It's not to us you should apologize, but to Abigail who was rightly most embarrassed by your uncouth behavior." Patrick's eyes met his in a direct and challenging way.

In Shamus' expression, they saw a faint bitterness, almost defeat, but he spoke with a prickly determination. "I know that, sir. We discussed it at length during breakfast. She has asked me to come here—ask you to explain the problems of the American colonies as they relate to the British Parliament, she used the word 'demands'. She has gone so far as to suggest that my twin brother, Sean, who stayed back in Ireland to carry on our Father's affairs, might find it easier to trade places with me."

His eyes again took in Maureen's slim figure. Then tearing his eyes away from her, he turned back to Patrick. "But I find I'd rather learn your ways. Your beautiful daughter has found my heart. I visualize the O'Toole and Tucker Plantations merging with Maureen as my gracious hostess."

Patrick's face took on an inscrutable look. "That will be Maureen's decision. She's much too young, and you have a long way to go." His tone turned just short of angry. "You have done *nothing* but amuse yourself as the gentleman playboy since you arrived. I see no signs of you trying to learn the rigors of properly running your late Uncle Thomas' plantation. Tobacco and wheat are commodities that take hard work. Your grandmother will keep me informed. And you can start to learn our ways by keeping informed. After Bryant and I are finished with it, I'll see that you get the Gazette."

A shadowy ironic sneer hovered about Shamus' mouth. "Don't bother," he said, sarcastically, "I learn all I need to know from the chaps at the Hunter Inn."

Patrick turned to Bryant. "We'll load the tobacco hands today. Captain Zachary is pulling the *Desiree* into our dock mid-morning. Maureen will back us up in the big barn…"

Shamus interrupted. His smug expression revealed an air of conquest. "I want Maureen to ride with me this morning. It's far too lovely a day for her to work like a slave." He looked at Bryant with disdain before adding, in a lower, huskier tone, "Besides, if I'm to court Maureen, we must be together often. Winter will be here before we know it and Maureen will soon be of age."

Maureen raised her eyes to find him watching her. He stared at her in waiting silence. His eyes alone betrayed his ardor. Maureen gave Shamus a smooth smile, betraying nothing of her annoyance. "Not today, Shamus. You just heard that I'm needed here, and Sabrina, Amanda and I have plans for this afternoon. Maybe tomorrow."

She glanced at Bryant, noticed his deep blue eyes surveying her with gentleness. Every time his gaze met hers, her heart turned over in response. A spot inside her stomach weakened, a passion sprang into the middle of her. She felt breathless and knew her cheeks colored. She said, "Wait for me, Bryant. I'll get my cap."

Shamus was livid. "Tomorrow then," he said as he turned on his heel and left the room.

Patrick grinned. "Don't work too hard, you two. I'll meet you at the wharf to help unload the drays."

Bryant softly ran his hand down Maureen's arm and took her hand as they leisurely walked toward the barn. "Don't, Bryant. You don't know who may be watching."

"I don't care who may be watching. I'll court you, too, in my own way. I'll have you, my fragile beauty. Shamus is wrong for you. Don't you get it?" He brushed the truant blond tuft of hair away from his face.

Maureen's stomach was tied in a knot that she didn't understand. She was pleased that she sounded so calm when she answered, "*You* don't get it, Bryant. Shamus has Papa's permission. You can't be one of us. We know nothing about you."

But when they got inside the barn, he took her in his arms. She felt liquid; she thought her knees would give out as he brushed her lips with his own. Maureen was shocked at her own eager response to the touch of his lips. She stood silent, churning inside before slowly lifting up her arms to reach around his neck. He deepened the kiss; she kissed him back. Slowly his hands moved downward, skimming either side of her body to her thighs, then he kissed the tip of her nose. "So sorry, my dear, we must get to work."

Her lips still warm and moist from his kiss, she stepped back. "Oh, Bryant, I so wish we knew who you are."

"Shamus has a twin brother. I, too, have a brother, Maureen. He called to me in a dream last night."

"Do you know your name? What did he call you?"

"He called me 'Bro'. We were near water; blue water rippled gently toward the shoreline. We were walking barefoot on the beach. We were so close we could touch. I reached out to him, but he vanished in a misty cloud before I could know him." Frustrated, he turned away. "I don't know my name, or his. I woke up with a jerk, calling him back."

"What did you call him? It may be a clue."

"I called him 'Bro'. I loved him. That's all I know."

* * * *

Winter passed quickly.

Busy as she was, Kathleen gave an occasional afternoon tea and attended quilting bees. She planned her work around one social day each week. Maureen and Sabrina were required to be present at these affairs. Maureen protested, "Mother, let Sabrina go with you," she begged, "I've plenty to do in the barns with Papa and Bryant."

But Kathleen was adamant. Kathleen was slender, reedlike, willowy. Her facial bones were delicately carved, her mouth full. Her thick dark hair hung in long graceful curves over her shoulders and her ebony eyes were as beautiful as black satin, brilliantly intelligent and her spirit was powerful. Except for a very occasional obvious expression of grief that flitted though Kathleen's eyes, her face was full of strength, shining with a steadfast and serene peace.

She spoke now with quiet, no-nonsense firmness. "Maureen, you will someday be mistress of your own home, probably a plantation. I have let you go your way far too long. You must learn how to plan and serve an elaborate afternoon tea, dinner parties and festive balls. It's time you learned to supervise the household staff and the coachman. I expect you to read the British magazines I receive, in order to learn how to dress in a more appropriate manner. The clothes you wear to the barns, and, for heaven's sakes, the fields, are intolerable for a mistress."

She smiled radiantly and held out her arms for Maureen to walk into. "I know all of this seems harsh, but we'll work with your needs, too. All I ask is for one day of your week and a promise that you'll learn what you need to know to run a proper home."

At Kathleen's side, Maureen and Sabrina spent their Thursdays together. Purely bored most of the time, Maureen got well acquainted with the young ladies that were her peers. She learned to quilt a bit and do delicate needlework, but she hated it with a passion. One thing she began to enjoy was learning to knit. She made a warm scarf for Patrick. She did well helping prepare the afternoon teas, supervising the house servants, and directing the coach driver, Jeb.

Shamus courted her properly. Maureen was strangely flattered by his interest. A vaguely sensuous light occasionally passed between them. Shamus teased her sometimes, brushed her lips with his, put his arms around her slim waist. They enjoyed the parties to which he escorted her. They danced well together, and played charades and checkers and euchre and, on balmy days, enjoyed sprint races with friends. But Maureen's whole being seemed to be filled with waiting for something she couldn't find, something she felt when she was with Bryant.

One evening as a crescent moon rode in the sky, they arrived at the Tucker Plantation. Shamus took Maureen's hand

and asked, "What are you thinking?"

She surprised herself when she answered, "That I'm growing up."

"I'm waiting for that." His dusky blue eyes held hers. "I'll have you, Maureen, and I won't wait forever."

Maureen shrugged. "We'll see." Bryant's name lingered around the image of her mind. Her blood soared with unbidden memories. She could see again mornings in the barn when he pressed her lips to his, caressing her mouth more than kissing it, or when he captured her lips with demanding mastery.

Patrick had become deep friends with Bryant. In September, Patrick had seen that Bryant had proper clothes and had taken him to Philadelphia to meet with the assembly that set up a Continental Association to shut off trade with Britain. In a Declaration of Rights they told Britain that the colonies would no longer be bound by Parliament's laws or the king's word when it infringed on their liberties. Since the tobacco and wheat had been sent to market and lightened the chores when winter set in, Patrick took Bryant to Williamsburg each week where they attended the Committee of Correspondence meeting for the colonies.

Bryant and Patrick played chess several nights a week. Maureen served them tea and often sat quietly listening to their conversations. They discussed the Boston Tea Party with glee, and talked about the sure probability of a revolt against the Brits. They discussed books and history's highlights. Bryant had occasionally accepted a cigar and a brandy, but as she had that first night, Maureen always walked Bryant to the back door while Patrick relaxed with his pipe and a glass of brandy before retiring for the night.

She recalled again the very first time Bryant kissed the tip of her nose and the time he kissed her eyes and then planted a kiss in the hollow of her neck. She relived the velvet warmth of his many kisses, and shivered.

"So now what are you thinking?" Shamus' cynical voice cut through her.

Startled, Maureen hurtled back to earth as reality struck. And even more terrorizing, as realization washed over her. The admission was dredged from a place beyond reason and logic, and she couldn't deny the evidence any longer. She loved Bryant, was in love with Bryant, but could not have him—didn't even know who he was or what crimes he had committed.

Maureen sensed Shamus' disquiet. "I'm sorry, Shamus. My mind wandered. I feel achy and worn out. Please take me home now." Her exhausted eyes smiled at him, but her composure was a fragile shell around her.

His expression was grim as he watched her. A bitter jealously stirred inside him, but he feigned a concern he could not feel. It was his tone that shook her more than the words. "Of course, my dear."

The tenderness in his voice amazed her. She was humbled. Standing next to her, he looked incredibly strong and powerful. Maureen thought, *Maybe I will learn to love him—in time. I'll try harder; he's our kind of people; we're two nice people made for each other. Grandmama Abigail and Amanda would be delighted if we were to marry and I'd be close enough to spend hours helping Papa.*

Chapter 4

Besides the morning farming activities, Maureen and Sabrina learned music from the dance master. Isaac Hardwicke carried himself with a commanding air of self-confidence, with soft, dark watchful eyes that missed nothing. He came to the house on Saturday afternoon each week. Neither girl showed a talent for voice instruction, but Maureen favored the spinet, and Sabrina the harp. The sweetest music to Maureen's ear was listening to Sabrina master the beautiful chords of the harp. Both girls learned to dance the intricate figures of the minuet and became adept in other fashionable dance steps.

The other afternoons the girls attended Miss Matilda Lawrence's all-girls school, located in a local old-field schoolhouse. In the fall, Grandfather Tucker had insisted to Kathleen and Patrick that it was a must for the girls to attend the popular little school. Sabrina began to learn the fundamentals. Maureen went to enhance a rudimentary education in reading and simple spelling, for she could write fairly well and had learned arithmetic up through the multiplication tables. She added to her former studies a little history and geography, enough to give her a fairly good idea of the continents and countries. She studied grammar, rhetoric and composition.

She loved the study of literature and the lives of authors; biographies of many famous men drew her interest. *Next fall, I'll be ready to assist Miss Matilda with the teaching*, Maureen thought, and hugged the knowledge close.

Miss Matilda, whose large blue eyes were vibrant and questioning, was softly feminine, all natural and gentle, but serenely wise. Her dark hair glistened like polished wood. The girls loved her.

"After Christmas," Miss Matilda told the class, "we are going to have a spelling bee. I have talked to the boys' schoolmaster, Mr. Phillips, into bringing eight of his best boys to compete with eight of you. I hope you are aware that Benjamin Franklin suggested spelling contests a few short years ago, in 1750. For this one, I have chosen Colleen, Roseanne, Anita, Nancy, Sarah, Patricia, Felicia—and Maureen." In that space of a few seconds, Maureen held her breath before her own name was called. "You girls will be having advanced spelling lessons, and will be taking spelling lists home to learn. Ask your parents to help you study."

A low murmur of surprise and excitement filled the room. Maureen realized with numb astonishment what had just happened. She felt a bursting of mysterious bubbles in her head and the thrill of competition gave her a boost of vitality. She looked across the room at Sabrina, whose smile revealed open admiration for her friend, and joy shone in her dark eyes. Miss Matilda continued, "The spelling bee will be held at the town hall in Williamsburg on March 15; just imagine, it will be a new year. Good luck, girls."

That's my birthday, Maureen thought, *I'll be seventeen*.

* * * *

Christmas was upon them. Miss Matilda had dismissed

class for a five-day holiday. Maureen *loved* Christmas and was determined that Sabrina, and even Bryant would enjoy the activities surrounding the joyous commemorative celebration of Jesus' birth.

The affairs of the plantation had been set in order during the weeks before. The corn was in; the hogs killed; the lard tried; the sausage-meat made; mincemeat prepared; and the turkeys fattened. The servants' new winter clothes and new shoes were stored away ready for distribution. The wagon from the depot had arrived with the big white boxes of Christmas things.

The first cold spell that froze up everything enabled the icehouses to be filled. Shamus and Maureen had great fun with their friends at the ice-pond; he'd sat behind her on the big raft of floating ice. He had a wonderfully warm, cozy way of cradling Maureen with his arm. She felt deliciously alive, but even as she responded and seemed to be falling under his control, she hugged a wonderful secret close.

It had been only a few days before, on a gloriously brilliant sunny morning, when crystal-like icicles clung to the trees, that Bryant had asked her to walk to the river. They walked hand in hand, while the cold air stung their cheeks. But unaware of the cold, they watched the fluffy white clouds succumb to the sun and the feathery white flakes drift down to the silent world. They climbed on a huge slab of ice to be carried downstream. Bryant leaned forward and slipped his glove off; he touched her hand, her face and the tip of her nose. He pulled her around until his adoring bright blue eyes locked with hers. He touched her lips with quick little butterfly kisses. His touch sent ripples down her spine and at last, her lips parted to let his tongue slip inside her mouth.

Suddenly, the glacial coldness surrounded them, the ice float slammed into the bank and they both recovered their senses. "I must get back; we're hauling the wood," Bryant said. His low and husky voice was as gentle as the softly swirling snow.

"Thank you, my love, for the exciting memory." He grinned a crooked grin. "The ice seemed to know it was time for us to stop or we would freeze to death making love with each other." He kissed the tip of her nose.

Maureen was contrite and shocked at the depth of his feelings, and hers. She reminded herself she couldn't have him. When she spoke, she kept her voice noncommittal, not wishing to encourage false hopes. "It was a wonderful interlude on a glorious winter day. I, too, must get back. The Christmas cooking and baking has begun."

The kitchen was buzzing with the cooking. The baking was done in the huge oven outside the back door of the house. Maureen joined her mother and Sabrina, who were in the kitchen. She radiated her private pleasure as she smiled. "What are you two up to?"

Kathleen turned to look into her daughter's eyes. "More to the point, what were you up to? Your cheeks are a glowing blush."

"I've been for a short walk down to the river. Bryant took a few minutes off to escort me." Behind her mother's view, Sabrina winked at her.

Maureen shrugged. "What can I do to help?"

"You can whisk up the peanut soup," Kathleen replied. "I'm making the gingerbread cookies, and Sabrina is preparing the Holiday Wassail. Have you everything you need, Sabrina?"

"I've got the cider, pineapple and the tea; I found the

cloves and the other spices, but I can't seem to find the cheesecloth sack."

"Help her, will you, Maureen? It's our year to entertain visitors on Twelfth Night Celebration. We need to be ready for about ten plantation families. I do hope the weather holds."

Outside, Patrick and Bryant put all the wagons to hauling wood. Hickory, nothing but hickory was used at Christmas and the woodpile was heaped high with the logs. After they were satisfied, the two men went to gather the evergreens and mistletoe for the parlor. The hall and the dinning room were to be "dressed" and glowing in the soft candlelight.

The holidays went smoothly, except for Christmas night when Abigail, Amanda and Shamus dropped in to surprise them. The girls greeted each other excitedly. Delighted, Kathleen and Patrick hugged Abigail. Bryant stood up to welcome the visitors. Shamus' face molted with fury.

"What are you doing here," he exploded. Turning to Patrick, and pointing to Maureen, he erupted angrily, "don't you see what this man is doing? He's taking advantage of you. He's trying to take a place in this family so he can steal Maureen away from you, and me. Come on Grandmama, and Amanda. This is *not* a place I wish to spend the evening. We'll go to the Harrison's; they aren't so foolish as to invite their indentured servants to Christmas."

Patrick put a gentle hand on Abigail's arm. "It's probably best to leave quietly with Shamus."

Then he turned to Shamus. "You and I must have a talk." He smiled wickedly. "If your past pattern holds, you will no doubt be here in the morning to apologize; that seems to be your style. We'll talk then."

Indentured Love

* * * *

When Shamus showed up at the back door the following morning, he knew he had disgraced his family. He looked acutely embarrassed. The little blue seeds of his eyes showed worry. He acknowledged Bryant affably, also Kathleen and Sabrina. He drank in Maureen with a gentle smile. Her features softened; the irritation and resistance melted from Maureen's face.

Patrick stood. "We'll go to my office."

Shamus followed in self-conscious silence.

Whatever went on in Patrick's office was never discussed, but Shamus was ever after visibly, if not kind, reasonably tolerant of Bryant when Patrick was around. They would never become friends because they knew they were rivals for Maureen's affections, but a contrite Shamus left Patrick's house.

The Christmas holidays moved quietly into January, February and, quickly then, into March. Patrick, Maureen and Bryant sewed the minute tobacco seeds in seedbeds. The seedlings were then raised in carefully selected and tended seedbeds where they were protected against heavy rain and excess sun. Although Maureen was often frustrated, Patrick patiently taught her to take over the books. In time, she became proficient, and proud.

Maureen studied long and hard for the spelling bee. Patrick and Kathleen spent hours with her; Sabrina encouraged her daily. "You'll do it, my friend," she said over and over.

Bright and vivid sunlight painted the scene as Maureen and Sabrina set off for school. The yellow stubble fields were bathed in the cold early spring sunshine, and a gentle breeze came out to play among the old weeping willow trees along the riverbank. The girls' excitement skipped between them. The spelling bee was scheduled for two o'clock in the afternoon.

Everybody who knew any of the students would be there. Maureen knew Kathleen and Patrick would arrive early to meet Sabrina as she finished up her studies. The Town Hall was filled with enthusiasm. Supportive parents and siblings of the participants and all of the students in both classes jam-packed the room. The spelling bee began on time. Each participant was introduced. The girls sat to the left of the audience: Colleen, Roseanne, Anita, Nancy, Sarah, Patricia, Sophia, Maureen. The boys sat to the right: Arthur, Gavin, Clifford, Henry, Fletcher, Eugene, Wendell, Robert.

Roseanne went down on "architectural;" Patricia went down on "familiarize;" Gavin went down on "plagiarize;" and Sophia went down on "mercurially." Maureen groaned inside. *Three girls are already down. The rest of us will have to work that much harder.*

But when Clifford went down on "occasionally" by leaving out one c and adding an extra s, and Robert went down on "jaialai," the teams were even once more. Anita went down on "itemization;" Arthur on "irrecoverably;" Nancy on "unequivocal;" Eugene on "tiptoeing," he left out the e. The last six students seemed invincible, but slowly went down—Collent and Sarah first, and then Fletcher and Wendell.

Maureen and Henry Custis were, finally, word to word until Henry was asked to spell "kohlrabi."

"Kohlrabi," Henry repeated, "k o h l r a b e, kohlrabi."

"That is incorrect, Henry," Mr. Phillips said, "Miss Maureen come forward. For the win, you must spell 'kohlrabi.'"

Maureen stood up. She surveyed her family sitting in the

front row. Shamus and Amanda and Grandmama Abigail sat behind them. She looked directly at Shamus. There was a spark of some indefinable emotion in his eyes. Maureen glanced over the crowd. She paled. Bryant stood in the far back of the room, just inside the door. *How did he get here?*

Maureen remembered the feel of his strong muscular body, how he'd held her tight and kissed her, a kiss that had felt like an undying pledge when he'd wished her good luck. She felt the air go out of her lungs—the knot in her stomach spiraled desire inside her. Bryant reached up to brush the errant hair away from his forehead. His whole demeanor screamed pride. His steady gaze bore into her and beamed adoring approval.

"Miss Maureen?"

Startled and confused, she abruptly looked over the sea of faces. "Could you repeat the word?" she asked.

"Are you all right, Miss Maureen?"

No, she thought. "Yes," she said, "I'm fine."

The crowd buzzed. Miss Matilda held up her hand to quiet them. She turned to Maureen. "Your word is 'kohlrabi.' You must spell it now, or forfeit the spelling bee."

"Kohlrabi," Maureen repeated, "k o h l r a b i, kohlrabi."

The burst of applause was deafening. She had won! Maureen looked at her mother and papa, and Sabrina. They were beaming. She looked to the back of the room. Bryant had disappeared. The family, and many of their friends went with them to the Hunter Inn to celebrate Maureen's victory, and her birthday.

* * * *

When the sickness began, Patrick begged his wife to take the girls and go to the city. "You can stay with Grandfather

Tucker in Williamsburg until it's safe to return."

But Kathleen would not.

When the influenza climbed to epidemic proportions among the slaves and servants, and the plantation children, Kathleen set aside the everyday chores to take care of the ill. She sent Sabrina to the woods and the river to gather tuber root and red sage, catnip, wild cherry bark, marigold, red raspberry leaves, slippery elm, sarsaparilla, and numerous other forest and field remedies.

Kathleen herself worked from early morning to late at night over the beds of the suffering victims. She administered medicines and food. She prepared the herbs, sponged the patients with tepid water, gave enemas and laxatives to keep the bowels open and herbal teas to soothe sick stomachs. No one knew all of the many visits she paid to the cabins of her sick and anguished servants. Often at the end of the day, in the dead of night, she slipped down one more time to see that her directions were being carried out.

By her very cheerfulness, Kathleen inspired new hope in her patients, by her strength she gave them courage, and her very presence kindled faith. In her soft voice she told to dying ears the story of the suffering Savior. With her own inherent, optimistic hope she quieted troubled souls, and by her own faith lit the path down into the valley of the dark shadow of death.

In their own time, first Patrick and then Kathleen succumbed to the fever. They lay prostrate and spent in their beds. Side by side, Maureen nursed her papa and Sabrina nursed Kathleen. Around the clock the girls worked together or took turns, giving each other short periods of rest. They bathed them with soft cool cloths and encouraged sips of nourishment and otherwise tended to their feverish loved ones. They changed the sweat-soaked beds and put extra blankets on when their shivering bodies called out.

Kathleen and Patrick moaned and dreamed, sometimes sitting up jerkily, or calling out boisterously. Three weeks out, Patrick seemed to be coherent as he reached for Maureen's hand. "Marry for love, my dear daughter. Take your time; don't take second best. Trust..."

"Trust who, Papa; trust what? Oh, Papa, just get well. I can't stand it when you're like this. *Please*, get well."

But Patrick had sunk back to his bed. His limp arm fell back and lifeless fevered fingers fluttered over his face. Maureen watched as a final inhuman sound gurgled up from Patrick's throat. Still holding his hand, she cried hysterically, begging him to come back, before she went to her mother's bed. Tears coursed down Sabrina's cheeks as she moved aside.

Maureen laid her cold fingers on her mother's hot forehead. Within minutes Kathleen's eyes took on the unfocused glaze typical of the fever just before the final husky rattle of death. There was no final moment of recognition.

It was a warm and sunny April day when Patrick Maguire and Kathleen Tucker Maguire were laid to rest in the family cemetery beside the three babies they had buried together.

A few days after the funeral, Grandfather Tucker had left the farm and gone back to his work, and to his home in Williamsburg. They talked over breakfast before he left. "You'll be fine, Maureen. I trust you to take care of things here. You know your papa completely trusted Bryant. I can't tell you why exactly, but he is bright and knowledgeable. When he accompanied Patrick to the Committee of Correspondence for the colonies, he was eager to help. He was well accepted by

John Adams, William Smyth, Edward Blye and John Burwell. We'll do well to keep him on here as your foreman."

Grandfather Tucker held out his arms and Maureen went to him. "Grief is a terrible burden, but in time you will find your way." The beginning of tears stung the corner of his eyes. "I've lost a daughter and a wonderful son-in-law. You've lost your parents. We'll have to help each other through."

Maureen's own green eyes blurred with tears, but she held him tight. "We'll do it," she said bravely. She stood on the doorstep and watched him ride away through the dogwood trees stretching tall against the sky and bursting open in spectacular bloom.

Chapter 5

Sabrina had long since eaten breakfast and left to tend the bees. When Bryant arrived for breakfast, as he had everyday since the first morning Patrick had asked him, Maureen was already seated. She had selected a bowl of hominy and milk, heated and sweetened with molasses; a tiny dish of battered eggs and a thin slice of baked ham from the sideboard.

Bryant kneeled beside her. She *loved* the outdoorsy smell of him. He leaned forward and in a low voice said, "Promise me you'll wait for me, my love."

His gaze was riveted on her face, then moved slowly over her body. He wrapped his arms around her and she was content to rest against the warm lines of his body. "How are you doing, Maureen?"

A flash of wild grief ripped through her. Her gaze was clouded with tears that rolled down her face. Surprised at herself, the words seemed to fall out of her mouth. "How can I live without them? It has been a year. Without Sabrina—soft, gentle Sabrina—I couldn't survive. She's taken over Mother's work. She cries with me at night. Mother's gone. Papa's gone."

Bryant reached out and lifted her to her feet. She sobbed.

He enfolded her in his arms until she quieted. She took a last shuddering intake of breath. "I don't know why I'm telling you this," she said.

"Because I love you, Maureen, and you well know it. I think I loved you the first time I saw you from the auction block."

Maureen jerked away and sat down at her place at the table. She picked her food apart and pushed it around the plate. "What did you do, Bryant? You *have* to remember."

He rested his hands on her shoulders and massaged her back softly. "I don't know, Maureen, but I don't think I murdered. It doesn't feel right inside me."

She believed him, but he went on. "I dreamed about water again last night—a lot of water, like an ocean—blue water rippled gently toward the shoreline. A road ran past the beach; I was across the road watching the easygoing waves roll in. A young man about my age, barefoot and walking along the shore, waved at me excitedly, motioning me over. I started across the road, but he was wading through the swirling fog that billowed around his feet and swallowed him up into the thick black misty distance. I don't know where it was. I wish I could answer your questions." His brows drew together in an agonized expression; he brushed at the golden hair that fell on his face, then whispered a touch along her cascading curls.

Maureen stood. Her face was firmly set in deep thought. Inside, she ached, hungry for his touch, but knowing she must not have it, must not encourage him. "It's okay, Bryant. Shamus is courting me. He wants to marry me and merge our plantations. He said you could stay on to manage Tucker Plantation. Of course, you are indentured for three more years and I told him I would not let you go."

She didn't tell him the icy blue eyes radiated hatred nor that Shamus' voice was cold and lashing when he told her Bryant could finish his indenture before he would send him on his way with no acreage and no money. Maureen knew, however, that Bryant was skilled enough and educated enough to make his own way.

"Don't! He's wrong for you, Maureen. Don't do anything until I return. Promise me that much, Maureen."

Surprised, the blood drained from her face. "What do you mean until you return? Where do you think you're going? Do you forget you're indentured? You're my servant."

Abruptly, almost angrily, Bryant answered. "I must leave you for awhile. God knows I don't want to leave you, but I must." His voice softened, faded to a hushed stillness. He put his arms around her waist and laid his cheek on her silky hair. Nervously she responded by running her fingers through the errant tuft of his blond hair, pushing it back as she had often seen him do.

He pulled her close then, put his hand under her chin, and turned her toward him. He moved his mouth over hers, devouring its softness. Burying her face in his neck, she breathed a kiss there. His kiss sang through her veins. Standing on tiptoe, she touched her lips to his. Reclaiming her, he crushed her to him. "Promise me you won't do anything brash until I return."

Maureen left the circle of his arms and sat down at her place. "Get your breakfast. We need to talk."

When Selma went to order his eggs, he sat down opposite Maureen. "Your papa told me I could help the colonies fight for freedom. One of the men from the Committee of

Correspondence sent a horseman to look me up. We just got word that Paul Revere and Charles Dawes, and others, rode all night on April eighteenth to warn the people that the Brits were going to attack. The first shots burst out a few days ago in Lexington and then Concord. Our people heard the news by express from Philadelphia. Ted Anderson was the rider from Philadelphia, but he had to return home today to get on with his work. This morning, before he left, Mr. Custis and Mr. Harrison sent Ted here to ask me to ride to New Bern, Northampton County, North Carolina to spread the news. The last time I attended the meeting with Patrick, I volunteered to help the revolution effort any way that I can. If I leave right away, with good luck, I can be there in a few days."

Maureen drew his face to hers, then kissed him, lingering, savoring every moment. There was a dreamy intimacy to their kiss now, but before she could start to move away, he gently lifted his lips and kissed the tip of her nose. Their contact left her weak and confused.

She said, "Of course you must go. But I must tackle the books. Tell Joshua I will be out at ten o'clock to help with the planting. We must have it done by the end of the week."

She tilted her chin up, wiped at the tears in the corners of her eyes, and turned away. "Go now. Papa would have wanted you to go. Take Papa's horse, Ebony. You do ride, don't you? Chester is more gentle if he would suit you better."

Bryant stroked her arm sensuously, then clamped his hand over her trembling chin. His mouth twitched with amusement. "How do you think I got to your spelling bee if I didn't ride Ebony?"

She loved the gentle sparring. Her green eyes lit up. "Oh, you were there? I looked to the back of the room when I won but the apparition I had imagined was you had vanished."

He threw back his head and let out a great peal of laughter. "Don't ever change, my love." His gaze traveled over her face and searched her eyes. His hands brushed softly down the wisps of golden-red hair that framed her face. Regretfully, he said, "I must leave you now, but I'm already counting the days until I shall return."

When he left, Maureen felt an extraordinary void. Impatiently, she pulled her drifting thoughts together and went to Papa's, now her office to tackle the bookwork.

* * * *

Late in the afternoon, Shamus found Maureen in the midst of the rows of newly planted tobacco. His eyes raked boldly over her, taking in the smudges scattered across her face. His tone was fairly civil in spite of his anger. "What are *you* doing here? Did you forget we are to meet our friends at Hunter Inn for dinner and dancing?"

His blue eyes captured hers. They looked into each other's eyes as if they saw something new and very nearly serious.

He was so handsome in his silver gray cloak and breeches, accented with a raspberry-red, long-sleeved shirt and matching silk stockings. His cravat wrapped around his throat and loosely tied in front was of white linen. Maureen's breath caught in her throat. His vitality still captivated her and she thought there was some tangible bond between them. Shamus stood, pensive now, seemingly not disturbed or angry.

"I lost track of time. We're trying to get the tobacco starts planted. We need to be finished by the end of the week and we're short-handed."

He snapped back. "Why are you short handed, and where, may I ask, is that scoundrel, Bryant Taylor? If you treated him like the servant he is, you wouldn't have to work in the fields like a slave."

She suppressed the anger that singed the corners of her control. "I beg you not to speak of my overseer with your nasty superiority. Bryant was Papa's friend, and he works hard and well, but he is gone on a mission now and won't be back for several days—"

He interrupted, but tempered his anger with amusement, "What do you mean, gone? What kind of a *mission* did he make up in order to run away?"

The tension was gone from Maureen's face when she looked up at him. She met his accusing eyes without flinching. She spoke with quiet firmness, explaining why Bryant had left and assuring Shamus he would return.

Shamus sneered. "He'll never come back. You are a fool to think otherwise. The chaps at Hunter Inn are laying wages about how this rebellion will come out. They say the Declaratory Act stated that the Americans are subject to Parliament—that between liberty and taxation their liberty could be destroyed as easily by one as by the other."

"I would like to ask you a question, well, two questions: What no one has showed us, and few have attempted, is why Parliament should have a right to either tax Americans or legislate here in the colonies. Why do you think Parliament has any authority in the colonies at all? And, two, why do you take the word of the 'chaps' at the Inn, instead of reading the Gazette and doing the research for yourself about what we need here, on our plantations, to survive?"

Shamus peered down at Maureen with ill-concealed disdain. "First off, this is men's business. The men I meet at the Inn waste a lot of time reading and researching. I have better things to do." His face darkened with defiance. "Parliament has the authority because they announced that they have it. Satisfied?"

"I'm not going to argue with you about the Sons of Liberty, but if you still want to go to Hunter Inn to be with our friends, I can stop working now. We were almost finished for the day. You may wait in Papa's office while I bathe and dress."

The smile in his eyes contained a sensuous flame. "I certainly don't think you want to go like that. You're dirt-splattered. I'll wait."

* * * *

Maureen took her time, basking in the wondrous fragrance of the luscious flower, attar of roses, that Minnie, her late mother's maid had put in her bath water.

"Better hurry, now, Miss Maureen. Mr. Shamus will be getting restless. Let me get you dressed." She picked up a towel and helped Maureen out of the tub.

An hour later Maureen walked slowly down the curved, stairway. Shamus watched her and took in his breath. "The wait was worth it," he said as he looked over her, then stepped forward and clasped her body tightly to his, her soft curves molding to the contours of his lean body.

Maureen's heart thudded once, then her breathing began to settle down to a more even beat.

Shamus stepped back. His stare was bold and assessed her frankly. Slowly and seductively, his gaze slid downward. Maureen was tightly laced in stays. Her anglaise gown was leaf green. The stomacher attached to the skirt was a separate white decorative triangular bodice. Also stitched to the bodice of the gown, was a cascade of ruffles, as was the flowing front of the petticoat skirt. White ruffles attached to the sleeves matched the bodice. Her only jewelry was a lace ruffle stitched around the neck of her gown. The green gown brought out the color of her golden-red hair, hanging loose under a white ruffled cap.

Maureen raised her chin with a cool stare in Shamus' direction. She flattened her palms against her dress and stood motionless at the bottom of the stairs. He offered her a sudden, arresting smile, and his arm.

"You're beautiful," he said, "ready to go?"

The golden light of early evening was on the land as they stepped into Shamus' coach and began the trip to Williamsburg.

* * * *

On Bryant's first day on the trail south, he surveyed the landscape skimming by on either side. He gloried in a free and limitless expansive opening out into vast distances. He rode through segments of the immense quiet of empty country and through fields of waving wheat. The unparalleled natural beauty included May's panorama of the colorful splash of blooming wildflowers. Sometimes he saw trees stretching tall against the sky on the horizon or found himself in a deep shade under low-hanging branches of trees that arched thick over the dirt pathway.

Bryant's mind slid into the harbor of his dreams. His thoughts filtered back to the day he met Maureen. Her face haunted him—smiling, serious, or thoughtful. He savored the feeling of satisfaction she left with him. She was gentle and loving, with an eager warmth, a whisper of wonder, a taste of paradise. He relished the memory of his mouth on hers. He could almost smell the warmly romantic essence of rose water that she used in her bath. He wanted to give her more, but he couldn't—not yet.

By sheer will and effort, he jerked back to reality. He didn't know who he was or what crime he had committed that caused him to become indentured. He had taken an instant dislike to Shamus O'Toole and now jealousy crept into his thinking as he saw the contrast between his own life and Shamus'. Shamus had everything: the O'Toole Plantation and permission to court Maureen. He had the freedom of the countryside and the friendships of the best families between the plantation and Williamsburg, and camaraderie with the fellows at Hunter Inn.

But something was wrong. However brutal and coarse everything was, and no matter that his world seemed outrageously unjust in order to survive, Bryant hoped for, and would find a solution. He inhaled the soft scents of the spring countryside.

Ebony's hoofs thudded, hollow. Bryant had ridden Ebony hard and long before he stopped at Thurston Tavern for rest and food. He tenderly took care of the horse before taking a room. Ordering shepherd's pie, he sat at a corner table and listened to the talk around him. "There's going to be a war," he heard the man someone called Alec say to the room in general.

"Yah," said the man called Thatcher. "I can hardly wait."

"We'll be called 'rebels.'" said a third man.

Bryant joined in the conversation. "Have you all heard that two men, Paul Revere and Richard Dawes rode at midnight and all through the night warning the people that the Brits were about to attack? Then there were outbreaks in Lexington and on the North Bridge at Concord. For sure, the war has already begun. I hope you're all on the side of the American Colonies."

Thatcher walked over to Bryant, held out his hand and said, "Name's Justin Thatcher." Justin's ruggedly handsome face rearranged itself into a grin. "In this here room we all are on the side of the colonies. What *you* doin' 'round these parts?"

"I came from a tobacco plantation up around Williamsburg. I was asked to spread news of the war. I take it upon myself to recommend that all of we who are able join in."

"You got me," Alec said.

"Me, too," the unidentified man said.

A chorus of "yeas" were confirmation. Bryant inclined his blond head. "That's good, chaps. Pass the word. We'll be a free nation before we're old men. I think I'll turn in for the night. I've got a couple of days of hard riding ahead of me yet."

"Where ya headed?" Justin asked.

"South, to New Bern County, North Carolina."

"What's your hurry?"

Bryant's face brightened. "Got me a girl back at the plantation. She's got full lips and sparkling eyes. Her skin's the color of honey. Her hair is golden red." There was a slight tinge of wonder in his voice. "There's both delicacy and strength all through her. She owns the Tucker Plantation I work on."

Justin Thatcher slapped him on the back. "You better get home quick 'cause I might just take a notion to head up north and find that Tucker Plantation."

Justin watched cornflower-blue eyes light up with amusement. Bryant smoothed his windblown hair and chuckled. "Don't think I'd do that if I were you. The competition's strong enough there to keep *me* guessing. The chap who owns the plantation next is after her, but I can hold my own." He said the words with the certainty of a man who could never be satisfied with only a dream.

In his room, Bryant lay in the bed wanting to escape into dreamless sleep. But the: *Who am I?* had wrecked a peaceful sleep and terrorized his dreams. The nagging question marks were gnawing in his mind. Then unexpectedly, out of the nowhere a light began to tremble on the horizon of his mind. The scene came vaguely to his eyes in a hazy half sleep.

It was the water. He was on an island the size of the Tucker Plantation tobacco barn floor. Tidewater seeped into his footsteps. A whiff of pungent sea air filled his nostrils. His bro was shouting, anxious, but suddenly faded away in the muted glow of dusky, shadowy darkness. When Bryant awoke the next morning, that water tugged at his mind. *I've got a piece of the puzzle*, he thought. *Someday it will all come back to me.*

Chapter 6

Three days later, dead tired and riding an exhausted Ebony, Bryant arrived at the North Hampton County office. He tied his late friend's horse to the hitching post and went to see Samuel Harris. "It's pleased I am to meet you, Mr. Taylor. What can I do for you?"

"Call me Bryant. I've come with the news of the midnight ride of Paul Revere, William Dawes and the other messengers who spread the word of the coming attack of the Tories. It's happened—we're at war."

"Ah, yes, we heard by ship from Newport a few days after it happened. We've been waiting for a courier to arrive—that would be you. It's been told to us that you are to travel, post haste, to the Shenandoah Valley."

At first, Bryant was too startled to offer any objection. His composure shattered, he pushed the tuft of blond hair up off his forehead and drew in a deep breath. "Oh, but I cannot. I need to get back to the plantation. The planting will be done, and by the time I get back the caterpillars and earth worms that devour tobacco leaves will need to be picked off. They're undermanned as I am the overseer."

"Golly, I'm sorry Bryant, but my orders are to send you on

to the Valley."

"How far is it? My horse is about tuckered out."

"Three good days will get you there. Tonight you can stay at the Harris Inn. My brother runs it. We'll send along enough hardtack, and dried meat and cider to get you to the Prescott Tavern—you'll have to sleep in the rough 'til you get there."

"You're saying there's no place to stay before the Prescott? How do I find it?"

"I'll draw you a map; you can't miss it. Come on with me. The stable hands will take real good care of your horse. We'll get you a hot meal—today's special is veal chops with mushrooms, thyme, and port wine. It's real good with the best dark ale you've ever tasted. Then we'll put you up in a comfortable bed."

Bryant left Harris Inn just before dawn. Shadows were yawning and stretching toward the searing light of sunrise. Headed north, bright vivid sunlight enhanced the country scene before him. He struggled to wake up. Sleep crusted in the corners of his groggy eyes. Ebony took it all in stride. Bryant pushed.

During the next two days, horse and rider galloped as one over miles and miles of nothing but miles and miles, stopping only long enough for brief rests, short grazing times for Ebony, and water wherever Bryant found a creek or a spring-fed pond. He built the campfires long after the harsh bright sky turned a deep purple velvet.

On the third day, fog sat like a lid on the valley ahead. The misty atmosphere rolled and churned around them, but Bryant and Ebony forged on, relentlessly, seemingly tirelessly. As the day grew late, clouds were weaving cobwebs across the sky when Bryant saw a corral and the roof of a barn in the distance.

Indentured Love

"Go, boy, we're almost there," he said, giving Ebony a gentle spank on his rump. Lightening flickered against the sky to the west and a thunderclap pealed as fat raindrops began to spatter down.

Ebony stumbled. Bryant held fast. He wasn't thrown, but he knew by the horse's limp that they were in trouble. He slid to the ground. Ahead, horses nickered; cows lowed. Forty-five minutes later, Bryant led Ebony to the stables behind the Prescott Tavern. He rubbed him down and settled him for the night before going inside to secure a room.

"I'm Murdock. What'll you have, stranger?"

"The name's Bryant Taylor. For now, I need feed for my horse, supper, and a bed. I'm a messenger of the war that's started up in Boston. War between the Brits and the American colonies."

"What does that have to do with us here in the Valley? And, by the way, a message came that one Bryant Taylor is to ride north and west to carry the message to the Ohio Valley."

Bryant Rory Taylor was exhausted and desolate. He knew he must go, but he felt his life was over. Maureen would never wait for him. He gathered his wits about him and said, "Tell you what. Let's talk in the morning. I'll be here awhile, a couple of weeks at best. My horse is lame. Let's start with food and rest. What's your special?"

"Fried oysters with hot sauce and beer with rum. Jake'll take care of your horse."

After supper Bryant went straight to his bunk. He was sick at heart, knowing Maureen would think he ran away, or worse, abandoned her. Her slim body and deep green eyes lingered around the edges of his mind as he finally slid into a thin sleep.

By the next evening, the whole valley was talking about the

war. A week-old paper had arrived and they read that the Congress had unanimously elected George Washington to be commander in chief of a Continental army. Many had already decided to go east to volunteer for the war.

Two weeks dragged by. Bryant massaged Ebony's leg every day and rubbed it down with liniment. Tonight, he was restless; he wanted to leave Shenandoah Valley, but Ebony was still slightly lame and needed more time to heal completely. Bryant thought about hiring another horse and returning for Ebony at a later date, but he was afraid to leave his horse's care entirely to Jake. Discouragement, and depression—like pain and loneliness walked through him and left him in a dark mood. It led him to take to his bed early where he tossed and turned until an uneasy sleep stole over him.

Suddenly he was caught in the throes of a monstrous nightmare. He stood in the middle of a burning lake, unable to break away. The horror gripped his whole body. Although he tried to escape, he was simply hanging on to survival. The water was swirling around him—engulfing him, consuming him; he would drown. He could hear his heart battering against his ears and the uncontrolled sounds of a crowd anticipating his end. Maureen smiled at him with tears streaming down her delicate face. A secretive smile softened her lips as though out of pity for him. "I think I know this man," she said as she reached out trembling fingers to lend a hand. But a hand descended on his shoulder from behind. Bryant didn't know who it was, but a voice, thick with Irish brogue, said, "Come back, Bro."

Bryant gasped, panting in terror; fear knotted inside him. He choked back a frightened, electrified cry as his eyes opened and recognized the familiar room. Not asleep, but not moving, a memory opened before him as if a curtain had been ripped aside. The water was the Galway Bay; the island of his last dream was the smallest island of the Aran Islands, just off the shore. He had grown up in Galway Bay. Bryant thought, *I'll write a letter to the Taylor family in Galway Bay as soon as I get back to the plantation. They'll know me; my brother will come here to help me regain my memory. If I can get back in time, Captain Zachary will take the letter back with him in the spring when he auctions the slaves. I'll have my answer, maybe my brother, when the Captain returns in October.* He drifted into a silent darkness, a dreamless sleep.

* * * *

Four weeks had melted away. *Where is he?* Maureen asked herself repeatedly. "Sabrina, where is he? He left weeks ago. He should have been back last week."

"Sure and I don't know any more than you. Did he tell you how long the trip would take?"

"A week, ten days at most. It's June."

The girls lay on their beds after a long, hard day. Sabrina had begun spinning a new supply of muslin for the slaves' shirts, and dresses and caps. The worms and caterpillars were profuse. Maureen was giving hour for hour to the slaves who were removing them.

"I can take tomorrow afternoon off," Maureen said. "Joshua is doing a really good job. He's going to pull Tim out to help and Jeb said he'll work the tobacco leaves so I can get away. I want to visit Grandmama O'Toole and Amanda. You need to get away, too. The bees will need you in a day or two. Come with me, Sabrina."

There was no answer from Sabrina's bed. Sleep had nudged in among Maureen's words. Maureen smiled to herself. *Ah, well, she needs the sleep. I'll tell her my plans in the morning. But where oh where is Bryant Rory Taylor?* was her last thought before his face came to her, and his kisses came into her mind. She felt the tug of emotion and could feel the physical waves pulling at her. She tingled for him. The morning he left flooded back in her memory.

Maureen remembered the fresh, outdoorsy smell of Bryant when Bryant had kneeled beside her. He'd ask her to promise to wait for him. He'd called her "my love." He'd caressed her with his eyes, wrapped his arms around her and pulled her against the warm lines of his own body. She'd cried in his arms during a flash of fierce grief for the loss of her parents. Bryant had lifted her to her feet. "I love you, Maureen," he'd said. "I loved you the first time I saw you from the auction block."

They had talked of Shamus, but Bryant had insisted, "He's wrong for you, Maureen. Don't do anything until I return. Promise me that much, Maureen."

He'd pulled her close then, put his hand under her chin, turned her toward him and moved his mouth over hers. Even now, that kiss sang in her heart. He had asked again that she promise not to do anything until he returned.

Then he explained why he had to leave. Maureen had drawn his face to hers, they had kissed, lingering, savoring the moment. Then he'd kissed the tip of her nose and they had joked before he left. When he was gone Maureen felt an extraordinary void.

She felt it now, the void, and emptiness. Could she have been wrong? Shamus had assumed Bryant made up the "mission" in order to run away. He'd sneered at her. "He'll never come back. You are a fool to think otherwise," he had said.

Shamus had continued to be attentive. They often took leisurely, very early morning rides together on Black Warrior and

Little Princess. Shamus was usually delightful, always a gentleman, even when he would have asked for more than Maureen was ready to give. "I must be sure about my feelings," she would tell him.

But there was one thread of contention between them. Shamus was always sarcastic about Bryant, always derogatory about "your indentured criminal—a murderer, no doubt," and always with a secretive glint of amusement.

Maureen thrashed about; she changed positions and fluffed her pillow until, finally, drowsiness stole over her and she slept.

* * * *

"We've come." Maureen said to Abigail the following afternoon. "Me to see you and Amanda; and Sabrina to see Joy."

Abigail laughed heartily. "Sabrina may have found the best company of all." She turned her attention to Sabrina, and giving her a kiss on the cheek, said, "Would you mind taking Joy for a walk? Amanda and I can't keep up with her and she loves to romp and fetch her ball and run."

"Thank you, Grandmama O'Toole. I would love to take Joy outside."

"We'll call you in for tea after awhile, my dear."

"Not to hurry," Sabrina said. Joy, already at her heels, bounded out the door ahead of her.

Abigail turned back to Maureen. "Amanda is taking her rest. We'll have tea when she gets up, but I really welcome this time to talk privately with you." Although she spoke with a quiet dignity, an anguished tone, a strange reluctant note had come into her voice. She seemed sad.

Maureen looked at her, startled. "Is something wrong? Are you ill, Grandmama?"

"Oh no, nothing like that. I'm fine, doddering, but fine."

She grinned, but the smile didn't reach her eyes. "It's Shamus I want to discuss with you. He is not taking over the work of the plantation. He is behaving like a 'gentleman' plantation owner. When he is not with you, he is most often at Hunter Inn. He talks terrible about we colonists who are concerned with the taxes on our commodities, and with our freedom."

"I know," Maureen said, "I've tried to talk to him, but he can't see it. He's so sure that the fellows he chats with are right. They believe we need the British Parliament to help make our laws and oversee our American Colonies. Shamus says the odds are all against America. He says this infant nation is matching itself against the world's richest power, the world's strongest army and navy. They can't find objections to the unfair taxes."

Maureen sighed. "But you and I know if Parliament continues to tax us, we can't survive, we can't be free and we can't move on."

"Did you know I met the twins when they were knee high to their pa? Did you know my sons were also twins? Thomas and Timothy." Abigail's voice was soft with memories so vivid, so close. Thomas decided to come here and establish a home and a heritage. I came with him to care for Amanda as her mother had died of the fever when she was tiny. Timothy stayed in Ireland to care for their heritage there, the heritage my beloved William had worked so hard to leave to them. Timothy sent the fare for Amanda—she was six—and me to visit his growing family. There were the twins, three-years-old at the time, and two older children, the girls—Genevieve was nine years old and Bridget was twelve; their mother died after the twins were born." She hesitated. "Ah, my mind swirls with memories, but I've gone off on a tangent and wandered off the point."

"It's okay, Grandmama. I'd love to hear more."

"They were darling boys, so blond and fair. They sat in my lap and listened to the stories of *Gulliver's Travels*. Shamus said, even then, 'When I get big as you, I come to America, Grandmama. I live with you and Mandy. Can I, can I?"

Abigail struggled with the uncertainty that had been aroused. "I was so proud, and when Thomas died, I sent Shamus the message to come to me. It was what he always wanted, he said in his letter, but so hard for him to leave Sean. But he did it, and now I don't understand what's come over him. Have you any suggestions, my dear, to get Shamus interested here at the plantation?"

Maureen sat thoughtfully before she answered. "I've tried to get him to read the Gazette, but he just laughs at me."

"Oh, my dear, I'm so sorry. I've tried to get him interested in a game of chess or a discussion of books, but he refuses. I can't imagine that Timothy and Sean don't play chess and I know they read a good deal. The twins went to Trinity College in Dublin. It just doesn't make sense."

"Maybe he could sit with Amanda and learn the books. If he could see the results of the horrible taxation, he might begin to get the real picture."

"I do wish that would work, but he seems arrogant around Amanda. He loved her as a child, but he doesn't treat her at all well now. He acts like she is an embarrassment. I don't know what his problem is, but when he received a letter from Galway Bay, from Sean, he threw the letter at me and told me to read it."

"Did you?"

"Yes, of course, I read it out loud to him and Amanda. It was so sweet. They miss him, but their farm and investments are doing well. Timothy is so happy that Sean stayed to manage the farm, says he misses Shamus, but hopes he is loving being in America. Sean is looking forward to visiting us as soon as the war has settled down here, said he hopes to bring his pa with him. He told Shamus to fight for the colonies' freedom, that things would be better when we could get independent from the British king."

"What did Shamus think?'

"He thought Sean didn't know what he was talking about, that he didn't know the whole situation. Shamus stormed out of here to go to his friends."

Maureen put her arms around Abigail. "We'll work together to convince him about the truth."

Amanda joined them. "Wow. I'm so glad to see you, Maureen. Have you heard from Bryant?"

"No, but I expect to very soon."

Abigail looked lovingly at the girls. Let's call Sabrina in and have tea. We'll adjourn to the dinning room"

The four women, and Joy beside Abigail, had "tea," coffee really, because they, along with many colonists were abstaining from tea in order to support the boycott against the British tea tax. The women feasted on small meat pies, cheese, delicate little cakes, sugary confections and chocolate.

When Maureen and Sabrina left for home, it was late afternoon. Clouds scudded playfully across the warm June sun.

Chapter 7

It was April, 1776. Winter had passed. During the fall months, Maureen had helped harvest the tobacco, a bumper crop. She had helped load the tobacco on Captain Zachary's ship at their dock.

Sabrina and Maureen always ate breakfast together now that Kathleen and Patrick were gone. Zachary had come to the house to join the girls for breakfast. He first held Maureen. He stroked her cheek. "My dear Maureen, I am so sorry for the death of your parents. Patrick was a dear friend of my pa, Alfonzo, and he was very helpful to me after his death. I hurt for you; if there is anything I can do..." His embrace was warm and comforting.

Zachary then turned to Sabrina. His eyes brimmed with tenderness and passion. She was entranced by the silent sadness of his face. He opened his arms and she slid inside them and leaned lightly into him, tilting her face toward his. His lips feather-touched her cheek. His voice was soothing. "And you, too, my dear, have lost your parents. Someday, I promise that I will take you home to visit them. Your mum and pa will be proud to see how you have grown up. Your life is here, and I hope your heart will be with us in America. When the time is right, you can go with me one April day and return with me in October. I'll take good care of you."

Maureen and Sabrina had attended school five afternoons a week during the winter—Maureen as Miss Matilda's assistant, and Sabrina to further her own education. Isaac Hardwicke had continued to teach the girls music and dance each Saturday afternoon. They were both advancing and loving it, even though Mr. Hardwicke was a somber taskmaster.

Maureen had given up ever seeing Bryant again. Whenever she thought of him, she felt as if a hand had closed around her throat; her chest felt as if it would burst; a cold knot formed in her stomach. She knew in her heart he hadn't abandoned her. Maybe he was ill, maybe he had joined the war. Maybe he was dead. The thought cut through her like a saber.

Shamus and Maureen continued their friendship. They visited friends frequently. Maureen had talked to Shamus until she was weary, but she kept trying for Abigail's sake.

"Don't you recall, Shamus," she said, "when the Continental Congress set up a Continental Association to shut off trade with Britain? When they told Britain the colonies would no longer be bound by Parliament's laws or the king's word when it infringed on our liberties, and demanded repeal of *all* the offensive acts passed by Parliament twelve years ago?"

"My friends say plans have been laid to raise an army, funds, and supplies for that crazy George Washington." Shamus replied. "I repeat my views. It's a program bordering on revolution. The odds are so obviously against the colonies. It's an infant matching itself against the world's richest power, against the world's strongest army and navy. And, yes, I heard about that stupid Patrick Henry howling out... 'give me liberty or give me death.' He should be shot. That would give him 'death.'"

"Shamus, forgive you. Don't you read anything for yourself? Let me give you a copy of Thomas Pain's *Common Sense* pamphlet. It explains in everyday language what our needs are and why we call for a separation from Britain."

"But Britain is our parent country. Forget the pamphlet; the chaps told me all about it."

"Don't you know these American Colonies have been the asylum for the victimized lovers of civil and religious liberty from every part of Europe? Didn't you listen when your twin brother wrote and told you to support the colonies? Why *are* you here, Shamus?"

"Come here, my love. I don't want to discuss this insufferable subject any longer. It does no good and may harm our courtship." Shamus' blue eyes flashed a gentle but firm warning as he laid his hand on her shoulders.

He was so compelling; his magnetism was so potent that she felt the electricity of his touch. He projected an energy and power that undeniably attracted her. Her feelings toward him were becoming confused; she wanted to hurt him and to make him want her at the same time. *I must be calm,* she thought. *I can help him learn. I owe that much to Grandmama O'Toole.* Shamus brushed his lips against hers; parting her lips, she raised herself to meet his kiss.

* * * *

Bryant and Ebony moved unhurriedly across the whispering fields. They had begun their trip weeks before, but they traveled at a slow, leisurely, pace to make certain Ebony's healing leg was protected. Bryant was apprehensive about his return to the plantation. He ached to see Maureen. But would she accept his explanation or would she be so angry she would reject him? Could he hold her warm, slim body close to him again? Kiss her lips; kiss the tip of her tiny pug-nose?

He turned Ebony across the dark bare tobacco fields through slowly changing patterns of sun and shadow. Ebony neighed contently as Bryant brought him to a halt at the stables of Tucker Plantation. Jeb welcomed them home and took Ebony to his stall; Bryant went to his hut and drifted into a dreamless sleep.

* * * *

This day Maureen and Joshua would plant the seedlings. She was wide-awake at once and before the last quivering chime of the clock had died on the air, Maureen Maguire was getting up. It was her custom to rise at seven o'clock, although everybody else at Tucker Plantation was up by five. She went to a bedroom window and looked upon the awakening Virginia morning.

The sun was comfortably above the horizon. Its slender level rays gilded the tops of a grove of peach and apple trees and danced across the brown fields beyond them. The fresh mist green of foliage on the flowering dogwoods made intricate patterns against the ashen whiteness of the sky.

Behind the house, in full view from her room, was the little village of tiny slab-wood huts with gray smoke coming from their clay chimneys. The black slaves lived in them. Nearby, the stables and the kitchen garden separated the huts from other small houses built for the white indentured servants. Between the garden and the orchard were a dovecote and a dozen beehives.

Slow moving white and black servants went about their tasks with the sedate and dignified aversion of unpaid labor. Phoebe, a Negro girl, came from the cow shed with a wooden pail full of milk.

Maureen looked toward the border of an adjoining field where a white man was hitching a horse to the harness of a plow. He wore a raccoon skin cap with the tail hanging down his back, and knee-length leather breeches stretched tight around muscular thighs. From the knees down his legs were bare. He wore no coat; his gray shirt was of a coarse cotton cloth. Maureen watched his motions—his powerful well-muscled body moved with easy grace. His face was bronzed by wind and sun. His long and thick tawny-gold hair kept falling down on his face. Now and then he dusted off his hands and swept it back with a swift gesture. As he worked over the buckles of the harness he glanced boldly, but without impudence, toward the windows of the house. Irish by birth, he was an indentured servant with another full year to serve before his freedom was due.

Maureen had seen Bryant ride in the night before. She tried to keep her heart cold and still. She was determined not to reveal the joy she felt when she saw him. "It's all over the plantation that you are sweet on Mr. Bryant. What made you chose him to be in your service, Miss Maureen?"

Maureen whirled around. "Oh. Sabrina O'Connor, you startled me. How often must I tell you not to sneak up on me like that? And don't call me 'Miss'. Whose business is it anyway that my overseer met with me each morning to take his orders for the day?"

The warmth of Sabrina's smile echoed in her voice. "I do be sorry to frighten you, Miss, but you was so lost in looking you just didn't hear me coming. Do you be ready to dress?"

Turning back, Maureen looked down again, straight into eyes that sent her a private message. She suffered the dull ache of desire, and with a shiver of vivid recollection wondered again if she and Grandfather Tucker had made the right decision to keep him on. She moved away from the window. *I'll think of the problem later,* she decided as she turned to the pewter basin on a stand in the corner. "Yes, Sabrina, I'm ready to dress, but for heaven's sake, you don't have to help. Minnie will do it; here she is now, and don't call me 'Miss.'"

She turned to Minnie and said, "Forget the panniers and whalebones. I can't get the work done wearing such uncomfortable garb; just hand me the indigo Lindsey-woolsey."

Sabrina said, "But what of school? You won't be going a-teaching without proper dressing, will you?"

Maureen reached up to smooth an escaping curl. "We'll talk while Minnie is tending to this tangled mass of hair."

She pulled off the soft flannel nightgown and slipped the dress over a silk chemise, barely disguising full, young jutting breasts. The supple material flowed over her narrow waist that flared into agile rounded hips. She stood quietly while Minnie fastened the tiny buttons up the back, then sat before the long, wooden-framed mirror. Minnie brushed Maureen's golden-red hair until it gleamed with shadows of deep gold. Then as she curled the long locks around her two fingers, Maureen said to Sabrina, "Did you know it's the anniversary of the very day we met? Papa let me accompany him to the docks in Williamsburg on an April day just fine as this."

"Sure, and I know. Me mum and me pa put me on that ship hoping I'd find good people to care for me, and that I would meet and marry a fine young man from the colonies. But they didna have money to come along, and there were so many babies to care for at home…"

Maureen watched Sabrina's eyes fill with a deep longing

and reached up to touch her hand. "Oh, my dear, you were so young. Don't look so sad."

Sabrina looked into Maureen's face in the mirror, and flashed her a smile of thanks. "It's all right, Miss Maureen. I was lucky you found me. Me mum will be proud when she know an Irishman, Patrick Maguire, and his good wife Kathleen took me in. I wrote them a letter a day ago. You can give it to Captain Zachary next week when his ship comes to dock."

"You can give it to him, yourself, Sabrina. He will be so proud to know you have done well in your new land. And, we will find you the young man of your dreams as soon as we properly join society in Williamsburg. Grandfather Tucker will have our 'coming out' and Grandmama O'Toole will be his hostess."

"Sure an' 'twill be soon enough, but tell me about Mr. Bryant."

Maureen studied her friend in the mirror. Her features were dainty. There was both a glow and now a confidence in her clear oval face. She was slender with smooth velvety skin. Her thick dark hair tumbled carelessly down her back. *We've both lost our parents, even if for different reasons. It brought us close—like sisters,* Maureen thought.

Aloud, she said, "Shamus O'Toole first caught my eye. I thought he was the most charming man I had ever seen."

Sabrina said, "And now we know he thinks you is the most "ravishing" lady he ever seen in the whole of his life."

For a moment before she continued, Maureen felt a stab of pain. "Silly goose, you know this story as well as I."

Sabrina's jet-black eyes sparkled with mischief. "Then there was Bryant *Rory* Taylor, bigger than life—with more golden hair and startlin' blue eyes…"

Maureen couldn't help laughing aloud. She said, "Yes,

there was Bryant. The coastal guard had snatched him up out of the water and Papa bought him for twenty-five hundred pounds of tobacco, the same as twelve pounds of sterling."

Sabrina's eyes widened and caught Maureen's in the mirror. "So much? That be a lot of silver, Miss Maureen."

Maureen's expression stilled and grew serious. "I never could understand why Papa took such a liking to the man, but a few days before he died, Papa said, 'You will know what to do about Bryant.' I, with Grandfather Tucker's blessing, kept him as our plantation overseer, but I have no idea what Papa meant. Oh, Sabrina, that's over two years past. Will I ever quit missing Papa and Mother?"

Minnie gently pulled Maureen's hair back to her right side and let the long curls hang down her shoulder.

Sabrina asked, "Has Mr. Bryant ever told you what your papa wanted you to know about him?"

Maureen remembered the tortured dullness of disbelief that passed through his blue eyes when she had asked him. When his expression had clouded in a scalding fury, she had felt suddenly weak and vulnerable. "No, and he says he won't. He's got a torture inside him that I cannot break through..." Biting her lip, she looked away.

"Minnie, hurry. I must go downstairs. He'll be here soon and I've a hundred things to attend to before I change my dress and go to Miss Lawrence's to help with the sweet little monsters. Will you join us this morning?"

Sabrina regarded her with amusement. "So now you be a 'silly goose'. You know I be up before first light and now I be finishin' me cloth I started a fortnight ago."

Maureen groaned. "Ugh. I'm happy it's you that has taken over the spinning," and added gently, "you're an angel of the spinning wheel. You remind me of my mother sitting there so sweet and serene."

"Thanks be to her. *She* was the angel of patience to teach me. But I wished I had learned better the chore of the weavin' and makin' the garments. And I gots many other things to learn, too."

Maureen stood up and patted Sabrina on the shoulder. "You are doing fine. After all, you are already reading those retched pamphlets about measles and smallpox. You wrote that letter to your family all by yourself. I'll see you after mid-meal and we will walk to school together."

Maureen picked up a soft, pale blue silk apron and tied it around her middle as she glided gracefully down the wide curving stairs to the first floor. But Bryant had arrived ahead of her. He was no longer barefoot, but had donned thick woolen stockings that reached to his knees and a pair of square-toed shoes. He lounged casually against the wall and watched her intently as she descended the stairs. Once again, his arresting good looks totally captured Maureen's attention. She felt the power that coiled within him as he stood quietly in an attitude of self-command, a picture of studied relaxation.

She thought again that he had the craggy look of an unfinished sculpture. Although pleasure now softened his granite-like features, Bryant's face was bronzed by the same wind and sun that caused age lines about his mouth and eyes to mute his youth with strength. Her face grew warm as she watched the light of desire illuminate his blue eyes. The tall figure stepped forward to meet her at the center of the bottom step. He reached out to let his finger tenderly trace the line of her cheekbone and trail across a splash of freckles on the bridge of her nose. His greeting was a husky whisper. "My lovely Virginia planter and mistress, how long has it been since I told you I dream of your silken hair and emerald green eyes. They catch the sparkling golden lights of the sunshine or candle light…"

"Bryant, not now." She smiled to take the sting from her words. "How can you walk back into my life without a word of explanation or remorse? We must have a serious talk, but first breakfast. Come."

Without a word, he put his hand on the small of her back and guided her toward the dining room where they took their accustomed places in the high back chairs at the long oak table. A young white girl stood at the fireplace stirring the contents of the cast iron pot. She quickly dished up two bowls of thick hominy and placed it before them with a pitcher of fresh thick cream sweetened with molasses.

Bryant and Maureen didn't speak as they took turns pouring the cream over the hot hulled corn. "What be your pleasure, Mistress Maureen?" asked a soft voice at her side.

Maureen realized she was hungry for the first time in months. "We'll have battered eggs, Selma, and while they are prepared, we'll help ourselves to the side board."

They selected generous portions of the various dishes—baked ham and broiled partridge. They spread hot corn hoecake and wheat biscuits thick with butter. Bryant poured himself a tankard of cider and Maureen chose a tin cup of sassafras tea. Seated again, Maureen spoke first. Her eyes drank in his powerful, sensuous physique. She looked away, needing a moment to reorient herself. Fury almost choked her. "How does this happen? You come waltzing in without a care in the world, without an explanation, and expect to take up where you left off. Do you forget you are indentured and that you have another year to serve?

Chapter 8

Bryant faltered in the silence that almost engulfed them. "Of course, I didn't forget I am indentured. I only hope you will give me the courtesy to listen."

"Make it quick. I have much to do today. I must order more seed and get the vouchers ready to take to Williamsburg on Monday next. The *DESIREE* will most likely dock within the week, and I have to pick up my order, and place another, and take care of other business before I go to Miss Lawrence's. There are seeds to be tended for this years' planting, and the planting of those that are ready."

Bryant's gaze roved lazily to appraise her. Slowly and seductively, his eyes slid downward to the low neckline that laid softly across the top of Maureen's proud rounded breasts. "Come for a walk with me."

"Maybe later, Bryant. Didn't you hear me? I must work." In Bryant's eyes, Maureen saw a tenderness.

"His voice was uncompromising yet oddly gentle. "You work too hard, Maureen. You should hire a bookkeeper. A plantation the size of this is no place for a young lady to run by herself. Take a walk with me, my dear. I have much to tell you."

"We've been over this before, Bryant. Papa taught me well, and Grandfather Tucker needs me here. Besides, I love it, and well you know it."

Maureen was sick with the struggle within her. Her bearing was stiff and proud, but her spirit was in chaos. She found his nearness disturbing and exciting. Some of her anger evaporated, leaving only confusion. "So, where have you been for almost a year?"

Bryant unraveled his long crossed legs and rose in one fluid motion. "Come on, walk with me. I'll tell you all, then I'll help you with that order and the planting." He reached out and caught her hand in his to help her up. Bryant leaned forward and lowered his voice. Deep and sensual, it sent a new flutter of desire through her. "Don't fight it, Maureen."

They walked to the river while Bryant told her where he had been and the why of so many delays. "And," he said, "three days west of here I met Chief Sky Bear of the Toyhonka Tribe."

"However did you communicate?"

"He has mastered a little English and we did the rest with signs and pointing." Bryant's firm mouth curled as if on the edge of laughter. "I came upon them without warning when I was looking for a place to camp for the night. Fortunately, he and his tribe were friendly, and I made a friend. The Chief first sat me down beside him around the circle of fire and offered me the peace pipe. After that ceremony, we ate wild turkey stuffed with cornpone, beans, and a small bite of some kind of cake dribbled with syrup, and, of course, there was plenty of rum. The Chief insisted I sleep in his teepee and Little-Star, his son, took care of Ebony."

"What an exciting adventure. Were you frightened when

you first came upon them?"

"Not nearly as frightened as when I had the dream a few nights before I left the Shenandoah Valley. I was drowning and you were there and couldn't help, and my bro called me back. I don't yet recognize who I am, but I know where I lived. I know I have a brother of whom I'm very, very fond. I'm quite sure I lived in Galway Bay. I'm going to write a letter to the Taylors there. I'll send it next week with Captain Zachary. When the family receives my letter, they'll answer. I'm going to ask my brother to come in the fall with the Captain so that he can help me learn more about my life; surely something will find it's way into my mind so that I can remember everything—everything about my family, if I am really a criminal, where I got my education, where I learned to play chess and read. Please, Maureen, trust me."

"How did you learn where you are from?"

"It was the dreams; they keep coming and coming. Maybe I'll learn more before my brother arrives. I have to believe that."

Maureen looked up and her heart lurched. His cornflower-blue eyes riveted her to the spot. He held out his arms to her. His look was so intimate a shudder passed through her. She moved toward him, driven involuntarily by her own passion. In one forward motion, she was cradled in his arms. She dropped her chin on his chest with a sigh of pleasure. She felt the heady sensation of his lips as he kissed the pulsing hollow at the base of her throat. Maureen felt the intimacy of his kisses as his mouth grazed her earlobe. Standing on tiptoe, she raised herself to meet his lips. She felt his lips touch her like a whisper and she kissed him with a hunger that belied her earlier anger. His lips were hard and searching, urgent and exploratory and, finally, soft and sweet. It was a kiss for her tired soul to melt into, leaving her mouth burning with fire.

Bryant reluctantly pulled away, then brought her close to his side and they walked on together. Old weeping willows sat along the bank above the shimmering waters of the river. Maureen noticed elm trees that were beginning to show their buds, live oaks wrapped in strands of Spanish moss and the colorful splash of blooming violets.

Bryant spoke. There was a quiet dignity in his voice. "I was able to convince many men to join the army; they're being signed up for six months service. Newspapers were scarce while I was traveling, but I heard General Washington is offering a twelve dollar bounty to join, sixty dollars a year in pay, and 'the opportunity of spending a few happy years in viewing the different parts of this beautiful continent' and returning home 'with his pockets FULL of money and his head COVERED with laurels.' Can you imagine the excitement?"

Maureen stopped. "She took his hand into both of hers. Do you want to join General Washington's Army?" Bryant bent down and kissed the tip of Maureen's nose. "I'm indentured. You are my mistress and I am your servant. Do you forget?"

Maureen giggled. "It's likely you have remembered and are quoting your 'mistress'."

"Actually, my love, I would consider it an honor to be your slave for the rest of my life. I sorely regret that at this time I can only ask you to wait for me."

"Seriously, Bryant, Papa cared for you and trusted you. You went with him to all of those meetings, and volunteered. I don't want to stand in your way if you decide to join the war for our freedom."

"The truth is, Maureen, I can't kill. I could not carry a musket to kill another man, no matter where his loyalties are. There is another reason. At the House of Burgesses, and in the other colonies, we have reached the conclusion that each colony must defend its own borders. If we all go north to join the army, we can't defend against our land becoming battlefields for British troops to invade. Also, there are lurking Indians so our people need us to protect against them. There are other things I can do for the war effort; we'll talk about them as the war progresses." His large hand took her face and held it gently. "Besides, I don't want to leave you; I can't leave you in the clutches of Shamus O'Toole."

"But he comes from a very good family. I'm trying to help Grandmama Abigail show Shamus our side of the war. But he is stubborn; he won't take over the work of O'Toole Plantation because he spends too many hours with the chaps at Hunter Inn. But there is one other thing, maybe something you could help me with. Grandmama needs a new overseer. Charlie is getting too lame with the lumbago to work. Shamus says it's up to Grandmama to hire someone. I thought you might help me find someone for her. When Captain Zachary comes next week, I'm going to the auction block to try to find someone who might be able to be trained for that job. Will you go along with me?"

"You know I will, but please, Maureen, stop seeing him."

"I can't, Bryant; I promised Grandmama I'd help her and I can't let her down. Also, as you know, Papa gave him permission to court me. We're practically pledged. Grandmama and Amanda think the union would be suitable, and delightful."

Bryant draped an arm lightly about her shoulders. Her

senses throbbed with the strength and feel and scent of him. His brilliant blue eyes showed the tortured dullness of disbelief. Cheek muscles stood out on his clenched his jaw. "You can't be serious. How do you feel about it, and him? Do you love Shamus?"

The questions that hung between them unanswered needed a thoughtful answer. All of her loneliness while Bryant was gone and her confusion about him welded together in one upsurge of devouring yearning to his gentle loving look now directed at her. "I don't know for sure how I feel, but I promise to think on it and let you know as soon as I can."

* * * *

As was often his habit, Shamus showed up at the tobacco field where they were planting late in the afternoon. He saw Bryant across the field and approached Maureen who had arrived home from Miss Matilda's school and was properly dressed. "I see you are decent, so let's leave for the Inn to spend time with our friends."

It came as no surprise to see him there. With Shamus, Maureen had come to recognize her own needs and the strong passion within her. *Why,* she thought, *must his every movement remind me of his sexual attractiveness?* Too tired to argue and seeing an opportunity to plead once again with Shamus, Maureen went to the stables and asked Jeb to saddle Little Princess.

Mounted, and riding side by side, Shamus measured her with a cool appraising look. "So," he said, "what excuses and lies did your servant Bryant offer for his absence of the past year?"

"It's really no concern of yours. But he has consented to go with me to the auction block and help me find Grandmama O'Toole an overseer."

Shamus turned to look directly at her. For a long moment she looked back at him. "Will you go along?"

"Why should I? You seem to be in control of the situation."

If Maureen had expected a yes or no, she had underestimated him, again. "Why *are* you here Shamus," she asked. "I thought you are the twin that always wanted to come to America to live with your Grandmama. Now that you are here to run the O'Toole Plantation, you show no interest."

He replied with reckless anger. His cynical voice cut through her. "And what's it to you? I did come and I own the plantation. I don't have to work like a slave. That's your desire, not mine."

Her stomach knotted and she stiffened under his condescending glare. She had reached a point where their relationship had to be resolved. She needed to be alone with her thoughts. "I'm turning back, Shamus. Give our friends my love."

Before he could speak, she wheeled around and without a backward glance, galloped toward home He didn't follow, but yelled after her, "Get rid of Bryant. He's trouble between us. People are beginning to talk."

* * * *

The next morning at breakfast, Maureen said, "We've got to quit seeing each other so much, Bryant. Shamus says people are beginning to talk, and Sabrina told me only yesterday the servants are whispering about us."

"Let them, my dear. In fact, let's give them something to talk about."

His fingers were warm and strong as he grasped hers and a spurt of hungry desire spiraled through her. Her body ached for his touch. She was more shaken than she cared to admit. Bryant said, "We don't have to concern ourselves with rumors and half-truths. I've written my letter to Galway Bay. Could you give it a listen and see if I've left out anything important?"

Maureen wrinkled her nose and inclined her head in a small gesture of agreement. Before he began, he gave her a smile that sent her pulses racing. *Concentrate,* she thought to herself.

Bryant's expression stilled and grew serious.

Dear Postmaster:

I have lost my memory due to a fall from the stern of a ship, the Desiree, that brought me from Dublin, I am told, to America. I am called by the name of Bryant Rory Taylor. Although my memory of the incident and of my family and of my former life has left me, I have had strong dreams and frightening nightmares that I am sure are pieces of my life. I know I am educated. I read well and write. I play the gentleman's game of chess.

I am somewhat certain, due to the reoccurring dreams, that one scene was the smallest island of Aran off the coast of Galway Bay. The others were always of water, which I believe were the waters of the bay. In every dream there is a chap who is calling out to me, calling me Bro. I feel love from the image, but he always disappears in the mist or is behind me so I cannot see his face.

My humble request, Sir, is that you forward this missive to any and all Taylor families in Galway Bay or its county. If indeed I have a brother, and he is able to come to me in October via the Desiree, I will be forever grateful. If he cannot come in person due to financial consideration, please ask him to reply to this letter giving family details that might restore my memory.

I must be completely honest with you, Sir. For reasons that don't make sense, due to my apparent educated state of being, I am at this writing an indentured servant because I arrived with one suit of cheap clothes on my back and no money to pay for my passage in April, 1773. I thank you in advance and will pay you in tobacco once my indenture runs its course, one year hence.

In your debt, sincerely, Bryant Rory Taylor.

"Perfect," Maureen said, but her faint smile held a touch of sadness. "I do so hope, and pray that your letter will bear fruit."

Thinking it was Shamus, coming to apologize once again, Maureen cringed when they heard a rap on the door. "I be gettin' it," Selma said as she hurried to answer.

When she returned, she said, "It be a man called himself Justin Thatcher, Mistress Maureen." He be askin' if Bryant Taylor be about."

Bryant's infectious grin set the tone. "By your leave, Mistress Maureen, please let him enter."

Seeing the change on Bryant's face, she was curious. "Of course, if you say so," she said. "Selma, please bring him in."

Bryant rose to his feet. Maureen looked up to see a small-boned, of medium height, timid young man pause just inside the door. Bryant went to him, slapped him on the back and said, "So what are you doing in these parts, Justin Thatcher?"

He held out a beautiful, long-fingered, and strong looking hand to Bryant. His gray eyes were like silver lightning. His appreciative eyes roamed over Maureen's figure and he gave her a conspiratorial wink and a broad smile. His mood was buoyant. When he spoke, his voice, though deep, was crisp and clear. "I told you, Bryant, that I might take a notion to find the Tucker Plantation and check out your beautiful girl."

Bryant chuckled. "And so you have. It's good to see you. Are you headed north to join the war?"

There was a trace of laughter in Justin's voice. "Nothin' so brave as that. I'm lookin' for work and I thought there might be some around these parts you spoke so highly of."

Bryant grew pensive. "There just might be." Bryant thought Justin might be the answer to Maureen's dilemma for Abigail O'Toole. He found the thought very satisfying.

"What you got in mind, pal?"

Bryant looked over at Maureen as if he were weighing the question, but she was surprised to hear his words echo her own first thoughts. "Our neighbor next, at the O'Toole Plantation, is needing to retire their faithful overseer; he's done his time and is lame with a bad back. The job is tough to learn; the work is hard and the days are long, but the books and the ordering are being taken care of by the granddaughter, Amanda O'Toole. You'd be working with her. Maureen, what do you think?"

She looked at Justin. His sandy-red, unruly hair was ruffled by the breeze. He was an agile, freckled, rugged-looking fellow, plainly dressed in kaki breeches, and a coarse white shirt. She had thought there was something special about him from the first moment he'd entered the room. "I think it is an answer to our prayers. Get your breakfast at the sideboard, Justin. We'll talk a bit, then I'll take you over to meet Grandmama O'Toole. She'll have the final say."

Justin mused on some private thoughts, then grinned at

Bryant, before he blurted out, "Isn't that the plantation the competition owns?"

An unwelcome blush crept into Maureen's cheeks, but Bryant was quick. His touch was reassuring. When he spoke, he was sure of himself and his rightful place in the universe. "For the moment, I'm at a disadvantage, but it will be corrected in due time. When my memory returns, or my indenture runs out, the contest will be over. I'm doing my own courting and I am pursuing my identity."

Justin's gray eyes sparkled, swept over Maureen's face approvingly, "I haven't met this man, Miss, but I'd bet my last wooden nickel on Bryant."

"And a good bet that would be," Bryant countered. His laugh was triumphant. "But what you are going to do with two wooden nickels is beyond my imagination. Why don't you two go on to the O'Toole Plantation. I want to start Tim on the plowing. I'll help get the rest of those seedlings planted, and I will see you, Maureen, in the library after the noon meal. We'll finish the vouchers and plan our trip to meet the *Desiree*."

Chapter 9

Maureen still marveled at the warm cozy feeling of the library that had been her papa's, and now was hers. She had asked Selma to serve her a bowl of turtle soup, a small dish of custard and a chocolate drink. She sat down on the small sofa and reminisced about the morning.

She and Justin had ridden in companionable silence over the rolling, sunlit countryside.

Justin had been well received by Grandmama O'Toole and, in fact, he charmed her. He reached down to take her lined hands in his. "Where have you been all my life?"

Abigail laughed, then countered, "I was old and wrinkly before you were born."

Justin turned to the old dog sitting by Abigail's feet. "And what's the mutt's name?"

"Not a mutt. Can't you see she's a Labrador Retriever? Her name is Joy."

Justin grinned. He reached down to pet her. "Of course, I'm seein'," he commented as if the answer were obvious, and without taking his hand from Joy, he continued, "and I like what I'm seein', but I got to get serious. I'm needin' a job and I understand from Bryant and Maureen that you're needin' an overseer. I'm here to beg for the job."

A few minutes later, Abigail was satisfied. She had been grateful to have the problem solved, and had immediately called Amanda and asked her to work with Justin everyday so he would learn the gist of the ledgers and ordering.

When Amanda had limped into the room, Justin had stopped petting Joy and walked toward her. He took in Amanda's mass of silvery gold ringlets cascading down her back and the loose tresses that softened her face. With his eyes on her, Amanda's cheeks flushed like the flush of an early evening sunset. Her eyes were fixed on Justin as he took in her dainty, petite figure.

Maureen smiled when she recalled his quick response to their introduction.

"And to think, I was just flirtin' with your grandmamma. You *are* beautiful."

Then Abigail called in Charlie and asked him to train Justin. Her voice was gently loving when she told Charlie it was time for him to rest. Charlie hung his head, "What be gonna 'appen to me Mistress O'Toole? I ain't got no place to go, ain't got no kin neither."

Abigail took his big hands in hers and looked into his big black eyes. "You are going to stay right here with us. You can sit in that big old rocker of yours and tell stories to the little ones. They will love you for it and so will their mamas. And I'll just bet Justin will be asking you questions for a long time. And on days when you're feeling able, he will find something for you to do, as will old Henry in the stables. You don't go worrying any more. You will live here until the Master calls you home."

Charlie looked mollified. He managed a faint grin. "I be

thankin' you ever day, Mistress."

"You and Justin go get to work now. He's got much to learn from you."

* * * *

Maureen ate her lunch and, too restless to begin work, surveyed the room with a new interest. On an outside wall was one of the mansion's four fireplaces. At its far end stood the iron poker loggerhead. A fire of cedar logs laid directly on the square stones of the hearth blazed, taking the chill from the crisp spring day. The pungent odor reminded Maureen of walking through a forest in summertime.

Across the chimney was a thick heavy oak mantel, an unlighted candle in a silver candlestick on each end. Displayed across the mantel, and on bookcases that covered the rest of the wall and reached the high-beamed ceilings, were curios from foreign lands. Patrick had acquired the mementos from sea captains of his acquaintance. Maureen gingerly picked up the shrunken head of an African savage. It had been her papa's favorite.

"A ghastly relic," Maureen said aloud.

With a shudder, she set it back and looked over the rest of the collection—several small figures of carved wood, a ceramic Buddha, a leather flask from Spain, a gold and silver goblet from France and chinaware on which festive scenes were painted.

A bamboo chair from Jamaica and an oriental flowered screen had been placed in one corner. Facing it all was a sofa covered with bright flowery splotches of designs. Maureen turned to the soft mohair chair facing the center of a second wall and a large double window where she often relaxed. Her window view included the spacious, sprawling barns to which the tobacco leaf was taken to dry. It overlooked the creek running into the York River, and the Tucker Plantation dock.

Alongside the creek were the plantation sawmill, the brickyard, a distillery in which peach brandy was the specialty and a carpenter shop where the cabinet and coffin making took place.

She walked to the tall narrow mahogany desk at which she worked. Its narrow writing surface was hardly wide enough for two sheets of paper. The upright portion rose to the height of about six feet with glass doors and several shelves for papers and books. The drawers in the lower part of the desk were locked.

From a recess on the same level as the writing surface, Maureen picked out a container of ink and filled the ornate inkwell. She selected a goose-quill pen from an adjacent cubbyhole and a silver shaker of fine sand for blotting freshly written sheets of paper. But abruptly she replaced the writing tools and walked to the center of the room. *I really should move my things to Papa's larger desk,* she thought.

She ran her fingers over the small round, finely polished mahogany table and impatiently removed the six candles from the large candelabrum in the table's center. She replaced them with newly-molded tapers.

Patrick Maguire's bowl of long-stemmed pipes, a silver tobacco box and a flint-and-steel still lay where he had left them. Maureen picked up the fire-maker that he had used for lighting a pipe when the candles were not yet lit, and there was no fire on the hearth. She cocked the hammer, pulled the trigger, and let the spark it created fall into the little metal box filled with fine wood shavings. Her soft, tiny hands gently cradled Patrick's favorite pipe. She thought, *How many evenings*

Indentured Love

I watched him transfer the burning shavings to the bowl of his pipe. While he and Bryant smoked together, each studied the board as his opponent moved the elaborate chessmen —belonging to a set that Captain Zachary's Father had brought Papa from India.

She moved away from the table and sat on the sofa to wonder yet again how a poor indentured servant had made such an impression on her papa. And how had this man, obviously a criminal, learned to play the gentleman's game. *Papa said I would know what to do, but what did he mean?* Maureen wondered. *Maybe I should have Bryant teach me to play chess,* Maureen thought.

Confused, she shook her head, stood up and walked to the bookshelves where Aphra Behn's novel, *The Nun* and Bunyan's *Pilgrim's Progress* were prominently displayed. Maureen smiled and thought, *Papa's favorite book of all was Jonathan Swift's Gulliver's Travels.* A character in Gulliver's Travels gave it for his opinion that "whoever could make two ears of corn, or two blades of grass, to grow upon a spot of ground where only one grew before, would deserve better of mankind, and do more essential service to his country, than the whole race of politicians put together."

"Captain Lemuel Gulliver of Milton, Massachusetts," Patrick loved to tell Maureen over and over, "was a most prolific teller of queer yarns. I am told that this redoubtable captain was a native of Ireland and took delight in astonishing his listeners with accounts of the monsters he had seen, and his hairbreadth escapes. His friends did not take him seriously, but humorously, and asked him to talk at numerous drinking parties. Captain Gulliver returned to Ireland in 1723 and met one Jonathan Swift. Gulliver told him the stories of frogs so large that they reached to a man's knees and had musical voices that sounded like guitars; of mosquitoes with bills as long as darning needles; and of grass that grew as high as a house and was so tough that it could not be cut. It is believed that his tales inspired Swift to write this book."

Maureen ran her finger across the rest of the books as she scanned them. Her Papa had often poured over the four law books and her mother had used the medical texts to treat the plantation sick. Maureen sighed. Much as she had loved her beautiful, delicate mother, she cared nothing for the life she lived. Kathleen Maguire was ecstatic when Sabrina showed interest in her work and before she died she had taught Sabrina almost as much as she knew about the treatments of diseases.

Other books on the shelves were handbooks on agriculture, building, hunting, fishing, horses and horsemanship, gardening and raising silk worms. Maureen then skimmed over titles by Homer, Horace, Shakespeare, Milton, and Pope, her papa's favorite poets. Plutarch, Bacon, and Aristotle were his philosophers. Maureen recalled that he knew their teachings and tried to pattern himself on them. He was also keen on Nathaniel Ames' almanac, and Ben Franklin's, *Poor Richard's Almanac*. Maureen opened the small volume at random and read, "Where there's marriage without love, there will be love without marriage."

Papa told me to marry for love. He said I must wait for the wisdom that I would be as happy as he and mother, but how does one know?

As Maureen placed the book back on the shelf, she heard the faint squeak of the library door. She swung around to face Bryant and watched his eyes search her face. They seemed to reach into her thoughts while at the same time bathing her in admiration. He closed the door quietly behind him and bolted the lock.

Maureen felt a pulse beat and swell at the base of her throat as if her heart had risen from its usual place. She moved toward Bryant driven involuntarily by her own passion, but stopped a few yards in front of him. She fought the dynamic vitality he exuded. "I can't let you... make love to me, Bryant. I don't know anything about you. As far as I know you are a criminal who tried to escape indenture. I don't know your crime—before."

She stood silently as he moved toward her. It was like a bad dream. She tried to step back, but her body wouldn't respond. He took charge with quiet assurance. "Shush, my love. I won't hurt you, or embarrass you. Trust your instincts. You know you love me. I won't be an indentured servant forever."

"But you tell me nothing."

"No. I can't yet." A momentary look of discomfort mixed with confusion crossed his face. "Soon, I hope. But that has nothing to do with our love. Come. Let me hold you."

Maureen felt the magnetism of his smile as two deep dimples appeared in his cheeks. She watched the glow spread to his eyes until they contained a sensuous flame. It made him look even younger than his years, which she figured to be in the late twenties. When she asked him, he had changed the subject. Of course he couldn't know. Nervously she moistened her dry lips, but his tawny eyebrows arched mischievously. "Come," he said again, "I won't harm you."

Bryant did not move, but held out his arms with an open invitation. Her vow shattered. She lowered her eyes so he couldn't guess the love in her heart. Maureen had pondered the wonderment of desire since she first glimpsed Shamus and then Bryant at the docks three years before. She had only recently begun to recognize the strong passion within and it was her own driving need that startled her most. She couldn't resist another look at him. She knew he had not taken his eyes off of her. His gaze was as soft as a caress.

As if sleepwalking, Maureen moved into the circle of his arms. Bryant cradled her gently, rocking her back and forth, then picked her up and carried her to the sofa in front of the fireplace. He gently laid her down and sat on its edge beside her. His mouth covered hers hungrily, sending new spirals of ecstasy through her. Then his lips left hers to nibble at her earlobe; they seared a path down her neck and shoulders. She was hypnotized by his touch, but dismayed at the magnitude of her own eager response to the brush of his lips as he continued to explore her soft warm flesh.

Burying her face in his neck, she breathed a kiss there before he recaptured her lips, more demanding this time, but still surprisingly gentle. Bryant turned Maureen slightly away from him. She did not protest when his hands sought the tiny buttons down the back of her dress. He slid the gown off her shoulders, down her arms. His hands explored the soft lines at her waist and hips. She closed her eyes. Aroused, she drew herself closer to him. His tongue explored the rosy peaks of her breasts. Her nipples firmed instantly under his touch.

Bryant slipped the chemise off. Then lifting her lightly, he eased it downward past her thighs and gathered her against his warm pulsing body, but abruptly left her. Maureen's eyes popped open as a soft gasp escaped her. She watched fascinated while he pulled his shirt up over his head, untied the rope at the waist of his breeches, then pushed them to the floor and stepped free of them. "Another of the many differences between Shamus and me, Mistress Maureen," he said.

"I'm a gentle, patient lover."

"Shamus has never—"

"I know, but he will. He will want his women practiced."

"Are you going to be my teacher?" she asked.

His eyes captured hers—drank her up. "Yes, my love, I'm going to be your teacher, but for me—not for him."

Maureen's felt her smile fade as she lifted her arms to cover her breasts. "Grandfather Tucker was generous to allow you to oversee the plantation, but he expects that I will marry Shamus."

Bryant's hand smoothed stray tendrils of hair away from her cheek and brushed the reddish-gold curls back from her ear. An easy smile played at the corners of his mouth and Maureen felt her body smolder with craving as Bryant knelt above her. "Oh what are we to do, Bryant? This seems so right and yet so wrong."

In a deep, husky whisper his voice echoed her own longings. "It's not wrong for us to love each other. I'll be free in a year; then I'll court you properly, but we can't deny ourselves for all those months. It's British to want a marriage in order to merge lands, but this is America. Here in the colonies we will eventually cut through that caste, class system."

His lips burned on hers; his fingers flamed where they touched her skin. His kiss stirred to life torrents of desire that raced through her. There was no will left in her to resist. Parting her lips, she raised herself to meet him; his tongue explored the recesses of her mouth. His hand lightly touched her hardening nipples—almost unbearable in its tenderness. He moved over her, leaned forward and clasped her body tightly to mold her soft curves to the contours of his lean body. Crushed in his embrace, she gasped as her breasts met the hardness of his chest and melted into the thick mat of golden hair.

Slowly his hands moved downward, skimming either side of her body to her thighs. They explored her thighs then moved up to her taut stomach. In a corner of her mind Maureen felt the warmth of the fire flickering and heard the ticking of the sweet-scented cedar log burning in the fireplace. She closed her eyes, realizing her own hands were caressing the length of his back. Instinctively, her body squirmed beneath him, arched toward him. The moist tip of her tongue crept into his mouth. She could feel the healthy physical craving soaring full to the surface and knew he could feel her wanting intensifying in waves.

A pounding at the door pierced their senses. A groan escaped Bryant's lips as he pulled away and rolled to the floor. "Double drat!" he said under his breath as he reached for his breeches and shirt. "Who's there?" he demanded in a loud voice directed towards the door.

"It be Miz Sabrina," came Phoebe's timid voice from the other side of the door. "Jeb, he see her be snatch by injun."

"I'm on my way. You come in here and take care of Miss Maureen."

Maureen and Bryant stared at each other across a sudden ringing silence. A smile trembled on her lips, as she felt the heat stealing into her face. "You can't leave me undressed. Here, I've done everything but button up the back. Please, Bryant, there's enough talk."

Bryant fastened the buttons quickly, then turned her around, and touched her cheek in a wistful gesture. "Soon, my love..."

In three strides he was at the door. "Ride over to get

Shamus. Tell him I'm heading up towards the Pamunkey River. I'll take Joshua with me. You take Jeb with you…promise me you won't go anywhere, not *anywhere*, without Jeb."

Maureen hungered from the memory of his mouth on hers. She fought feelings of irritation and frustration. In no mood for games, she knew she snapped, "I'm going *with you!* Jeb can get Shamus. Let's hurry. Oh, poor Sabrina. Phoebe will give me a hand getting into my riding habit. I'll meet you at the stables."

He gave her a brutal, unfriendly stare. "This is no job for a *lady,* if that's what you are. I asked you to get Shamus. In case you have forgotten, there are Indians out there. Now, do you promise to stay close to Jeb, or do I tie you to the bedpost in your room?" His glare burned through her.

She bit down hard on her lower lip. "You don't have to get nasty. I'll go with Jeb for Shamus. Please hurry to find Sabrina."

Maureen heard the impatience and determination in his voice. "If she's alive, I'll find her."

Fear and anger knotted inside her. Despite her anger she struggled with an overwhelming need to be close to him. "Be careful, Bryant. They're savages—beasts."

She saw a flash of tenderness in his eyes before he turned away abruptly. She found herself wishing that the prolonged anticipation were not so unbearable. He unbolted the door, disappeared. At the same time Phoebe slipped into the room.

Chapter 10

"Phoebe, what are you doing here?"

"Jeb, he send me. I's be helpin' you lak mis'er Bryant tole me if'n ye be wantin' me."

"Hurry, then. Go tell Emmie to pack provisions—food, flint, a couple of extra blankets. Ask Jeb to saddle Little Princess, and Chester for himself, and a pack horse. Then come upstairs and help me into my riding habit."

Maureen had grabbed her riding habit and put on the pale green waist. She was struggling into the long, clinging forest green skirt when Phoebe appeared at her side. "Let me be doin' tha', Miz."

Phoebe deftly straightened the skirt and fastened it. Then she handed the matching cloak around Maureen's shoulders, clipped the fastener at her throat and started to place the tight-fitting cap over Maureen's disheveled curls. Stopping in mid action, Phoebe spoke eagerly, "Ye wants me to smooth tha' hair some 'fore I puts the hat ober the top?" She lowered her eyes, but not before Maureen saw amusement flicker in them.

She was angry at herself for being embarrassed, but her face burned as she remembered the flame of passion that had ignited within herself and Bryant. "Phoebe, can you be discreet?"

"Wha' be descreet, Miz Maureen?"

"I have Minnie, but Sabrina needs someone to help her—someone who will not carry stories to the rest of the servants about either of us. Do you understand?"

"Yez, um, ma'am. If tha' be descreet, I no lak carryin' tales to them nosy fiel' han's or them uppity white domestics, *no how*."

"That's good enough for me. When I return home, I'll see about bringing you inside the big house. Now smooth my hair. I must hurry over to the O'Toole Plantation to ask Shamus to help with Sabrina's search."

Maureen watched Phoebe's ebony black eyes sparkle in the mirror as she deftly put her mistress's reddish gold curls back in place. *We can trust her*, she thought, *she'll do just fine.*

Stopping in the kitchen, Maureen took the basket from Emmie and ran to the large horse barn. Jeb was waiting. He took the heavy bundle and quickly loaded the backpack on the extra horse. He helped Maureen mount Little Princess before he climbed on the back of Chester.

The O'Toole and Tucker plantations ran together. As one approached the tidewater outside of Williamsburg, the woods gave way to great fields of tobacco. In season they were alive and glowing with the yellow-green leaves.

This quiet road that ran from Williamsburg to the northern counties was fairly well-traveled. Following the York River, it meandered to the northwest and the Pamunkey River road. Maureen burst into a gallop as her thoughts focused on the disappearance of Sabrina and the Pamunkey Tribe. Despite their usually gentle ways, some of the Indians were still bitter.

At her side in an instant, Jeb broke into her thoughts. "Ye better be payin' attention, Miz Maureen. Could be dangerous sittin' side-saddle on Little Princess. Frisky she is, bein' you don't be ridin' her ever day. Thet pure white filly truly do need mor' exercise, Miz. "

"I know, Jeb. I'll try to get her out a little more often, but I love the walk to Miss Lawrence's school, and we've got to teach Sabrina to ride; I'll get her a horse of her own soon."

Looking up at the new green arch of flowering dogwood trees, Maureen spoke to Jeb in an awed voice. "Look at the budding spring leaves. They have the clean, smooth freshness of youth, as yet unspoilt by dust or decay." Abruptly changing the subject, she said, "Do you think Bryant will find Sabrina before dark?"

"If'n he don' be findin' her afore dark, he can be stayin' the night at Stegg's Inn."

"I've never been that far north."

"The Stegg's is inside de woods at the side of a road dat runs down to de ferry on de Pamunkey River. Bryant, he won't be thinkin' to git on dat battered flat-bottom scow till firs' light. An'way, I don' be rememberin' dat big Ben be runnin' the ferryboa' 'ceptin' a' dawn an' agin af'er de midday meal."

Maureen patted Little Princess and settled back to enjoy the ride, quiet except for the piping of the birds and the clopping of the horses' hooves on the hard dirt road. She looked into the distance where the O'Toole manor sprawled across the horizon. It was like her own; built of dark red brick. The front steps led up to a terrace that ran across the front of the house. Grandfather Tucker had explained that all of the houses in the early Eighteenth Century were built with the same red brick and in much the same manner as these two.

"I was a wee lad," he said, "when father built the Tucker mansion and William O'Toole's brother built his manor. In a strange land, they struggled for survival together and helped each other."

The striking features of them, she thought now, *are the twin chimneys, one at each end of the house, and the imposing door frame of white marble.* She remembered Sabrina's violent reaction the day she arrived at the Tucker manor. "I canna go to the inside of that huge house, Miz Maureen."

"But why ever not, Sabrina?" she'd asked.

"Me mum work in a gran' house. She say it be not comfortable."

"You will learn to be comfortable." Maureen smiled as she recalled Sabrina's learning, then sobered when she remembered her mission. She looked up. Shamus and his cousin, Amanda O'Toole, stood side by side on the veranda watching them approach. *Shamus's features are so perfect, so symmetrical, that any more delicacy would have made him too beautiful for a man*, Maureen thought, not for the first time.

* * * *

Beside him, Amanda waved at them. They were too far away to see her small crippled leg, or make out the delicately carved facial bones and full smiling mouth, but her silvery-golden hair gleamed in the sunlight. Shamus called out across the terrace. "Hi yo! To what do we attribute the honor of this unexpected visit?"

Close enough now to see his blue eyes pierce the distance between them, Maureen saw pleasure soften his handsome reserved face. His steady gaze bore into her and the double meaning was obvious. Ignoring the bold stare, Maureen jumped down unaided from Little Princess and rushed to her childhood friend. "Oh, Amanda, I'm so scared. They have taken Sabrina. Bryant went to find her."

Remembering it was Shamus she had come to find, she turned back to him. "Hold it, Maureen," he said, "Calm down."

He put his arm around her waist in a possessive gesture. "Who took Sabrina? Where did Bryant go to search for her?"

"Indians." Maureen tried to pull away, but Shamus tightened his hold. He pulled her roughly, almost violently to him. She wrenched herself away and glared at him, eyes burning.

Maureen's heart squeezed in anguish as she realized she could feel the compelling, potent magnetism that made him so sure of himself. She was by no means blind to his attraction; in fact, was strangely flattered by his intense attention. Tormented by confusing emotions, she stiffened, momentarily abashed. "Shamus, for heaven's sake, act like a gentleman. It's bad enough that we need to make the most haste, but there are others around."

Ignoring Amanda, he crushed her to him and pressed his mouth to hers. He stepped back and looked her over seductively. Alarm and anger rippled along her spine. Struggling free, she faced him furiously. "Shamus, what's gotten into you? Bryant needs your help."

She hated the cold, lashing tone in Shamus's voice. "Be sensible, Maureen. I'm not going to chase after Indians. They're dangerous. Sabrina is merely an indentured servant. Bryant, too. I'm late with the planting. You know it's time to get the tobacco planted. I'm a busy man."

His eyes and voice softened, "I love it when your green

eyes blaze. Did you remember the Custis dance is Saturday? You'll be going with me, won't you?"

Furry almost choked her. "You talk about dances and tobacco. Sabrina is missing. What's the matter with you? You've never cared for the planting or anything else around here; Justin and Charlie will do the work here. And I *was* planning to attend the dance, but now I'm not certain."

Amanda, her face paled with anger, joined the couple. She looked up at her cousin. "Shamus, you can't be serious. You wouldn't let Bryant go out there alone. The two of you can protect each other."

"Mind your own business, my dear cousin," he replied with a contempt that forbade any further argument.

As one the girls turned toward the house, but Maureen remembered Jeb before she entered the house. Panic rose in her throat, but after a pause long enough to gain a fragile measure of self-control, Maureen spoke. She heard a light bitterness in her voice. "Have Little Princess saddled and waiting for me at the back stoop."

Tossing her hair across her shoulders in a gesture of defiance, Maureen lifted her chin and met Shamus's icy gaze straight on. He waited, challenging her to speak, but she swallowed hard and squared her shoulders as she brushed past him. Amanda held the door open for her to go inside ahead of her. "Why did you ask Jeb to saddle the Princess? What in the world are you thinking of?"

Maureen stood motionless in the middle of the room. "Amanda, I've got to go to him."

"To Bryant? You're out of your mind."

"Come on, Amanda, you must see that he needs help—someone to help watch out for signs of Indians, or Sabrina. He will get exhausted alone; it's dangerous. Two of us can work together. Besides...oh, Amanda, I think I love him."

"You can't. Bryant's a criminal. Anyway, you are practically promised to Shamus."

Maureen looked into her friend's rounded blue eyes, then dropped her head. "I know, but I can't help what's in my heart." She turned away and headed for the stairway. "Right now I haven't time to think about it. I need breeches and a shirt. I can't ride out dressed like this. Please, Amanda, give me one of your papa's outfits."

Limping, Amanda followed Maureen up the stairs. "You're serious, aren't you?"

"Never more serious in my life." She looked back at her friend.

In Amanda's bedroom, Maureen slowly began to remove her riding habit as she watched Amanda pace from the bed to the fireplace, and back, then squeal as if hugging some wonderful secret to herself.

"Whatever are you thinking, Amanda?"

"I have it." Her words tumbled over themselves. "You're about the size of Henry. I'll ask him to get his extra suit of clothes and find you a coonskin cap. You can hide that brilliant hair. You'll look like an innocent boy—an indentured servant on an errand."

Maureen watched Amanda's expression change to one of deep concern. She said, "Oh, Maureen, I'm afraid for you. What if something happens to you like it did to Sabrina? I'll never forgive myself for helping you."

"Forget it, my friend. I'm going with or without your help. I'll tell you all about it at the dance."

An hour later, standing beside Little Princess, Maureen

threw her arms around her friend and confidant. She looked down at the square-toed shoes and giggled. "Just call me Sir Lancelot. I'm off to save my friends."

Maureen saw Amanda's eyes glisten with unshed tears. "I wish I could go along or that Shamus were going instead. Be careful, Maureen."

She gathered Amanda into her arms and hugged her tightly. "It's all right. Really." She looked toward the big barn. No one was in sight. "Tell Jeb to go back to the plantation. I'll be at Stegg's Place before nightfall and Bryant will be there. I'll be safe."

With a half-salute she mounted up and galloped off toward the northwest.

* * * *

Lost.

Maureen gasped, realizing a shiver of panic. Out of Amanda's sight, she had circled around the back of the fields and returned to the O'Toole Plantation stable to exchange Little Princess for Amanda's bay roan. She decided the exchange of horses was far more suitable for the young boy she pretended to be.

Little Princess might be recognized, or the brilliant white might draw attention to me, she thought as she selected the small roan called Gwynne. She stripped the packhorse, put the supplies in two burlap bags, saddled up to ride astride and was back on the road within minutes. She had traveled for an hour or more before the sun suddenly slid behind a black cloud. When a light drizzle threatened to blur her vision, Maureen lowered her head against it. A slow, moist heavy coldness sank inside of her.

The hours dragged by. The road in front thinned to a trail

and disappeared altogether into a deep woods as the monstrous darkness approached. Maureen continued to watch for tracks, or a lane leading toward the river, but they eluded her. No sign of Stegg's Inn.

She backtracked. Birds and insects fell silent. She shivered and searched anxiously for signs of life in the desolate unmovable background as full darkness settled in. A screech owl pierced the silence and the roan stumbled just as Maureen made out the shape of a hut straight ahead.

She dismounted and tethered the horse at a nearby tree. The persistent rain pelted steadily now. She reached up to find some of her hair had escaped from the coonskin cap. Droplets that perched momentarily on the fringe trickled down her face. She walked toward the hut, a dome-shape design with a roof of straw and bark thatch. Maureen looked for another horse or any sign of life, but if there had been anyone in the vicinity lately the steady rain had washed the foot prints away.

An animal skin hung over the doorway. The place seemed to be abandoned. As she reached out to lift the skin aside, Maureen felt a momentary dread and her mind jumped on, a crazy mixture of hope and fear. Inside, everything was wrapped in black. Nothing moved.

Maureen called out, softly at first, and then again, but her voice sank into the shanty as into black ash. She went back to Gwynne. She un-strapped the saddle and bags and carried them with the blankets into the hut. *I can't start a fire*, she thought, *but I'll eat a hardtack biscuit and a strip of dried meat. If the sun shines in the morning I'll find my way.*

Setting the provisions just inside the door, Maureen rummaged in the scratchy bags for a candle. But she failed to find a flint to light it in order to explore the inside of the hut.

She ran into wooden crates and fell over something soft and furry. A terrified squeak emitted from her throat until she realized it was a pile of furs.

Getting her bearings once again, Maureen finished eating a small portion of the food. Then she spread furs on the hard-swept dirt floor in a small space between the hut's wares and the outside wall. She laid a blanket on top and rolled up in it to try to sleep.

Her stomach was clenched tight. She tossed. The fact she had found a trapper's hut or a trader's stash was far from comforting. Trappers and traders were a rough, tough group of men and sometimes Indians stored bounty in these huts. Maureen felt numb with fear. Sleep wouldn't come.

She wished Brian or Shamus was with her. *But who would disturb me tonight,* she thought, as her muscles began to relax. *I'll wake up early and can be gone from here before anyone comes this way.*

Maureen smelled a spicy fragrance in the damp air and listened to the hum of the rain, gently now, invading the thatch. She summoned up the memory of her first encounter with Bryant after he joined the servants at Tucker Plantation. They were picking the threadlike tobacco worms on opposite sides of the rows. She had found him vaguely disturbing, as his eyes seemed to probe into her very soul. He said, "I can't picture you spending your life growing tobacco, Miss. Shouldn't you be doing the spinning or…"

She smiled when she recalled her answer that she was her papa's girl and had always followed him through the planting season. Maureen felt the drowsiness steal over her before she finished the cherished memory of his tender concern and she drifted into a dreamless sleep.

* * * *

Maureen awoke with a start. She stepped quickly out of the hut to see bright sunlight bobbing through the dense tangle of oak and pine. She tucked her hair into the raccoon cap and hurried through the packing. She mounted Gwynne.

With the blazing sun guiding her, they headed northwest. She figured it was mid-morning—she had forgotten Patrick's pocket watch—when she spotted Stegg's Inn.

Once inside, Maureen lowered her voice and asked after Bryant. "You missed him, young man. He's searching for a young lady caught up by an Indian. He left before dawn."

"Which direction did he take?"

"The ferry took him across the Pumunkey River. It was big Ben who took him," the desk clerk said, pointing to the only other person in the room.

"He was headed west," Ben broke in, "said he had a friend, Chief Sky Bear of the Toyhonka Tribe."

"Thank you, Sir," Maureen said. "Can you take me across?"

"It'll cost you, young man."

Maureen pulled a silver coin from her pocket. "Will this be enough?"

Ben's eyes lit up. "I reckon so. Are ye havin' a bit of dinner?"

"Oh, no; please, can we be on our way?" Ben stood up and led the way.

Once across the river, Maureen headed west.

Chapter 11

Bryant and Ebony entered Chief Sky Bear's camp at noon on the third day. "Welcome," the Chief greeted him. "Pleasure, mine."

"I've come for help," Bryant finally got across to the Chief.

Chief Sky Bear was dressed in deerskin. His hair, long, straight and loose was held by a headband. His face was painted black around his eyes, red cheeks and a slash of red across his forehead. He shrugged his shoulders. "What help?"

"A beautiful," he motioned slim curves, "hair black like squaw. Missing!"

"Ah, I know. She be with my squaw, Little Flower, teepee."

"I thought you friendly. Where did she come from?"

"Brave Kit Dog, bitter; he want white squaw."

"Did he harm her?"

"No harm. Brave Crow Fox protect as they come home to tribe. Kit Dog a mean one. I take you young white squaw to Little Flower."

"May I see her?"

"Little Flower," Chief Sky Bear called out in his own language, "bring white squaw."

Bryant ran to meet the trembling Sabrina. "Have you been hurt?" he asked, raising his eyebrows inquiringly.

His words didn't register on her dizzied senses; her eyes darted nervously back and forth. Fear, stark and vivid, glittered in her onyx-black eyes. "N-n no," she stuttered, "but I be so scared. I not know how to get home. Chief Sky Bear say he take me."

She shuddered. Bryant smiled at her as if she were a small child. He moved in an instinctive gesture of comfort and drew her into his arms. "You're safe, now. I won't let anything happen to you."

He turned to the Chief. "We start home. Long trip to Tucker Plantation,"

"No! You stay night," Chief Sky Bear said to Bryant. "Chief Mongoo Rock with fierce Lippian Indians near about. Live in Smoke of the River—how you call? Nomadic? With morning light, I send Eagle Sun and Crow Fox to protect friends."

Little Flower coaxed Sabrina back into the circle of women.

Once again Bryant sat with the Chief and his braves, sharing the peace pipe and eating homily and roast pork. An approaching horse caused a commotion among the tribe's horses during the middle of the hunters' ceremonial dance; the braves would leave in the morning to hunt buffalo and deer.

Standing at the edge of the circle of squaws, Maureen took several moments to let her eyes adjust. She watched the dancing braves, the vivid colors of their faces and feathers. She cast her eyes downward, then blinked and focused her gaze on the Chief. She was able to study him freely, outwardly, until as one, all eyes turned toward her. She froze, mind and body benumbed.

When she spotted Bryant sitting next to Chief Sky Bear, Maureen was unwilling to face him and unable to turn away. Bryant stared at her, baffled. He turned to Chief Sky Bear. "Let me talk to the young man in his own language."

Chief Sky Bear nodded his consent. "Take to teepee of Big Bird; he got two young braves. That one," he said pointing to Maureen, "stay there the night. You think what to do with him. Vicious Indians might harm him if be alone. Great Spirit with him so far."

Bryant approached Maureen and guided her to the back of the teepees where they could talk in private. She turned away, her hands clenched stiffly at her sides. He halted her escape with a firm hand on her arm and turned her around to look directly at her. With a pang, Maureen realized just how angry he was. His vivid blue eyes blazed with anger. He frowned with cold furry, his tone was velvet edged with steel. "What in the name of all that is sane are you doing here?"

Maureen remembered to lower her voice. When she spoke, her voice was deep and dusty, spoken in a broken whisper. "Shamus wouldn't come to help you. I thought you might need help with Sabrina. I followed you here."

His deep voice simmered with barely checked passion, but his tone had a possessive desperation. "Are you aware what could have happened to you? There is a band of angry, vicious nomad Indians lurking in the country you just came through."

Maureen swallowed hard, lifted her chin, and boldly met his eyes. She answered in a rush of words. "I didn't mean to upset you. I just thought…"

"You just *didn't* think!" His words were as cool and clear as spring water, ground out between his teeth.

She met his accusing eyes without flinching. "It's over Bryant. I'm here, but you haven't even told me if Sabrina is all right. Was she harmed? I just glimpsed her, so I know she's here. Please tell me, Bryant."

His eyes didn't leave her face. When he spoke again his voice was warm. "She's very well. She knew raw fear. Kit Dog wanted a white squaw. Seems he followed me home. He waited until no one was near and snatched Sabrina when she was tending the bee hives—stripping the honey. Fortunately, Crow Fox was near by. They had been hunting wild turkey and small game; Crow Fox protected Sabrina 'til he could get her to Chief Sky Bear. Chief's squaw, Little Flower has been taking care of her."

Maureen felt a warm glow flow through her. Tears of joy found their way to her eyes. "When do we leave for home? Captain Zachary will dock the *Desiree* soon. We need to go to the auction to get more help. Grandfather Tucker says…"

Bryant's glance was bemused. His mouth curved with tenderness. "Whoa, my dear. We have to get you out of this mess first. Chief Sky Bear told me to talk to you—to tell you how dangerous it is with the Lippian Indians in the vicinity."

Maureen looked out, watching the dark come on as night swooped over the tipi village. "Can you tell him I'm going back with you and Sabrina in the morning?"

"Yes, of course, but I think it's important that you travel as the boy who came into camp. You are to sleep in Big Bird's teepee; he has two young braves about your age, the age you look." Bryant grinned. "We'd better join the others."

Maureen shivered with chill and fatigue. "Do you think I

could get a change of clothes from one of the Indian boys? I've had these on for three days."

"Better not chance it. If you undress in front of them, they'll discover you're a girl. We'll be home in a few days; dream of a hot bath and that rose water scent. Come on, my love."

* * * *

The trip to Tucker Plantation was not destined to be uneventful. Crow Fox and Eagle Sun kept watch the first night. Bryant slept fitfully between Sabrina and Maureen. His body ached with wanting Maureen. He mused on private memories—how he was drawn to a height of passion when he held her in his arms; how a deep feeling of peace entered his being when she put her arms around his neck; how her eager response matched his; and how her mouth became softer as he kissed her.

In the morning of the second day, the five moved on. Sabrina rode the better part of the day on Ebony behind Bryant. Maureen followed on Gwynne. Crow Fox and Eagle Sun led, keeping close watch ahead. The sun dipped and rose and, finally disappeared in the misty clouds. Steady rain blew across the rolling plains.

Sabrina, aching and exhausted cried for a break. It was mid-afternoon. "We must stop, Bryant. Please, I cannot go on."

Bryant called for a halt in a grove of sycamores, oaks and pine; a small, spring-fed pond was nearby. They built a fire to brew coffee and heat up the vegetable soup, thick with corn and turkey. Bryant brought water to wash up the cups and the kettle. The braves went off to circle the area.

Bryant said, "Rest now, you two. I will take the watch."

He gazed at Maureen. "Where did you sleep, young man, on your trip west," he said, almost angrily.

She gave him a devilish grin. "The same as you, I reckon; under the stars."

Bryant frowned and sighed heavily, his voice filled with anguish. "Did you not know it was risky?"

"I had my musket beside me. All young men are taught at an early age to shoot to defend themselves and their land. Papa taught me." She looked at Bryant tenderly and said in a low voice, "Did you not know it was dangerous to travel alone?"

Bryant returned her gaze. Blue eyes met emerald green eyes straight on. "I've been too angry to know you followed me. Why didn't you come directly to Stegg's Inn so I could send you packing? I knew where to go for help to find Sabrina."

Shocked comprehension dawned on Sabrina's face. She said, "Now I know why you look so familiar. Maureen?"

"Shush, now. It is better if the braves think I am a young man. Bryant recognized me immediately. What took you so long?"

Sabrina giggled. "You make a fine looking young man, but strands of golden-red hair have slipped from your cap. If you want to keep up the pretense, you best fix it."

"Help me, Sabrina, It's a tangled mess."

While working with her hair, Sabrina asked, "Where did you get the roan? She's not in Tucker's stables."

"I traded Little Princess for Amanda's Gwynne. When we get to auction, Grandfather Tucker told me to buy you a gentle roan and teach you to ride. Jeb can teach you. By fall, we can ride to Miss Matilda's school."

Sabrina's face fell. Her soft voice trembled. "I be scared to learn."

Bryant cut in. "You are doing fine at my back, Sabrina. Tomorrow you can ride in front and I'll give you your first lesson."

A curdling war whoop broke into the conversation. Bryant was on his feet in an instant. "You girls stay put behind that pine tree! Don't move!"

"Trouble," shouted Eagle Sun, "kill fire!"

Maureen poured the kettle of water on the fire, then reached for her musket from the gunnysack and followed Sabrina.

Three large, painted braves were coming over a hill from the north. Bryant crouched low beside Crow Fox. Eagle Sun stepped forward, hand up, and calling to Chief Mongoo Rock. Ignoring him, they raised their loaded bows. Eagle Sun was quicker; he hit one of the Indians, disabling his right arm with an arrow through his shoulder. The other two galloped on toward them.

Weapons ready, Bryant and Crow Fox stood up to meet them. The Chief's bodyguard missed, but Crow Fox caught him in the leg and sent him groaning to the ground. Chief Mongoo Rock aimed at Bryant. Maureen stepped out from behind the tree. Her musket exploded in a wild primitive blast; the bullet hit the Chief square between his eyes. He dropped. His braves, one managing to slump over the back of his steed, and the other holding his wounded shoulder tight to his body, turned tail and retreated.

A pale sun swept through the rain, which was beginning to slack off. "We go on," Eagle Sun said. "We kill Chief. They bring back more braves."

Bryant, with a sense of astonishment, looked at Maureen with unabashed affection. "You saved my life. Are you okay?"

Maureen hugged him impetuously. "I've never killed before, but I couldn't watch you die." There was only room for one man in Maureen's thoughts. "I'll be okay when the shock wears off. It was either you or him."

"We have to go," Bryant said. "We should be at Stegg's Inn before sunset. I'll ride ahead and signal the emergency code for big Ben to come for us. Crow Fox and Eagle Sun, stay with the young man and Sabrina."

* * * *

Amanda was frantic. She pleaded with Shamus. "Please, Shamus, go after Bryant and Maureen. They've bee gone five days. Something terrible may have happened.

"So, you have decided to tell me that Maureen followed him. First you tell me she must have gone to her Grandfather Tucker's. Now you tell me she followed Bryant. What am I to believe?"

"I'm begging you, cousin. You can go to Stegg's Inn. Nathan Stegg will tell you which direction they took."

Shamus frowned with cold fury. He said in a nasty tone, "I would rather see Bryant dead, and I certainly don't know where Stegg's Inn is."

Amanda felt the irritable desperation of hopelessness. Her tone hardened and she retorted tartly. "Don't you care for Maureen either? Don't you care that they might need help? I'll draw you a map." She flung out her hands in despair.

Abigail spoke up. "If you don't go, Shamus, I will personally send you back to Ireland."

Shamus felt like he'd betrayed himself, but he roared, "I'll be damned if I'll go. You, an old lady and Amanda, a cripple, cannot run this plantation. And as you well know, there may be a band of dangerous Indians about. You may need my expertise with a gun."

Abigail bristled. She said, "Do as you please then, but we've been doing fine without you now that we have hired Justin Thatcher as our overseer and all you've been doing is gambling our money and hanging out with the chaps at Hunter Inn."

"Very well. If that's the case, maybe I'll join up with our mother countrymen and help blow this rabble-rousing independence babble to bits. But there is one thing you've forgotten that will keep me here. I plan to marry Maureen. You want that, don't you?"

Abigail wilted. "Yes, Shamus. Professor Tucker is a very dear friend of mine. I would very much like to see you marry Maureen. She is a lovely girl and most likely could help you take care of our plantation."

Shamus felt as if he had won a victory. "So it's settled. I promise I will stay right here until Maureen returns."

* * * *

Crow Fox and Eagle Sun turned back when they arrived at Stegg's Inn. Eagle Sun said, "We go now. When time comes right, we go to war for independent nation."

"Thank you," Bryant said giving each man a hug and a kiss on each cheek. "We will let you know when the war is ready."

Eagle Sun poked Crow Fox in the rib and grinned mischievously at Maureen. "Me bet you beautiful little squaw when hair fall down and you dress like Mart'a Washington."

Maureen took off her coonskin cap and let her tangled hair cascade down her back. Her smile lighted her from the inside. "You knew?"

Eagle Sun smiled back. "Me know. You shoot good, too." The braves mounted their spotted pintos and with a flourish and a wave, rode off in the ever-shifting panorama of sunset.

Bryant got two rooms, one for the girls and another in which he slept alone.

The dream that teased Bryant when he awoke in the morning was not of water. He was walking the long empty corridors of a huge school. The classrooms were vacant. He reached the library where books were lined down both outer walls and down the center; the shelves were stacked to the ceiling, ladders extending to the top in order to access the books. A man behind another stack of books called to him, "Come here, Bro. Look at this!" But before he could find him, the image disappeared.

In the morning, a great ecstasy filled Bryant's chest to bursting. The way he moved toward Maureen, where she and Sabrina were sitting at a table waiting for him to join them for breakfast, carried its own excitement. He announced without preamble, "Maureen, I know where I got my education. It was at Trinity College in Dublin."

"Wonderful! When we get home, you can write to the college also, and find out what years you attended college."

* * * *

Sabrina took turns riding behind Maureen and Bryant. They arrived at O'Toole plantation at teatime. Bryant said, "I'll go on to Tucker Plantation, Maureen. You and Sabrina let Amanda and your Grandmama O'Toole know you are okay. Have tea with them if you wish. Change out your horse. I'll let Minnie know you are coming so she can have your baths ready and I'll check in with you tonight." He gave Maureen a quick, but endearing kiss on the tip of her nose and started off.

Maureen's heart fluttered in her breast. She felt a warmth creep into her cheeks. She touched her nose. "One thing more," she called to Bryant. "Would you tell Phoebe to go to the house to tend me when we get home? I liked what I saw in her when you sent her to me. I promised to bring her into the house. Sabrina will have Mother's Minnie full-time now."

Shamus glowered at Amanda and took Maureen in his arms. "We've been so worried."

In spite of herself the idea of his eagerness excited her. Her feelings for him had nothing to do with reason, so she pulled away from his embrace. "Yes, but not worried enough to go with Bryant to help rescue Sabrina. We could have used your help when the Indians attacked."

Maureen turned then to hug Abigail and Amanda. "I'm sorry I took Gwynne without asking. I thought she would be less conspicuous than Little Princess. I hope it didn't inconvenience you too much."

Amanda curled into her arms. "None at all. Forget that. I've been beside myself with worry. Did you have any problems?"

Sabrina, petting Joy, laughed out loud. "Oh, you should have seen her. For two days, she fooled me into thinking she was a boy. Then she killed Chief Mangoo Rock with one shot between his eyes; saved Bryant's life, she did."

Shamus' eyes darkened. Fanning the flames of his hatred, angry words erupted. "Didn't that good for nothing criminal even try to protect you from those savages?"

His contemptuous tone sparked her anger. Maureen grinned spitefully. "Oh yes, he tried, but I'm hard to protect. I came out from behind that pine tree just in time to see the whole scene. I fired my musket at the perfect moment to save Bryant's life." She added sarcastically, "You could have done that if you had been there."

Shamus' voice was totally disapproving, and possessive, "When we marry, you will put away that gun forever; you *will* act like a lady at all times."

Abigail's wrinkled face creased into a sudden smile. "Seems to me, Shamus, you've met your match."

She turned to Maureen. "I'm proud of you, dear. When I was your age, I, too, could aim a musket. Father taught me, just as your papa taught you. But I'm sure you will grow into a fine lady."

Her tender looked encompassed Amanda, Sabrina, and Maureen, "But for now," she said, "tea is waiting. You, Sabrina and Maureen, need nourishment and a hot bath if you are to become ladies any time soon. Will you join us, Shamus?"

Shamus followed in silence as Abigail led them to the dining room for the tiny tea sandwiches, scones and hot chocolate.

Chapter 12

Shamus escorted the girls home. Bryant and Captain Zachary were waiting for them at the stables.

"Captain!" Sabrina said.

"Call me Zachary," he said as he swept her, weightless, into his arms and gently rocked her back and forth. "I've been absolutely frenzied. I've been here three days. I hope you don't mind, Maureen. Selma put me up so I could await your return. If I'd had any idea where to look, I would have started after you myself."

"I'm so glad you are here. Of course, you may stay with us. Selma did right. Tonight we will have a celebration. Will you join us, Bryant, Shamus?"

Shamus stiffened as if she had struck him. "If you prefer to eat with criminals and servants. Forgive me, Captain, but except for Maureen, you seem to have chosen indentured slaves to cohort with. I will be on my way to Hunter Inn; you are welcome to join me, Maureen."

Maureen dismounted Little Princess. "Enjoy your evening, then, Shamus," she said coolly.

Zachary put Sabrina down with deliberate care. "You two beautiful ladies go to your baths. Bryant and I will be waiting in your office, Maureen." Turning to Bryant, he said, "I understand you play a mean game of chess; could I challenge you to a game while we are waiting?"

Bryant and Maureen gloried briefly in a shared moment, before Bryant answered, "By all means, Zachary. What's in it for the winner?"

Zachary's laugh was an affectionate, rich sound. "Let's leave that up to the girls. Will you buy that?"

Bryant felt a wave of warm gratitude for the friendship with Maureen's Captain Zachary. "With trepidation, I accept."

The homecoming celebration was a gala affair. Bryant had won the chess game, and his prize was an invitation to the girls' Coming Out Party in October. Because Zachary lost, the girls mandated that he be *forced* to attend the event. "How is it the winner gets to go and the loser must go?" Zachary asked in mock confusion.

Sabrina smiled shyly at Zachary. "You are lucky is me guess."

The evening ended in easygoing, sociable laughter.

Maureen, as was her custom, walked Bryant to the door. She said, "I think the Captain and Sabrina are finding each other much to their liking."

Bryant pulled Maureen out into the soft quiet night. Maureen thought night had never smelled as fragrantly sweet as this one. Bryant said, "It will be fascinating to watch their courtship unfold. But enough about them."

He bent and kissed her gently. At last, as they clung to each other in the darkness, her lips parted and he tasted her sweet mouth. When he straightened, he said, "I'm getting closer. We'll soon know who I am. Wait for me, Maureen."

"Hurry, Bryant. We are available to each other on borrowed time. Shamus will ask Grandfather Tucker for my hand straight away after Sabrina and I have our party."

"We'll fight him. I will ask Grandfather Tucker for your hand before the ball. Zachary will be back by then with answers to my letters, maybe even with my brother."

* * * *

A couple of weeks slipped past. Zachary had left the morning after their celebration party. He had taken the letter from Sabrina who was looking at him with open admiration. He proudly beamed back.

"Just think what this letter will mean to your mum and pa. I will deliver it in person. I grew up in Dun Laoghaire, which is near the part of Dublin where your people live."

Zachary picked up a lock of Sabrina's silky jet-black hair and caressed it gently, then boldly moved his mouth over hers and felt the eagerness of her body. Maureen and Bryant saw Sabrina's face flush before Zachary stepped away.

Bryant, Maureen, Sabrina and Justin Thatcher with Amanda rode off to the auction two days later. While Bryant and Justin were selecting their pick of needed slaves, the girls went to the stables. Sabrina said, "I wish Zachary were here to help us decide on a horse."

A soothing voice beside her said, "Your every wish is my command." Zachary winked when he caught her eye.

"How can you be free?" Sabrina asked.

"How can I not? When I saw you all come in, I turned the auction over to my friend and followed you girls over here because I know just the horse for you. Bryant told me you are going to learn to ride."

He turned to Maureen, "By your leave, Maureen, this

chestnut filly is three years old and perfect for a new rider. And she'll *love* Sabrina's gentle ways."

"Thank you, Zachary. Would you make the arrangements? We'll need a side-saddle and...well, you know what we need."

Zachary helped Sabrina off from behind Little Princess and took her to pet the horse. He took a lump of sugar and a carrot from his pocket and said, "Give her the carrot first and when she's finished with that give her the sugar—like this." Zachary guided Sabrina's hand and then together they stroked the softness around the ears of the filly."

"What be her name?" Sabrina asked.

"The owner told me they had always just called her "Filly," so it's time she had a real name. You can name her; she's yours. I will be off now to get the saddle and settle the sale."

When Zachary was gone, Sabrina said to Maureen and Amanda, "Her name is Jingles."

"Jingles? However did you come up with a name like that?"

"In Ireland, me friend's name was Ginger, but she spelled it with a J, she did. Before I could know it, I called her Jinger as in jingle. Me friend laughed so hard tears came into her eyes. But me mum was trying to teach me me letters and she showed me the J and said 'jingles—like coins in Pa's pocked when he be workin' good and we be rich.' So I come to Virginia Colony and you and you folks take me in and love me and that be me riches, and Jingles, me filly, be like coins in me pocket."

Maureen put an arm around Sabrina's waist. "It's you who brought riches into my life. I don't know what I would have done without you when Mother and Papa were sick, and since they've been gone, you have been extra, extra special. And who did you say you are going to marry?"

Sabrina's face colored fiercely, but her eyes shone. "As me recall, Humpty Dumpty."

"And if he has a great fall?"

Amanda couldn't stand it. "What's *this* all about?" she asked.

Sabrina and Maureen burst out giggling. Maureen said, "It's just a silly game we play. I'm going to marry the man in the moon. You may join us. Who are you going to marry, Amanda?"

"I think I'll choose Little Tommy Tucker; then I'll never go hungry because he'll sing for our supper." But, catching on in earnest, she said, "Sabrina, you didn't answer the second question. Who will you marry when Humpty Dumpty has a great fall?"

Maureen watched Sabrina shiver. "I could let you off the answer," she said,

"Oh, no, I don't mind," Sabrina said, recovering her composure, "I'll meet my true love at our Coming Out Ball in October."

"Good answer," Amanda said. "I wish that could happen to me, but I'm crippled and I'll never be attractive enough to catch a man of my dreams."

Maureen reached out and touched her shoulder. "Don't be so sure. I am going to be sure to ask Grandmama O'Toole to invite Justin to our party. Have you seen the tender way Justin looks at you?"

A flash of humor crossed Amanda's face. She said, "That must be typical of overseers looking at their mistresses. I notice Bryant often loves *you* with his eyes."

For a moment, Maureen became lost in magic dreams, but suddenly realized she was thinking with her heart again. "That may be," she said, fighting to keep her voice steady, "but Shamus is courting me for keeps. He's only waiting until after the party to ask Grandfather Tucker for permission to marry me."

Amanda said, "We'll be *real* cousins then; won't that be great?"

Sabrina chimed in. "But can't you refuse him?"

Maureen chided herself for her indecision. "It is a frightening and awesome muddle and I am so very confused. But I have time; I'll work it out. At least you two girls don't have double trouble." Changing the subject abruptly, Maureen asked, "Amanda are you getting tired?

"Yes, very tired, but I don't want to spoil your day."

"You couldn't spoil this day if you tried. Here comes Zachary with Jingles." Maureen turned to him. "Zachary, would you fasten the filly to Little Princess. We girls are going to Hunter Inn for tea and a rest. Would you tell Bryant and Justin we'll be staying for the night, and won't you join us all for dinner?"

Zachary looked directly at Sabrina. His features softened. "We'll be there by seven-thirty for dinner. Thank you, Maureen."

* * * *

Maureen had taken an early morning ride with Shamus on a mid-April day enlivened by a warm breeze and a candy blue sky. She was puzzling over why so many things irked this man who was so strong and powerful looking, and so handsome. He had a plantation and good help, for Justin was doing a marvelous job, and had, at auction, brought a bright young buck to learn from Justin, and help him. But Shamus seemed angry inside.

Shamus and Maureen stopped to tether the horses and walk along the river shore. "So," Shamus said, "I see you are still working with Bryant, and now with two of the new men. What's the deal? Is your white criminal getting so lazy you allow him to hire more help?"

"Come on, Shamus, don't you recall Papa was clever enough with the officials at the government building that they allowed him to acquire an additional twelve thousand acres south of our two plantations? It takes a lot of manpower to farm so much land. Bryant picked up five slaves at auction. Leon and Booker are extra bright; we're teaching them to work with Joshua."

"And where does that leave Bryant—an indentured criminal of leisure?"

"For heaven's sake, Shamus, Bryant will hardly be idle. Besides supervising the whole estate, he will be learning the books, the ordering and the office operations. You should be pleased. This should ease up my workload and give me more time for other things."

With a dazzling leap of logic, Shamus dared to dream of total success. He said, "And when we are married, it will all be ours. You'll have your men trained so that in two years Bryant can be on his way, but I'd be careful, if I were you, not to let him have full access to your business. He is a criminal, after all, and may take advantage of you with that knowledge."

Maureen remembered that she had expressed that same thought to Patrick when he purchased Bryant's papers. "You forget the land is Grandfather Tucker's. If Bryant decides to stay, we will pay him a decent wage. If he decides to leave us, we plan to send him off with two hundred acres and enough tobacco to start it properly."

Maureen had a sense that things were spinning out of control. She looked away to the east where Bryant was now an integral part of her life. The man with the cornflower blue eyes and the errant lock of blonde hair. Bryant was a wonderfully romantic man whom she thought had a proud and honorable soul, and he loved her. A sense of tingling delight began to flow through her.

A gentle touch nudged her out of her musings. She felt his hand brush the hair from her neck. His other hand came down over hers possessively, but amorously. Shamus was an endless surprise. His voice was low and smooth. "We'll see about Bryant when the time comes. Are you dreaming with me?"

He took his hand from hers, turned her toward the south and arched his arm in a full sweep across fresh, green, pastoral land, sun bathed with the prismatic light of spring glory happening. "This will all be mine—" Maureen was aware of the barely controlled excitement coiled in his body. He stopped short. He looked at her and the double meaning of his gaze was obvious. Shamus' voice dropped in volume. "Actually, ours," he finished unapologetically.

He said 'mine', Maureen thought. A terrifying realization washed over her. *He has no intention of working the plantations together. He would own the land after Grandfather Tucker passes because a married woman cannot own land. He would possess all of us: Grandmama O'Toole, Amanda and myself. He plans to get rid of Bryant. I wonder if his twin brother, Sean, will help set him straight.* She wondered if she should confess her doubts to him, and decided yes, she should and would.

Aloud, she said, "As a matter of fact, no Shamus, I am *not* dreaming with you. I know your dreams and I'm trying hard to dream with you, but I haven't decided for sure to marry you. I think all God's people have dreams. I know Sabrina does, and Amanda does. I have my own dreams and somehow they are not quite compatible with yours."

Suddenly, she wondered if she should feel some guilt for the relief she felt for saying those things to Shamus, and wondered just what she wanted from him. If she married him, it was certain she could be good for Amanda and Grandmama O'Toole. She could continue to do the office work for the Tucker Plantation. As far as that goes, she thought, she and Amanda could work together to merge the Tucker-O'Toole land.

This time her thoughts were interrupted by a very angry male voice. A sudden icy contempt flashed in Shamus' eyes. He snarled, "Believe me, you *will* marry me—no one, not even your Grandfather Tucker will deny me. If we don't have his permission, I will carry you off to be wed in Philadelphia or New York. Oh, what fun that would be."

Now his eyes sparkled and blazed down into hers. The smoldering flame she saw there startled her, gnawed away at her as a flicker of apprehension coursed through her. Nervously biting her lip, she looked away. She was actually trembling as he pulled her roughly, almost violently, to him and clasped her body tightly to his, molding to the contours of his lean body. He was as eager and erratic as a summer storm. He whispered in her ear, "Don't you know I love you?"

Maureen took a deep breath and tried to relax. A warning voice stealthily entered her brain. In truth, every fiber in her body warned her against him. She was suddenly anxious to escape from his disturbing presence.

Struggling free, she said quietly, "We need to talk more about our dreams; about the war and how the differences of our positions might affect a marriage; and about the way we are going to merge our plantations to make it fair to both of us; and more. But for now, I must get back to Tucker. I have work to do."

"All right, my love," Shamus said calmly, as they walked back to Little Princess and Black Warrior. "Let's get this war thing settled. Listen carefully because I've said this before and I don't want to repeat it ever again. Why in God's name would the congress send delegates to France before you folks are a confederation? It's absolutely insane to think France would fight on the side of the rebels..."

"Wait a minute, Shamus. Since we have declared British taxes not applicable to our interests and are exporting and importing our products to avoid those taxes, France is one of those countries, as is Holland..."

"Enough!" Shamus said. "Won't the colonies look ridiculous asking Europe's heads of state to support a union that doesn't even exist? If the colonies throw out Parliamentary supremacy, they will form kingdoms like England and Scotland."

Maureen sensed an odd twinge of disappointment. "Shamus, you are far behind the times. We did that a couple of years ago and in that relationship, we are able to mutually support and protect each other. We submit that Parliament has *no* authority whatever in the colonies. You really should read up on where we are."

Ignoring her suggestion, Shamus said irritably, "Well, it's

Indentured Love

not very smart to declare independence before you know you can achieve it. And, if you're all so smart, why would you warn Britain of America's intentions."

"It's obvious we're not going to agree about this today, but I would remind you that your Grandmama O'Toole and Amanda are hoping for our independence. And even your twin brother Sean told you in his letter that he is pulling for the American colonies."

"You are *all* wrong. Sean has no business trying to tell us how to think. I plan to be on the side of the winners. What's that?"

Looking ahead where Shamus pointed, Maureen said excitedly, "It's Grandfather Tucker's coach."

As she waved a farewell to Shamus, She spurred Little Princess to a gallop.

Maureen left Little Princess with Jeb and fairly ran to the house and to the office where Selma said he was, to throw her arms around her grandfather. She stopped short. With him, sitting on the brightly flowered sofa, were Nathan Custis and Grover Harrison. James Tucker's voice was gentle. "We need to talk to you about something serious that will affect us all."

Maureen shook the men's hands and welcomed them warmly, then spoke to Grandfather Tucker, "Would it be all right if I asked Emmie to fix us up some dinner, and then change out of this riding habit?"

"Of course, my dear, but you are a vision of loveliness for old eyes, no matter what you are wearing. Take your time; we are not in a hurry, but do you think we could ask Bryant in for the midday meal. What we have to tell you will also affect him."

"Certainly. I'll send Phoebe to fetch him, and I won't be

long, I promise."

Maureen appeared a few minutes later dressed in a forest green morning dress; the ruffles of the collar and sleeves, and the bodice and petticoat were of a pale moss green.

Bryant stood first, tall and straight *like a towering spruce,* Maureen thought. When blue eyes met hers, Bryant's captured and clung to hers. "You look lovely, Mistress Maureen."

Her smile was alive with amusement as she gave him a teasing half curtsey. "Thank you, kind sir."

Grandfather Tucker put his arm around her waist. "Selma announced that our vittles are ready whenever you wish. Shall we go?"

When the simple meal of vegetable soup, baked fish, and the dessert of stewed fruit mixed with custard, was set before them, Maureen asked, "Will you tell us the nature of your business, or must we wait in curious anticipation?"

"Enjoy your meal, my dear," Grandfather Tucker said. "We will tell you in a short while when we retire to the office."

Chapter 13

"Now, Grandfather, you've got to tell me what's going on."

The group was seated comfortably in Maureen's office. She sat behind the desk. Nathan Custis and Grover Harrison sat on the sofa and each lit up a cigar. Bryant had laid and started a fire in the fireplace. He and James Tucker, wielding pipes, sat in the two comfortable chairs by the window.

"I'm going to let Nathan begin, my dear. Keep in mind that we are all members of the House of Burgesses and have been appointed the delegates to the Continental Congress, which starts May 15. You may start, Nathan."

"The three of us have decided we want Bryant to go with us and take notes…"

Grover broke in, "There is a meeting of the House of Burgesses before the Congress meets. That is barely enough time to get him ready, although we think he could stay at the plantation, at least part time, for the next couple of weeks."

Nathan continued, "After the House ends their session, we will set off immediately to Philadelphia to do our work with the Congress."

As Bryant's and Maureen's eyes met, she felt shock run

through her. Her faint smile held a touch of sadness.

James' bushy white brows drew together in an agonized expression and quirked inquiringly. He offered Maureen a smile that pleaded for forgiveness. "There are many things that need to be settled before Bryant can accompany us," he said.

Nathan turned to Bryant. His hawk-like features were arresting and elegant. He sat, right foot on left knee. His voice was low and composed. He said, "Bryant, what do you think of our arrangement for your service? Better yet, think of it as an offer."

Bryant faltered in the silence that engulfed the room. His cornflower blue earnest eyes sought Maureen's. He glanced at her for a sign of objection. She watched the play of emotions on his face. She nodded her head in compliance without speaking. When he spoke his tone was filled with awe and respect. "I am honored, sirs," he said. "I hope I can live up to your expectations and confidence in me."

Maureen looked at him with reverent pride.

Grover said, "We don't doubt for a minute that you will do the job cheerfully and conscientiously."

James looked at his granddaughter. His smile was almost apologetic. "But there's more, Maureen. We need your permission. You will be short-handed here, and with the addition of that twelve thousand acres your papa acquired, there will be much more work. Bryant is indentured and we would need to have you sign a release stating that he is free."

Puzzled, Maureen said, "I have to ask some questions before I can release Bryant unconditionally. First, why did you choose a man who may be a disreputable criminal? Second, how do you know he will not escape from your company?

And third, could you tell me more of the nature of the duties he will perform and why the House of Burgesses will accept him in closed sessions?"

Nathan said, "I will answer the first question. Your papa, Patrick, was certain that Bryant is a scholar. His memory loss is certainly inconvenient, but your papa thought, and we agreed that his memory will return to find he comes from a good home. He certainly shows he has the breeding of a gentleman."

Maureen smiled playfully. "Yes, and he plays a mean game of chess. He's been teaching me, you know."

Bryant's tight expression relaxed into a smile. He spoke to all, but gazed only at Maureen. "And, she's about to tell you she beat me twice."

Laughter filled the room.

James, also enjoying their banter, but needing to get on with business, stopped them with a raised hand. "In answer to your second question, it is difficult to imagine such a talented and courteous, well-mannered young man turning out to be a criminal. We do not believe he would try to escape under any circumstances. If you will be reminded, Bryant was gone for most of a year working for the Sons of Liberty. He could certainly have left you then, but he returned," James finished, pointedly.

Maureen had to agree. Her mind turned to the night before when she had walked to the door after their game of chess. As she looked up to see Bryant studying her intently, she saw an instant of wistfulness steal into his expression, followed quickly by an invitation in the smoldering depth of his eyes. She recalled the ecstasy of being held against his strong body. Her blood soared and her lips tingled in remembrance of his kiss.

Grover injected, "The Revolutionary War has begun. Although Bryant is new to this country, he is already a strong, loyal colonist who feels as we do—that freedom and independence are the prime goals of this war, and that Americans are entitled to achieve a liberty and equal station. We need him, Maureen."

With a kind of unexplainable intuition, he said, "Did you hear me, Maureen?"

Surprised, she quickly chastised herself. "I'm sorry," she said, "my mind skipped away for a moment."

"No matter. My thoughts were a preamble to what needs to happen. With your release of Bryant's indenture papers, he will receive a little land to come back to when his duties are complete. As a freeholder who owns land outright, we will be able to support his right to be with us."

James said, "What we really want is to help Bryant climb the ladder of success. If Patrick had lived, he would have done everything in his power to make that happen. He once told me, 'my lovely daughter has followed me around all her precious life. She grieved with me when we lost a crop to a hailstorm or other problems, and she celebrated with me whenever we had a bumper crop. But Bryant is like the opportunity for the sons I never had.'"

Maureen's lower lip trembled slightly. Bryant and Maureen stared at each other across a sudden ringing silence. In his face caring and sympathy intermingled. She said, "I loved him so; I will always miss him and Mother, of course, and the babies." Shaking herself to stop the memories, she asked, "What exactly will Bryant's duties be? And how can he become a success if his memory doesn't return?"

"My dear," James said, "we all have to have faith that Bryant's memory will come around. But if not, he will be Bryant Rory Taylor, a landowner, and will be eligible to become a member in the House of Burgess. With us, his duties will be to record the proceedings and possibly help us to analyze the important items that are discussed on the agendas."

"I'm trying not to be obstinate, but we don't know if he will rise up politically, or that you men can influence his success. And if I release his indenture I will be left without an excellent overseer, supervisor, helpmeet."

Nathan stood and paced a few steps back and forth in front of the fireplace. Patiently he said, "We know this is difficult. That's why we are here to lay out the plans and come to a conclusion with the least amount of inconvenience or suffering and awkwardness to you. Bryant?"

Mixed feelings surged through Bryant. He looked directly at Maureen with adoring eyes, but he knew he must speak freely about what he was thinking. "I would like to go with the men; I think I can be of assistance to them and at the same time contribute to the war effort. But Mistress Maureen, I would do nothing to compromise your well-being. Also, I am confident that in the next couple of weeks, we can have Leon and Booker, along with Joshua who would supervise, of course, ready to take on the responsibilities of running the plantation. I will come back every chance I get, I promise you that."

There was tension among the men in the room. Only Bryant was relaxed and serene. Maureen had recognized the caress in Bryant's eyes, but she knew she could not afford to be distracted by romantic notions. A sense of strength came to her and her despair lessened. The anxiety was gone when she lifted her head to face the room full of men.

She smiled and spoke slowly. "You know, of course, that you are four against one, which doesn't make very good odds for me." She smiled more widely. "But, of course, you are right. It would be sinful to keep a good man down."

Maureen's jade green eyes lit up with a sly twinkle as she turned to Nathan Custis. "I presume that as the attorney of this persuasive band of conspirators you have the papers all drawn up and in readiness for my signature."

Nathan stood and bowed admiringly. He smiled with warm spontaneity. "You're quick," he said. "I just happen to have the papers."

Grover, too, stood and approached the desk. The gold-rimmed monocle gave the wealthy planter a scholarly look. "There is just one thing you must decide for yourself, and you will put that figure in the blank before you put your signature to it. That is the amount of the acreage you will give Bryant when you release his indenture."

James Tucker said, "Do you remember the figure we once discussed, Maureen?"

"Yes, Grandfather, I do remember, but something is niggling at my mind. Let me think a minute." The conversation dropped off; the words hung in the air. James motioned the men back to their seats.

Maureen sat back, momentarily swimming through a haze of feelings and desires. She tried weighing the whole structure of events. In order to vote, a freeholder needed one hundred unsettled acres of land or twenty-five acres with a house and plantation. These were the requirements for a voice in choosing burgesses or becoming one. Two hundred acres was the amount she and her grandfather had once discussed as Bryant's due. However, he had been much more adept and effective in the whole plantation operation than had once been anticipated. He had also become a trusted friend to Patrick, to these men and, finally, to herself. Slowly returning with difficulty from contemplation, she asked James: "Is this truly my decision? Do you want me to consult with you first?"

James looked into his granddaughter's eyes and walked over to stroke her fine, silky hair. "No, my dear. Do whatever your heart is telling you."

Maureen took up the quill and dipped it in the ink. She wrote slowly, deliberately, and when she finished she said, "Mr. Custis and Mr. Harrison will you please come and witness my signature? Then you will sign it as witnesses and I will read the results to grandfather and Bryant."

First Nathan's eyes widened in astonishment, then Grover's; it was a whole new documentation. Both men did as bidden without comment and returned to their seats. After a long pause, Maureen took a deep breath and spoke softly, but firmly as she read the document aloud:

> *On this 15th day of April, 1776, I, Maureen Maguire, hereby release the Tucker Plantation indentured servant, Bryant Rory Taylor, from his duties. Owing to his outstanding service during his indenture, I allocate five hundred acres of the far southwest section of the Tucker Plantation, sufficient for him to become a voting freeholder. Also, for his startup expenses, I gift Bryant Rory Taylor with chattel of ten hogsheads of tobacco and seeds enough to set him up next year. There is one condition on which this hinges: When he is available, Bryant Rory Taylor will spend the remainder of this year of 1776 on Tucker*

Plantation, in order to help us become independent of his services by January 1, 1777."

Duly Signed by Maureen Maguire, and witnessed by Nathan Custis and Grover Harrison

* * * *

The room was swallowed up by the silence until a weathered wood log sputtered and shot sparks as it hit the hearth with a thud. Bryant gave Maureen a sidelong glance of utter disbelief as he got down on his knees, poker in hand, to repair the glowing fire. When he stood, Maureen could feel across the room the surging power of his presence.

As he walked toward her, she studied him silently and the warm blue eyes studied her back. The woman inside of her started to come alive. A warm kernel of happiness wriggled into the center of her. At the desk, in front of her, sunshine broke across Bryant's face, his gaze steady. When he spoke, his voice was calm, but with a slight tinge of wonder.

"I am beholden to you, Mistress Maureen, but your generous offer must be discussed further. I believe you and your grandfather James should confer privately before finalizing the terms of the release."

James joined Bryant. In a voice that held depth and authority, and a trace of amusement, he said, "I have to admit I was momentarily speechless with surprise and I would like an explanation, but not privately." He gestured with an arc of his arm to include Nathan and Grover. "I am sure we all want to hear the reasons Maureen provided such generous conditions surrounding Bryant's release."

Maureen relaxed when she realized they weren't going to challenge her. She spoke with quiet assurance. "Papa's faith in, and friendship with Bryant was probably the basis for my deep pondering. However, you gentlemen have convinced me that you will be sponsoring Bryant for political reasons at social events, and for help during the war efforts. Therefore I came to the conclusion, and we all know it to be true, that a man with a large estate or plantation will be much more easily accepted in all areas of colonial life."

In all seriousness, Bryant said, "Thank you, Maureen, for your trust and faith in me, and for your generosity." He leaned over, touched her arm, and smiling benevolently, eyes dancing, he turned and asked James, "Does this mean, since I am a freeholder, that I may ask permission to court your beautiful, lovely granddaughter?"

With a tolerant chuckle and eyes that twinkled with hard merriment, James answered. "There are reasons, my friend, that it may be more prudent for you to wait for the formal courting until after the condition of the contract expires at the beginning of next year."

James and Bryant went back to their seats by the window and lit their pipes.

Nathan laughed appreciatively. His voice was cheerful and booming. "On the other hand," he said, "maybe arrangements could be made for you to join in the young peoples' party activities when you are available."

"Good idea," Grover injected, with a short, saucy smile. "As a matter of fact, my Laura is having a May Day garden party and an informal dance before we must leave. We want to include Amanda O'Toole as she gets out far and away too little; we thought Justin Thatcher, her overseer, might escort her so that if she tires he can see her home. Laura also asked if she might invite Sabrina—says she met her when all of you girls were learning to stitch. With that in mind, Bryant, you might escort Sabrina; the two of you could ride over with Amanda and Justin, which would give you exposure without showing your full hand."

Maureen had to fight her own battle of restraint. The question hammered at her until she ask, "Does this mean Bryant's indenture release is to be confidential?"

"Not exactly, my dear," James said. "But, for the time being, we would not want the whole of it disclosed. Bryant has been watching Shamus closely. There is something wrong that we can't put a fix on. If you will remember his explosion the night of Abigail's party, it was then she asked us to keep an eye on his activities."

Nathan continued. "We want Shamus to expose himself if he is not what he says he is. If he turns out to be the farmer he should be after he finishes his playboy act, we will try to work him into our system. We certainly need more upcoming young men to carry on the burgesses and the committees and congress' activities."

"And what about me? Papa gave him permission to court me."

"You are doing exactly right. If you are enamored with him, it doesn't show. If you learn anything we should know, we trust you will report it to Bryant, to us or to Abigail. But if you are enamored, we will do everything to the best of our ability to make it right for you."

"Shamus has a streak; he's a supporter of the King and the Brits, which is our strongest dissention and an obstacle to an otherwise pleasant friendship. He is consciously kind to me. He really tries to be patient with me." Maureen regarded Bryant and felt her blood soar with unbidden memories.

Bryant offered her a gentle smile. "At least I will be able to dance with you at Laura Harrison's party. I may even beat you at a game or two if we are competing groups, but," he sighed a long breath, "Shamus will have the pleasure of escorting you. Just remember, Mistress, 'this, too, shall pass.'"

James stood. "It's time for us to get back to Williamsburg. Bryant, your first assignment—appointment—is tomorrow at eleven o'clock at Sam Jones' place. He will measure you and pick out the materials for your new wardrobe."

Maureen giggled, and got up to hug her grandfather. "It seems you were very sure of yourself, Grandfather, to set his appointment without knowing the outcome."

James' tone was lightly teasing. "I know you, my dear. I knew you would see the merit of our quest. Besides, I was no more 'sure' than Nathan who drew up the papers ahead of time, or Grover who did such a thorough job of explaining it to you."

"As I said, earlier, I was outnumbered. It took four of you to do the job." She waved them away and finished with a jaunty salute.

Chapter 14

Two days later, Shamus stormed into the Tucker Plantation dinning room while Maureen and Bryant were having breakfast. He gave Bryant a brutal unfriendly glare before his accusing gaze riveted on Maureen. His expression was like someone who had been slapped back and forth across both cheeks. His face was a glowering mask of rage, a scalding fury spewed from his eyes. He spoke so viciously Maureen wondered how she had ever thought him kind.

"What is this I hear about your criminal going to Philadelphia to sit in on the Continental Congress? He's indentured, for damnation's sake. He doesn't own a blade of grass or have one stalk of tobacco of his own."

Maureen lifted her chin, meeting Shamus' icy gaze and his accusing expression straight on, without flinching. "I don't *have* to explain anything to you. But, not that it's any of your business, I will. Papa introduced Bryant to the committee in the House of Burgesses. After Papa died, Grandfather, Nathan Custis and Grover Harrison took him in friendship. Grandfather Tucker wants to borrow Bryant for a few weeks."

"He's a criminal."

"If that's true. Because Bryant lost his memory when he fell doesn't mean he's a criminal. Besides, it doesn't make sense. Bryant is educated and the committee wants to use his talents to record the meetings and bring an analysis back to the House of Burgesses."

Shamus, not bothering with the explanation, was incensed. "What do you mean it doesn't make sense? His papers were in order; they proved he was a criminal and was to be indentured for four years. Where did he come up with that stupid brain scheme that he is innocent?"

Bryant stood up to face Shamus. His voice was as cold as his eyes. "It's not necessary to talk about me as if I weren't here. It seems you know I'm going to the House and the Congress next month. Do you know I was measured for a suitable wardrobe yesterday? Now, what more do you question?"

"Of course, I know—how do you think my friends found out about you? They saw you going into Sam's tailor shop and made some inquiries."

Bryant's expression bordered on mockery, but his tone was casual. "Then of course you know that one of the new outfits I ordered will be appropriate for Miss Harrison's garden party and dance."

Shamus spun back around to Maureen. His voice, like a whiplash, was demanding. "You are going with me to Laura's party. Why didn't you tell me the criminal is going?"

Maureen smiled sweetly. "You are right. I am going with you. I didn't tell you Bryant is going because I haven't seen you since I learned of it."

"So, who is *he* going with?"

Bryant held up his hand. His eyes gleamed with mirth. "I'm still here, Shamus, and willing to talk. It just so happens that I will escort Miss Sabrina…"

"But…"

"Hang on a moment. I'm not finished. Your cousin Amanda will be escorted by Justin, your overseer, and the four of us will go together." Bryant's gaze roved lazily appraising Maureen before turning back to Shamus. "We would all be delighted if you and Maureen would ride along with us."

Shamus' brooding eyes held no warmth. He snarled at Maureen. "What *is* all this? A cripple, two indentured slaves and a servant? Going to a garden party of one of the most prominent families on the Virginia social register?"

Maureen spoke eagerly. "Isn't it wonderful? My two best friends, and being accompanied by two young overseer supervisors. That's what our independence will do for us, Shamus—it will release us to be equal individuals, no matter what our station in life. Let's go with them; it will be a wonderful, happy group."

Shamus scoffed. "Well, *we* won't lower ourselves to be seen arriving with them. Sabrina can't even ride—how does that work?"

Bryant said, "She'll be fine riding behind me, or maybe we'll take the coach. This summer Jeb and Maureen are going to teach Sabrina to ride Jingles, the new filly."

Wanting to put the pieces all together, Maureen touched Shamus' hand. "Shamus, Grandfather Tucker says we young people need to include all young people because we'll be the ones to take over the House and government committees. He said when you settle down, and get serious about your plantation, they will need you to help run things after the war. You have the land and the social status. The men working for our independence now are aging. The future is ours. Let's all go to the party together and prove we are worthy of their faith in us."

Indentured Love

She implored him with her eyes.

Bryant stepped back and sat down. Shamus's stepped forward and clasped Maureen's body to his. Without looking away, she backed out of his grasp. "As usual, my dear, I will bow to your wishes. I can't afford not to. But when we are married…"

* * * *

Jeb had hitched up the horses for their ride to Laura Harrison's May Day celebration. Bryant, dressed in blue breeches and vest, matching his eyes, watched the girls come toward him. Sabrina, also dressed in blue, a flowing afternoon frock, and Maureen, in a green frock that enhanced her eyes and cascading golden-red curls, look for all the world like princesses, Bryant thought. He said, "How lucky I am to be escorting you, my dears."

"But you forget," Maureen said, "there will be three others with us."

Bryant shrugged nonchalantly. "I couldn't forget that. And here they come."

Amanda, riding Gwynne side-saddle, was beside Justin who rode the O'Toole horse called Dom.

Shamus approached with a steady expressionless gaze. "Maureen, let the others take the coach; we'll ride our horses. We'll arrive in record time and can leave whenever we wish," he said.

"Not today, Shamus. You do what you want to do, but I've been so looking forward to being with our friends. The coach is plenty big enough for all of us, and we'll have Gwynne and Dom tethered behind in case Amanda tires and needs to go home early."

"Jeb, tether Black Warrior, too. In case I decide to leave

early, Maureen, you can ride behind me."

* * * *

The celebration, the grandeur of the games, was a resounding success. The first order of the day was a dance around the May Pole. Streamers held fast as they danced until they were dizzy and stepped away to make room for the next person in line.

Then Laura Harrison explained: "We're going to choose sides to play Paille-Maille, a French game that became Pall-Mall in English. Father brought the game here after a recent visit to England. It's played with sticks and wickets. The balls are blue, red, black, yellow, green and orange, and the object is for players to traverse the course forward and then back to the start/finish stake."

Bryant grinned as he chose the first ball of blue. "You can't beat me, Maureen."

She laughed, picking up the green ball. "Watch me," she said.

But she didn't. Bryant won the whole field. Shamus, awkward and embarrassed, pouted. Laughing and giggling the young people played the Pall-Mall tournament until teatime. After a delicious spread at the sideboard—of small meat pies, cheese, delicate petite cakes, sugary confections and tea, with lumps of sugar in the saucer, which was fashionably called the sip and nibble—the group retired to the ballroom where they began to dance.

Shamus held Maureen tightly, possessively. Although he looked at her with excitement in his eyes, she could feel the angry warmth of his nearness and her feelings of the contact ranged somewhere between disbelief and enchantment.

"Marry me, Maureen," he whispered in her ear. "I'll announce it at the end of this dance. Your papa would have been so proud if he could have lived to see us marry and merge the plantations."

Bryant cut in, his eyes mischievously merry. "May I have the pleasure, Miss Maureen?"

Maureen spun away from Shamus into the arms of Bryant. Shamus, his eyes a vicious glint in the flickering candlelight, said, "You may *not* dance with her. Tell him why, Maureen."

They stopped and Maureen turned to Shamus, giving him a prim and forbidding look. "I will not be coerced or intimidated tonight, Shamus. This is neither the time nor the place. Sabrina, Amanda and I will have our "coming out" at Grandfather Tucker's in October, but tonight is the celebration of May Day!"

Before he turned away, Shamus said. "I'm going to Hunter Inn to play billiards. Your *servant* friends can see you home. Please try to see reason. I'll see you in the morning for your answer and our ride along the river."

Bryant and other young men kept Sabrina and Maureen dancing the next hour away. The ride home was lively. Bryant sat between Sabrina and Maureen on one side of the coach; Justin and Amanda sat on the other side. Both men had their arms around the girls.

Maureen said, "I'm so proud of you, Amanda. You came in second to Bryant in the Pall-Mall tournament and you didn't seem to tire at all."

"I may be crippled," Amanda said dreamily, "but it's only a short leg. I have you to thank for encouraging me all of our lives. And now Justin has given me a new confidence despite Shamus' snide remarks about 'the cripple and the old lady.'" Amanda's soft voice shimmered with a steadfast serene peace.

Maureen was appalled. "Has Grandmama O'Toole ever heard him speak like that?"

"Oh, no, he would never dare act like that in front of Grandmama. She has warned him a couple of times that she may send him back to Ireland."

"And what does he say to that?"

"He threatens back that he might join the King's army."

Turning to include the others, Justin joined the conversation. "If Grandmama O'Toole sends him back or he joins up with the Brits, Grandmama O'Toole, Amanda and I will be just fine. Shamus is only an O'Toole figurehead. Amanda is a brilliant operations manager and I do the playboy's work. Did you know Amanda has taught me to read a lot better and is teaching me to write some and do the numbers?" His large hand took Amanda's face and held it gently.

Bryant turned to Maureen. "Didn't we tell each other Justin would be the perfect supervisor for the O'Toole Plantation?"

As the talk continued, Sabrina saw two couples whom she thought would find themselves in love. She smiled to herself. Then her thoughts turned to Zachary. The memory of his unexpected bold smiles and the touch of his arms around her waist or his fingers brushing her cheeks made her blush and look away. She was glad the late evening shadows would hide her face. She knew she was slowly but surely falling under Zachary's control. His continued absence was a constant reminder of how much she missed him. *But he'll be here for our coming out ball,* she thought with a warm, content smile. "Are we home already?" Sabrina asked with a start.

"Some of us are," Maureen said, "and it's time to say our good-byes to Justin and Amanda." Sabrina and Maureen hugged

Amanda. Bryant shook Justin's hand and bid them a safe journey home.

Bryant escorted the girls to the door. "Would you mind if I come in for a few minutes?" he asked Maureen. "Mr. Harrison told me we must leave in the morning."

"Of course," Maureen said, "you must have a farewell brandy."

"Sorry not to join you," Sabrina said, "but I'm exhausted and off to bed."

"Good night then, dear friend," Maureen said at the stairway as she and Bryant continued on to the office.

Bryant closed the door behind them and opened his arms to Maureen. Without hesitation, she walked into them, her eyes never leaving his. His face filled with love and Maureen knew Bryant was the answer to all her hopes, all her longings. "Oh Bryant, I so wish the mystery of your life was solved so we could know who you are. What if you are married? What if you have children? Let me pour you a glass of brandy."

"Thank you. I will sip a nightcap, but sit with me on the sofa." Against the chill of the early May evening, Bryant lit a fire in the fireplace.

He's leaving, Maureen thought, *I may be facing a lightless future.* Her eyes darkened with pain.

Bryant sighed heavily, his voice filled with anguish. "I am loath to leave you, Maureen. Shamus can't be trusted and I can't find my way back, but there is hope."

"How is that?"

"I am beginning to have serious headaches with the dreams. I talked to Dr. Julich. He said the headaches are a good sign when the memory has been taken away due to a blow to the head. He said I am probably very close to getting my memory back. Besides, the letters will come from Ireland when Zachary returns in October. Come here, Maureen. Let me hold you."

Maureen slid over next to him and hugged him impulsively. She could feel his heart thudding against her own. How quickly, but subtly this stranger had crept into her being. She could feel the physical waves pulling at her. Through some weird and wonderful chemistry of the emotions, all pretense seemed stripped away.

"You do know I love you, don't you, Maureen?"

"Yes."

"And you do love me, too, don't you Maureen?"

"Yes."

"Then it's time. I want to make love with you, Maureen." Maureen heard a deep longing in his gentle voice.

"I want that, too, but not yet. I want to be all yours and it's too soon, but hold me, love me in your arms." She leaned toward him and raised her face to his.

She could feel his uneven breathing on her cheek as he held her close. Then he kissed the top of her head, and his lips grazed her earlobe. He kissed her eyes, the tip of her nose and finally, his lips were tasting hers. The kiss left Maureen weak and puzzled. "I trust you in every way. Inside of me I know you are a good man, but there is so much we don't know. And the whole state of affairs is so complicated; Shamus would be a perfect solution, but I don't love him…"

"Shush, my love. That will take care of itself in due time. The way he feels, he won't stay around here for long. I wish we could meet his twin brother to find out what went wrong."

He gathered Maureen into his arms and held her snugly as he gently eased her down to the soft length of the sofa. His nearness wrapped around her like a warm blanket, and Maureen settled back, enjoying the feel of his arms around her. Then with a deliberately casual movement, she turned and faced him. Leaning slightly into him, she tilted her face toward his.

Bryant crushed her to him and pressed his mouth to hers with a savage intensity. The touch of his lips on hers sent a shock wave through her entire body. The kiss left her mouth burning with fire. He took her hand and pressed it inside his shirt against the hard, warm flesh and thick mat of blond hair. She felt the strong rhythm of his heart. "Do you feel it?" he asked softly. "You make my blood run like a shimmering moonlit waterfall."

She felt lost in the gentleness of his deep voice. As her fingers lingered inside his shirt, she stroked his muscular body, liking its feel. His breath was warm and a little unsteady as his lips brushed her forehead. Her curious fingers continued to explore his brawny chest. Emotion trembled between them. The silence was broken only by the sound of the crackling fire.

His lips caught her searching fingers, and she felt the tip of his tongue moving softly against them. She looked straight into his eyes, and saw the excitement in them. Silently, he examined her face. She knew she flushed. "Stand up, Maureen," he said at last. "I want to feel you against me."

As if without a will of her own, she obeyed him. He drew her so close she felt his forceful thighs. The muscles of his chest absorbed her soft breasts. She raised her eyes to Bryant's. "I...Bryant, I feel..."

His fingers pressed gently against her lips. "Kiss me," he whispered. "Don't think. Don't talk. Just kiss me."

His lips teased hers softly, causing a surge of passion that drew a moan buried deep inside her slender throat. She moved closer to help him, enticing him. Her lips parted under the passive strength of his mouth as he deepened the kiss. She felt his hands caressing her back, moving surely around to her rib cage. When he spoke again his voice was low and seductive. "There is so much more for us. I want you, all of you."

His hands rested on her shoulders, causing her flesh to quiver. Her whole body flooded with desire. She did not protest when his hands sought the fasteners of her dress and pulled it down off her shoulders. His fingers traced the gentle slope of her young breasts. He outlined the tips of them with his fingers, then suckled them to rigidity. Maureen stiffened intuitively as she felt his hardness brushing against her. She wanted to yield to the burning sweetness captive within her, but something held her back. She pulled away with a sigh and turned aside.

"It's all right," he whispered at her lips. "Don't pull away from me."

Her eyes opened, wide and curious, and a little frightened. "You know I've never been with a man," she whispered back.

His fingers moved higher, and he watched her face while they found the hard peaks and traced them again tenderly. His large hands embraced their softness and kneaded them gently with warm, sensuous movements. "How does it feel, Maureen," he asked in a deep-timbered voice? "Is it good?"

Maureen, feeling faint, remained silent. Bryant moved a step back. She sensed his fragile control. He was pensive, not distressed or annoyed. Bryant began to speak, slowly, as if to stroke her with his voice. His mellow baritone simmered with passion. "In time, we will be one," he said, "but I must leave before first light. Please walk me to the door."

Chapter 15

"Whatever are you doing up, Sabrina? I thought you were at the end of your energy and headed for your pillow."

Sabrina set her book down. "As you can see, I am propped up by my pillow," she said, but I be readin' works in the Oroonoko book by Aphra Behn. It was on your Papa's library shelves. It's a good book, and I think of all I learned with you, to be able to read these wonderful stories. But besides the reading, I thought you might need someone to listen."

"Oh, Sabrina, Bryant is leaving in the morning. Whatever shall I do without him?"

"Be patient, love. He will come back every chance he gets. He loves you, you know."

"Yes, I know, and I love him back, but what if he is a criminal or what if he belongs to someone else? His good looks have been bred into him. He…he's exquisite—there's no other word for him. Surely there is somebody out there to claim him."

"What do you think to do about Shamus? He be expectin' to marry you but he may be havin' a mean streak."

The questions and thoughts about Bryant and Shamus

hung between them and brought a hushed silence. Maureen could not help herself from pondering. Pensively, she went to the window and looked out into the darkness where Bryant had strolled out of her life for unknown months.

"Sabrina," she said, "tomorrow morning Shamus is coming for our usual ride. I'll not break things off because I must be cautious. But if you are free after school, let's ride over to talk to Grandmama O'Toole. Can you be free? You can ride Jingles for at least part of the way; if you get tired or frightened you can ride behind me on Little Princess and we'll lead Jingles."

Sabrina's face lit up; her black eyes sparkled. "I be free, and Jeb, he been coachin' me since we brought Jingles home. He says I be ready to ride with the best of you all. Joy be waitin' to see me."

"You have been sneaking around learning to ride behind my back? Good for you. Now, you better blow out that candle, dear friend. Let's get our sleep," Maureen said as she slipped into her bed between the cool cotton sheets.

* * * *

Maureen was eating breakfast alone when Shamus barged through the door unannounced. "I've had enough of your avoiding the details of our marriage. I plan to marry you. Set the date."

"Good morning, Shamus," Maureen said pleasantly. "It is not a good time to discuss a wedding. I have a full day, beginning with a ride along the river with you. Will you join me with a bowl of hominy for breakfast?"

Shamus' expression was grim. "Where is the criminal? He appears to be missing this morning."

Maureen was startled by the thought that burst through

her mind. *Papa told me to marry for love. Last night there were no shadows on my heart.* She said, "You certainly have a strange way of courting me. You have not said a kind word since you knew our friends would join us and ride with us to Laura's party."

"*Your* friends, my dear."

She shrugged in patient resignation. "It seems to me courtship should be filled with a joyous warm glow of two people in love. And that a marriage should be two people wrapped in a silken cocoon of euphoria. Papa and Mother had that. Papa told me to marry for love. I don't see that happening with us. Mostly, you are demanding."

Shamus showed no signs of relenting. "All that sweet, syrupy talk has absolutely no importance when we are discussing the wedding that I want to take place as soon as possible. You know I love you—that is what you want to hear, is it not? You know because I've held you and kissed you and wanted you, and you have responded. I've also been very aware that you have probably not had a man, and I choose not to spoil that for you."

It felt to Maureen as if the whole perception of love had been spelled out in fifty cold words, or painted in invisible brushstrokes. "I told you last night before you left in a huff that I'm not ready to marry you or anybody. You don't seem to understand that I am the other half of this undertaking."

With a visible effort, Shamus suppressed a retort. He looked deep into Maureen's eyes, searching, then answered with a wry smile. "Enough for now. Let's be off."

The sun had already burned the mist from the rolling hills when Shamus and Maureen mounted Black Warrior and Little Princess.

"I'd like to see that southwest corner of our new land. I am thinking we could put a cherry orchard down there and I am trying to figure out where we might put mulberry trees. If you have to bring Sabrina with you when we marry, she may enjoy spinning silk cloth for us as well as the cotton for the slaves."

Maureen became lost in her private reverie. *What astonishing ideas.* Since she knew whose land it really belonged to, Maureen wondered if Bryant would like to have some of his land planted in mulberry trees for the silk, and cherry trees. She smiled, then giggled deep inside.

"What do you think, Maureen?"

"I think you are a little premature deciding what you will do with land that is not yours. Jumping to speculative conclusions doesn't always make for happy landings. But your ideas are great and, yes, Sabrina will be with me as long as she wants to be with me; it's not a matter of having to bring Sabrina with me. She is my friend. Does all of this mean you are ready to settle down and work the plantation?"

"Don't be brainless. I don't have to work. Justin can buy more slaves. When we are married, the plantation will be huge and I can well afford to buy slaves to make all of my land productive."

Maureen did not respond, but they found the acreage to the southwest boarder more than adequate for the white mulberry trees, which had produced silk worms for over a century. She said, "Did you know, Shamus, that the coronation robe of Charles the Second was woven of Virginia silk. Mother always wanted mulberry trees enough to produce silk; I'm sure Sabrina will be thrilled with the idea. Thank you for thinking of it."

* * * *

That afternoon, Maureen and Sabrina enjoyed the short trip to the O'Toole Plantation. "You ride well, friend," Maureen said.

"I *love* it. Jeb be so patient, but he said I am a natural."

"And so you are."

Later, when Sabrina was running out the door with Joy, Amanda and Maureen sat at Abigail's feet. As they gossiped and chatted, Maureen finally broke in, "Grandmama O'Toole, I am troubled. I don't think I can marry Shamus. He talks of nothing but his land, even including the new land Papa acquired before he died. He is pressuring me to set a date for the wedding. I keep putting him off, but he's getting persistent. I've seized every chance to change Shamus' mind about our freedom, but he seems not to listen."

Abigail put her hand on Maureen's shoulder. "What can I do to help you?"

"I don't know, but I must tell you I've fallen in love with Bryant. He is the kindest, gentlest man I've ever met."

"I understand he is going with your grandfather, and Grover and Nathan, to help them during the House of Burgesses and the Continental Congress meetings. James told me you released him from his indenture so he could travel with them. I am so proud of you for that, my dear. He also told me they all like him very much."

Amanda said, "He is a wonderfully warm man, Grandmama. I can't think he's a criminal. I hope you can meet him soon."

Maureen winced. "I can't think he is a criminal either, but we won't know until, or if he gets his memory back."

Abigail said, "I wished so hard that you could marry Shamus and make an honest man of him. Also, I was looking forward to you being my new granddaughter." She shook her white head resignedly. "But, my dear, if that's not to be, I pray you will find true happiness.

Shamus strode through the door. "What's this I hear about Maureen 'finding true happiness?' Did she tell you the date of our wedding, Grandmama?"

"Quite the contrary, Shamus. She said you are pressuring her and she is not ready to be married."

"That's preposterous. Just this morning we were looking over our land trying to decide where to put a cherry orchard and a stand of mulberry trees for silk worms..."

"You are way ahead of yourself, Shamus. The land is not 'our land.' It is *my* land to do with as I see fit. We are not betrothed, nor will we be until I am ready, or not."

Shamus looked at Abigail. "You tell her, Grandmama. I thought everything was set; I would court and marry Maureen. How dare she talk like that?"

Abigail shook her head. "It seems you have spoken only from your own selfishness. Tea is ready. Amanda, will you call Sabrina and ask her to fetch Justin for tea? Will you join us, Shamus?"

"Not on your life," Shamus said as he turned away angrily and left the house.

* * * *

The days moved along busily. It was time to work on the worms that would eat up the tobacco leaves if left alone. Although Leon and Booker were ambitious and attentive, they weren't Bryant. Maureen felt alone. School had been dismissed for the summer, as students were needed to help out on the plantations. Sabrina was busy tending the bees and beginning the spinning for the servants' new clothes.

Maureen was waiting to discuss the idea with Bryant before surprising her with the hope of having a grove of mulberry trees for the production of silk worms, and weaving. She was almost too eager to spring the idea on Sabrina to wait, but she knew she must have Bryant's help to get started.

She and Shamus were pleasantly friendly and he had backed off, but Maureen knew that as soon as the October Ball was over, she would have to tell him the stark truth that she couldn't, wouldn't marry him. As for Bryant, she prayed he would soon know his identity.

This morning, Sabrina and Maureen were eating their battered eggs, fixed with fresh mushrooms and melted cheese. Selma placed a cup of steaming pungent coffee beside each girl just as a tentative knock sounded at the back door.

"I wonder who that could be," Maureen said, "Shamus comes in like he owns the place and I'm not expecting him or anyone else this morning. Get it quickly, Selma."

A moment later, Selma announced, "It be Jeb, Mistress. He say he must see you."

"It is all right, Selma. Bring him in."

Jeb entered half apologetically. "I be bringin' more than the paper, Mistress, an' I didna want to leave it in the kitchen like usual. You be getting' a special letter. Post Master Rolf tell me hand it to you direc'ly."

Maureen's heart raced as she held out her hand for the letter. "Thank you, Jeb. Whenever I get a letter, you just come right on in the house with it. It is a great help, since Papa is gone, that you collect the paper and the mail from the post. Stop by after your midday meal for the return letter you will post for me tomorrow."

"Yes um, ma'am," Jeb said, as he bowed and scurried away.

Sabrina said, "I must tend to the hives before I gather the roots to dry for the medicine cupboard and then sit down to the spinning. I will see you midday." She smiled a satisfied smile that reached her eyes. "Let us be ridin' the horses this day to get them some exercise."

Maureen waved her away with a laugh. "A short ride then when we finish with afternoon tea."

* * * *

Maureen asked Selma to fill her coffee cup to carry with her to the office. She put the cup on the table by the window and went to the desk to open the letter. Thrilled, she sat down, unfolded the page and read:

Dear Maureen, 15 May 1776

These are most exciting times. I don't have time to write to you every day, but I keep a kind of a diary with notes so I won't forget to tell you things when I have time to write. I first want to thank you again for the generous gift of land, and for my release from indenture. You have made me a rich man, and although it is not fully known as yet, I have been asked to become a candidate for the House of Burgesses at the next election, and to become a delegate at the Continental Congress. It is the nicest thing that has happened to me since I met you.

Oh, Maureen, I will never forget the moment our eyes first locked together. From the auction block, your green eyes glowed and pierced mine. The white lace at the throat of your chocolate brown day dress parted and I saw the hol-

low of your neck, the color of peach-tinted cream. The wind had whipped color into your cheeks; your oval face was daintily pointed. Your mouth was like a smiling rosy flower. Your stunning red-gold curls blew about you. You stood, exquisite, and I thought fragile. Today I chuckle at 'fragile.' You are very sensitive, but strong.

But I digress. I know you will read this in the Virginia Gazette, but this morning was phenomenal. I sit in awe of the men who are so enthusiastic, but who take their political duties extremely seriously. Over the past few days, in the House, the men debated and discussed and pondered, then voted to instruct its delegates in Congress to propose independence. And before the day was out we got word that Congress adopted a resolution sponsored by John Adams, advising the various colonies to assume complete powers of government within themselves. And, just think, I'll be a part of that future. Oh, Maureen, I so hope we'll be a part of it together.

And, guess what? I have two older sisters. I had a dream. In the dream I was just a wee lad. I don't know what I did, but the older sister swatted me behind. Bro was there, just about my same age. He stood behind me and laughed with the one who paddled me and they floated into the mist together. Then a younger one, but older than me, held out her arms and comforted me. I am sure it was a memory because I woke up with an awful headache and I missed the whole day of sessions at the House of Burgesses. It's coming, my love. Be patient for me.

If I could just hold you in my arms, this day would be perfect. Bryant.

* * * *

Maureen read the letter again, and again. *If I could just hold you in my arms, this day would be perfect*, Maureen read the phrase over and over. Then she stood, went to the desk, picked up the quill pen and wrote:

Dear Bryant, 20 May 1776

I am so sorry about your headaches, but one day you will be well and will know what we need to in order to move on, or not. I yearn to be in your arms. We could make a good team if and when you are able to work your plantation. I visualize The Taylor Silk Plantation. Oh, Bryant, I fun you.

Shamus and I rode to the southwest corner of the land—he to decide how to plant it and me to giggle inside because he didn't know the land is yours. He called it our land and decided to plant a cherry orchard and a grove of mulberry trees so "if Sabrina must come with me after we are wed, she could spin silk along with her many other duties." I set him straight about Sabrina being with me as long as she likes, not because I 'must' have her with me, but because she is my friend. I truly think, however, that she and Zachary will find they cannot live without each other.

But I really liked the ideas of a cherry orchard and the mulberry trees because I think he is right about Sabrina. I think she would dearly love to cultivate silk worms for the spinning of fine silk. I haven't ask her yet as I want to surprise her on her birthday with the idea and I decided to ask you for your advice as to where I might plant them, so as not to interfere with the tobacco fields that I will be developing over the next many years on the new land. Any suggestions will be appreciated.

Since our Virginia leaders have ask us to boycott English products, several things have become scarce, sugar being the worst. But Sabrina's bees are producing well; we have plenty enough honey and we are somehow making due where we thought we would not. The beeswax is enough for our candle making. Everyone on the plantation is cooperating. Leon and Booker are doing a grand job.

Grandmama O'Toole, too, is getting along on less but is a grand lady, and a trooper. Justin, as he said he would, is taking amazing care of the estate. I am watching Justin and Amanda falling in love, but I think they are not quite aware of what is going on with them at this time. Grandmama is at her wit's end over Shamus, but feels unable to settle it just yet. She said she will post his twin brother Sean when Zachary returns to Ireland at the end of October, after the ball.

I am so looking forward to the Ball and since Grandfather Tucker will be at his teaching post at that time, I feel certain that you, too, will be in Williamsburg, or here, and able to attend the ball. By then, let us hope you can announce your name and your land ownership.

Your work sounds enormously exciting. I am ecstatic for you and I am aware of how much it means to you. Keep those dreams coming, though maybe you could skip the headaches.

I wait patiently for the day I may find your loving arms waiting for me. Maureen

Chapter 16

My Dear Maureen, 10 June 1776

Thank you so much for answering my letter so quickly. I carry it over my heart.

You are such a sweetheart to set in a grove of mulberry trees for Sabrina, and cherries—I love them. My suggestion is that you take that piece of land just west of the house. It will be more convenient for Sabrina because it will be nearer the spinning cabin. Of course, the spinning cabin may need an addition, but I'll help take care of that when the time comes. The cherry orchard could be started out where the land has been used up for the tobacco; Cherry trees will be fine there, out in that acreage between the wheat and the corn. I hope I may be there to help celebrate Sabrina's birthday. I would love to see the look on her face when you tell her about the silkworm operation.

Oh, Maureen, I am learning so much. Before we came to Philadelphia, I was inadvertently educated in a matter that surprised my funny bone. Tory is an Irish word meaning 'pursuer.' It applies to Irish outlaws who preyed on English settlers and soldiers. Since last year a loyal colonist is a Tory held together not by organized political parties, but by a collection of special-interest groups. At Hunter Inn, the Tories meet on a regular basis, which explains, I think, why Shamus spends so much time there, and why I do not. We think we know I am not an Irish outlaw.

Actually, I was advised by your Grandfather not to go to Hunter Inn at all. But I have often gone to the Raleigh Tavern where I have been privileged to see Patrick Henry, Thomas Jefferson, George Wythe, Peyton Randolph and George Mason. I understand that before he was called to command the Continental Army last year, George Washington, too, was often seen there among these leaders.

And, of course, I loved touring Williamsburg and seeing all of the men's houses, gardens and orchards. I've been inside the Magazine where the mortars and gunpowder were stored before the battle of Lexington. Near the Capitol are the Public Gallows; I wouldn't care to enter the stocks or the prison to be in leg irons.

Curiosity took me into the Wigmaker's Shop, but do not worry. I will not be showing up in a wig. The best tour of all was with James, your beloved grandfather professor, and Nathan and Grover. They took me through the College of William and Mary. After Harvard, you know, it's the oldest college in the country. Can you imagine an English college set down in America's wilderness for the sole purpose of training ministers for the church and the conversion of the Indian heathen? Oh, how much it has changed.

But I ramble on. The exciting business of this letter was when Richard Henry Lee took the floor three days ago. Lee is forty-four; he's tall and lean, and red-haired like Thomas

Jefferson, but unlike Jefferson, he has a hooked nose and a Roman profile. He had a hunting accident and blew off the fingers of one hand; he covered that hand with a handkerchief before he spoke. Here is some of what he said: "That these United Colonies are, and of right ought to be, free and independent States, that they are absolved from all allegiance to the British Crown, and that all political connection between them and the State of Great Britain is, and ought to be, totally dissolved."

Then he suggested that Congress should prepare a plan of confederation for the colonies and send official delegates to France. Some said sending official delegates to France and drawing up a confederacy seemed sensible, but objected to declaring independence because that act would warn Britain of America's intentions. And, "wouldn't we look silly asking Europe's heads of state to support a union that didn't exist."

An Edward Rutledge of South Carolina hoped to postpone the discussion for three weeks, or for months if he could manage it. You know, dear Maureen, Americans do have to choose between their rights and their King, and in spite of everything the King has done or failed to do, the choice is not easy for people.

But today, Lee seemingly pulled the winning ploy out of his three-cornered felt hat. He won approval for appointing committees that would spend the next three weeks preparing drafts on Lee's resolution so that if Congress agreed on the concept, no more time would be lost. And because he is a Virginian and popular and a very good writer, Thomas Jefferson was assigned the job, or privilege of drafting a declaration of independence.

Oh, my dear Maureen, how I must bore you. In my mind

and in my heart I am holding you in my arms. Bryant

* * * *

Dear Bryant, 15 June 1776

It would be hard for you to bore me. I love your enthusiasm for the details of what is happening here and around the rest of the colonies, especially at the Congress.

And thank you for the help. I did a quick survey of the land you suggested for the silkworm operation; it is perfect. I also found a handbook in Mother's shelf titled The Silk Culturist. If Sabrina has seen it or read it, she didn't mention it, so I took it off the shelf to give to her on her birthday. I'm so excited. I'm going to get the mulberry tree starts from Grandmama O'Toole; she has several trees, but has never used them to produce the worms.

What I haven't told you was Shamus' reaction when I told him where I have decided to put the mulberry grove, and where we would get the starts. He said, "Those decisions are not for you to make. I already told you where I wanted them and the cherry orchard."

I had to remind him again that the land is not his. He looked at me aghast or maybe stunned, and asked, "Why are you being so obstinate? And why would you think to plant them between the plantations and so close when we have so much land? Just think how rich we will be when we are married."

I really wanted to tell him the land he chose is yours; needless to say I did not. For the most part, he is trying to be gentle and optimistic. He just kind of lost his composure *when I told him what I had decided on the locations, but then I did tell him that the ideas were his and I certainly appreciated them and felt they were exactly right for some of the land. That appeased him some.*

Sabrina and I have been busy planting the kitchen garden. We planted onions, squash, potatoes, corn and beans. The cabbage and greens will be planted in the fall, of course. We also planted the pumpkins and melons between the hills of corn and beans. I plan to look into the cherry tree starts; I think I will have to ask Zachary to bring them from across the sea unless you have a different solution.

Dear Bryant, despite being so busy in the tobacco fields with the planting, and the plantation books, the garden, and all the rest, my blood often soars with unbidden memories of being crushed to you, and held close in your arms. Maureen

* * * *

My Dearest Maureen, 4 July 1776

It has happened! I'm sure you have heard. Two days ago, the Congress resolved "that these United Colonies are, and of right, ought to be free and independent states." Congress made some changes in Jefferson's draft. But today the Declaration was adopted, and then printed. The text was read aloud to jubilant crowds, they say, throughout the states. Were you able to hear it in Williamsburg? Oh, I so hope you were.

After that brief preamble—oh, Maureen, listen to this: We hold these truths to be self-evident, that all men are created equal, that they are endowed by their Creator with certain inalienable rights, that among these are life, liberty and the pursuit of happiness…

Think of it, Maureen—"that all men are created

equal." The immediate application is that Americans are entitled to "a separate and equal station" among all the nations of the earth; a sacred creed; an elemental eloquence. Exciting years lay ahead as we take our new and independent way—we are Americans, Maureen—playing for keeps.

But, I have to admit, we have a big job to do.

You make me chuckle when you tell me about your Shamus. You are a delightfully naughty girl, and I love you. I will be anxious to hear how he takes the news of our new independence. Do you know how he feels about it?

I don't know when the Congress will have a break, but hopefully it will be soon.

I missed three days with the headache after my last dream of 20 June. I was on the Desiree. Pa and I were discussing the colonies pending independence. Pa's face was lost in the misty atmosphere that rolled and churned around us. I am sure we have had a somewhat similar conversation before I left Ireland. When Pa floated away, opaque fog billowed around his feet. Something cracked into, and splintered against my head. It seems I was lifted and launched up into the air. I woke up wet with sweat, clawing my way out of the cotton sheet that covered me. For the first time Bro wasn't there. The headaches are almost unbearable.

But in my daydreams, my love, I explore the soft lines of your back, your waist and your hips. My hands trace a path over your skin, my tongue explores the rosy peaks of your breasts and my lips trace a sensuous path to ecstasy. Wait for me, my love. Bryant

* * * *

Dear Bryant 15 July 1776

Oh, yes, how exciting this new Declaration of Independence is, but also sad. The fighting is frightening, but I was so proud of General Washington. The story was told this morning in the Virginia Gazette: As a show of force, a couple of British, a representative of General Howe met with General Washington and offered clemency for the American rebels if they want peace. He politely declined and left.

We got the news to gather at the House of Burgesses on 6 July to hear the reading of the Declaration. Amanda, Justin, Sabrina, Shamus and I rode over to hear the reading, so of course I got the full impact of Shamus' reaction. After the "We hold these truths to be self-evident, that all men are created equal," loathing was etched in his face, almost threat-like hate. He shoved his hands into his pockets and paced across the back of the room for the rest of the reading. He ranted and raved most of the way home. Justin and Amanda made faces behind his back, and Sabrina, riding Jingles, galloped on ahead. Oh, I forgot to tell you how well Sabrina took to Jeb's riding lessons. They did it on the sly to surprise me.

Anyway, the gist of Shamus' tantrum was that the British army will slaughter Washington's army; that if we had any sense we would surrender and learn to live with the homeland rulers; and that the colonies that had not yet voted for its adoption were the only smart Americans.

To me, Shamus said, "If it weren't for your Coming Out Ball, and the fact that we will be married at Christmas—since you won't set the date, I have done so myself—I would join the Tories in a heartbeat. What do you say to that?"

"I say," I told him, "that the way you feel, you might as well join the British forces now, and we can talk about marriage when the war is over and you arrive home."

"Then," he said, "I will stay at the plantation until after we are married."

Shamus went on to say that since I was used to running the plantation, I was to do so while he was fighting this "useless" war. He said I could handle both of them, but I am to live at the O'Toole Plantation and leave Sabrina at Tucker Plantation until we can merge them. By that time I was home and he kissed me lightly on the cheek, and rode off with Justin and Amanda.

But don't find this worrisome. I will not marry Shamus until you and I talk with Grandfather Tucker about what is in my heart. We hope, of course, that your memory has fully recovered and the whole thing has been solved. Come home soon. I long for your arms.

By the way, Sabrina's birthday is in five short days. I'm so excited to give her the surprise. I have the mulberry starts hidden away where she won't come across them. Take care of you, dear Bryant, for me. Maureen

* * * *

Soundless lightning flickered against the sky to the west the morning of the twentieth of July. The horizon lit with white light and thunder muttered far away and soon rolled over the plantation. Sabrina and Maureen were at the breakfast sideboard. When they sat down, Maureen said, "The rain will keep us inside today, but I have a surprise for you."

"For me?"

"Absolutely, friend. It's a very special day as you are having a birthday and I have a gift to keep you busy this day." Maureen handed Sabrina the handbook on *Silkworm Culture*.

A blinding flash followed instantly by a shattering crack of acoustical energy consumed the room. At that moment, a puppy, a tiny Labrador Retriever crept into the room and lay down next to the fire, ears down, tail tucked between his legs, and gave a tiny squeaky whimper.

Surprised, the book forgotten, Sabrina ran to the puppy and gathered him into her arms. "Oh, Blackie baby," she cooed, "don't be scared. It be all right."

Black eyes looked into black eyes, and up into Maureen's. Sabrina said, "He be mine?"

"Yes, he is yours."

Remembering the book, Sabrina carried the puppy to the table and sat him on her lap. Selma entered the room. "Someone to see you, Mistress. He seem in a hurry."

Bryant stood before them with a faint whiff of the intoxicating woodsy smell. He pushed a shock of wet blond hair away from his forehead, and looked quickly at Sabrina. "Happy Birthday, Sabrina."

"Oh, look what Maureen gave me. This beautiful puppy—Blackie be his name—and this book to help me learn about raising silkworms." She grinned. "I be reading the book over and over before it curiously disappeared."

"Did she tell you the rest of the surprise?"

"Not more surprise?"

Bryant looked at Maureen and motioned for her to continue. She said, "I have more than enough starts for a mulberry grove. Within a couple of years you will be spinning our silk and sewing beautiful garments. Bryant will help us set up the shed in which to raise the silkworms near the spinning wheel cabin."

Sabrina watched the look that connected Bryant and Maureen. She stepped between them to hug first Bryant and then Maureen. "I be thanking you from me heart, but I be taking Blackie to me room to help me plan for the silkworm farming."

When they were alone, Bryant crossed the distance that separated him from Maureen. Reluctantly, Maureen stood, her back to him. Her mind swirled with memories that still lurked in the secret places of her being. She struggled with contradictions in her heart as she tried to study the situation dispassionately. As much as she struggled to pretend aloofness, it was obvious their attraction to each other was all consuming. He could be the answer to all her longings, but she knew it might also be a hopeless love. Her eyes filled with blinding tears of frustration. She pulled back to catch her breath and collect her jagged painful thoughts.

Behind her, Bryant's arms encircled her waist. In a low, troubled voice, he cut through her pondering. "What is it, my dear?"

At the sound of him, she lifted her head and turned to him. She heard the bitterness spill over into her words. "Actually, I'm feeling wretched."

He eyed her with concern, pulled her to him. She knew she made a perfect fit inside his arms. If only she could let her feelings pour out. He turned her slightly and pulled her again into the circle of his arms. His cheek gently caressed her hair. With his mouth next to her ear, he said, "Is there anything I can do to help make you feel better?"

"In fact, you make me feel worse. I've dreamed of this moment from the day you left, but now I am stripped of energy, and struggling with emotions I should not feel."

Still holding her close, he pulled back a few inches and looked directly into her eyes. "How can that be when we are together at last."

Maureen felt her breath cut off, but she was determined to get this out. "I can't see you anymore. It's too painful for me. You know I love you, but there's too much between us that may not be able to be repaired. We don't know who you are or who may be waiting for you to return. You must move on, help Sabrina if you must, and then move on to settle your land, help with the war effort, and become all that you are capable of in this great country of ours—and then there is Shamus that would stand between us."

Sobbing, she spun around, but he caught her and whirled her back into his arms. She struggled wildly while he gently tugged the ribbon out of her hair and buried his face in the tumbling mass. Whispering words of endearment, he rocked her back and forth. When she quieted, he said, "We love each other. Things will work out. Let me make love to you!"

"But, what if..."

"Shush. I already know enough. How could I love you if someone were waiting for me? Wouldn't I feel it; wouldn't I know it inside of me?" Bryant's mouth twitched with mournful amusement. His eyes smoldered and probed her very soul. Maureen watched his tender glance travel from her tiny buckled shoes to her olive green dress, to the low neckline.

"It's flawless." His eyes flashed a familiar gentle humor. Maureen blinked, feeling suddenly lightheaded. She tried unsuccessfully to weigh the whole structure of events, but was swimming through a cloud of feelings and desires. He was so disturbing to her that she froze in limbo where decisions and actions were impossible.

Chapter 17

Bryant took Maureen's small hand in his large one and led her into the office. She was enjoying his closeness. When he finally spoke again, Bryant's voice held more than a hint of excitement. "Do you have pressing duties today, and how long do I have before Sabrina will come back."

"In a couple of hours, if the weather clears, Sabrina and I should put the mulberry grove in order while the ground is moist, and before nightfall."

His gaze, soothing as a caress and riveted to her face, now moved slowly over her body. The smoldering flame she saw in his blue eyes startled her, but he drew her to him affectionately. "Let's not waste precious time in idle chitchat."

Maureen's heart jolted and her pulse pounded. Just when she thought she would faint, Bryant pulled her down beside him on the sofa. "Drat, I must light the fire to take the chill from the room."

His appeal was overwhelming; the very air around them felt electrified as the blaze burst into the room. He was beside her quickly; she could feel his heart beat against her as he unbuttoned the back of her dress and began caressing her soft skin. His touch sent ripples down her spine.

She closed her eyes and sat very still. "Although I do not know what it means, I want you with my whole being. But I cannot come to you without marriage. Do you understand? Will you wait until all things are right for us?"

"Much as I want you, I promise not to take you by force. You are too precious, cherished one."

They shared an intense physical awareness of each other as he lifted her into the cradle of his arms and molded her soft curves to the contours of his lean body. She leaned against him with a sigh of pleasure. His kiss was slow now, unhurried. His lips pressed against hers, then gently covered her mouth, devouring its softness. The touch was a delicious sensation.

His tongue traced the silky fullness of her lips, delicately pried them open and explored the recesses of her mouth. Shivers of desire raced through her. His lips left hers to lightly nip her earlobe before searing a path down her neck and shoulders as they continue to peruse her creamy skin. Finally his lips recaptured hers, more demanding this time. Parting her own lips, she raised herself to meet his kiss. She gasped at her own eager response. His passionate fondling was surprisingly restrained. He moved slightly away and helped her sit up. He whispered in her hair, "I can't keep touching you. I want you too much."

"What will happen to us, Bryant?"

"God willing, someday we'll be together forever, but in the meantime we've got to get Sabrina's mulberry trees started and her silkworm culture business activated."

"How do I keep Shamus from spiriting me away? He has set a wedding date. He is determined to have me and merge the plantations. When will I see you again?"

Bryant's tone was warm, with a trace of laughter in his

voice. "You worry too much. Jeb, Leon or Booker are keeping you in sight at all times. In a week or two, I will be called back to duty, but nothing will keep me from your big dance in October. I wish I were the one escorting you, but that is impossible. You will go to the dance with Shamus, but he will never have your hand as long as there is breath in me."

Maureen knew she colored slightly under his gaze. "I've explained to Shamus over and over again that I'm not ready to give him the whole evening, that I want to dance with all the young men, and that I'm not ready to make the decision to marry him, or anybody else."

Desire brightened Bryant's sparkling blue eyes before his glance filled with amusement. "Did you know you lied?"

Maureen knew a sudden shyness inside her. She dropped her eyes before his steady gaze. "No…well, maybe, but it was not completely untrue, considering our uncertainty. I must confess, however, I agreed to let him squire me and have three dances."

"And how many will you promise me, my sweet love?"

"Go on with you. You're not a freeholder yet. I'll ponder on it."

"Don't ever change, love. You are a most refreshing, captivating, and magical creature in my life. I love you. But for now, we have work to do."

* * * *

Selma and Emily quickly cleared the table of the noon meal and dishes. Bryant sat at one end of the long table. Maureen and Sabrina sat on either side of him. Bryant had a sheet of paper on which to draw a sketch of the silkworm operation. He asked, "What do you need, Sabrina?"

"It would be really exciting to have the shed attach to the

spinning cabin with a door out to the mulberry trees. There seems to be two to three hundred starts, which will be ready to feed to the silk worms in a couple of years. They need to be kept pruned to bushes. The shoots grow from the stump-balls, and the whole shoots are cut to feed the worms. So if the trees could surround the shed, the process would be much easier. Inside the new shed, I need long tables and flat tables to keep the worms."

Maureen said, "Tell us about the whole process."

Sabrina smiled brightly. "Beside me reading the book, Miss Matilda tell me about a woman in Williamsburg where we can buy a few ounces of French silkworm eggs. The eggs are tinier than your tobacco seeds. Out of the eggs come the silkworms each spring. In the six weeks of warm spring weather the worms hatch while me feed the mulberry leaves non-stop, and then they magically spin the leaves into rich silk cocoons. Then I will smother the moths inside the cocoons with heat. The rest of the year me can reel the silk threads from the cocoons on to sticks to be spun at me leisure."

Bryant said, "It sounds to me like it's a lot of hard work. You are a brave girl to take on such an undertaking, but we'll get the shed ready and the mulberry trees planted, so you can be on your way when the time is right. When I told James, he said he had bricks enough to finish the shed to match the spinning cabin."

Maureen asked, "How long have you been studying silkworm culture, Sabrina?"

"Since me could read good enough to study your mum's book." Sabrina boldly looked from Bryant to Maureen. "Me be wanting to make your wedding dress of blue silk cloth that me spun and dyed myself."

From Sabrina's lap, the puppy wiggled and yawned. "It be time to take Blackie baby outside for he to be learnin' what he needs to learn."

Bryant said, "We'll be heading out to stake out the shed, and plant part of the mulberry starts before dark."

He held out his hand for Maureen and they walked toward the back door, just as Shamus came barging in. He glanced sharply around, his blue eyes blazing. His angry gaze swung over her then toward Bryant. "What in damnation do you think you're doing? Take your hand off my woman"

When Maureen would hastily withdraw her hand, Bryant halted her escape with a firm hand on her arm, and his free arm moved recklessly around her waist. His compelling blue eyes and the confident set of his shoulders, his attitude of assurance and studied relaxation exuded an air of command. His firm mouth curled as if on the edge of laughter. "To what do we attribute the nastiness of your outrage?"

Shamus stiffened at the question. His brows drew together in an angry frown. "You dare to so much as touch the woman I will marry? The date is set for the twenty-sixth of December, a few short months from now."

There was a slight tremor in his voice as though some emotion had moved him. His voice was uncompromising yet oddly gentle. "Maureen, come here this instant."

Shamus put his hand on her shoulder in a possessive gesture. His fingers dug into her soft flesh. Cupping her chin, he searched her face. Bryant's protective hand pressed her closer to himself. Maureen turned away then from both men, her hands clenched stiffly at her sides.

Shamus drove a fist into the palm of his hand, then grabbed her hand and pulled her back. "I want an explanation.

My friends at Hunter Inn say you released this criminal from his indenture. Is it true?"

Maureen said, "Yes, it's true. So that Bryant could be active with Grandfather Tucker and the other representatives of the House of Burgesses and the Continental Congress, his release was imperative; that was my responsibility."

"And just what is going on between you two?"

Bryant broke in. "That, Shamus, is none of your business, but for now we are headed out to stake out the shed for Sabrina's silkworm culture operation. Maureen has generously planned to set her up in the business. We would also like to get the mulberry starts set out before dark as the rain has softened the ground. You are welcome to help us. Any more questions?"

Hands resting on his hips, Shamus' eyes flashed a familiar display of impatience at Maureen. "Yes. What is that good-for-nothing pup doing with Sabrina? Maureen, you are collecting too much garbage to bring with you when we are married."

Maureen smiled indulgently. "The puppy's name is Blackie and she was one of my gifts to Sabrina. Today is her birthday and she so misses her home and her own black Labrador, I thought it would comfort her to have a 'pup' of her own. And, it has *not* been established that you and I shall marry. So far, you have taken a lot upon yourself."

"I told you that since you wouldn't set the date, I would do so myself. I've arranged for Parson Charles Moss to marry us. Bryant, would you leave us alone? You are no longer needed or wanted. Pack your bag and get your miserable self out of here"

Maureen's eyes darted nervously back and forth.

Again, the mischievous look came into Bryant's eyes and he winked at Maureen. "Well, Shamus, since you think you know so much, I can fill you in a bit. There was a stipulation in the release document that stated I must help Mistress Maureen at Tucker Plantation until the thirty first of December. If I leave before that, it will be considered a breech of indenture and I can be sent back to Ireland. I don't wish for that to happen."

Shamus shrugged, appearing bored. "Not that I am captivated with your story, but if you don't leave Virginia, what do you plan to do once you are free? Since Maureen will be wed, you will have nowhere to go and will be unable to pester her further."

"Believe me, I have plans to help with the states' war efforts for as long as I am needed. My plans after that have not been released. Apparently, even your 'friends' have not been able to sort out the whole of it. Tell them to keep on the lookout."

Bryant turned to Maureen. "I must get to work. I'll leave you two, now."

Maureen said, "Wait, Bryant, I'm going with you. We must get as much done as we can. You'll be gone soon and I promised Sabrina a birthday tea. Grandmama O'Toole, Justin and Amanda will be here at four. You are welcome to help us, Shamus, and join us for tea."

"Thank you, but I think not." He held out his hands to Maureen, offering an apology. His voice was a little awkward. "Would you stay here for a few minutes, Maureen?"

She dropped her eyes before his steady gaze and remembered her promise to his grandmother. She had no intention of permitting herself to fall under his spell, and struggled to maintain an even, amiable tone before she turned to Bryant. "It's all right, Bryant. Go out to the plot with Sabrina. I'll be with you in a few minutes."

His own mouth curved with tenderness. "By all means, stay. Take your time."

* * * *

Shamus was sure of himself and his rightful place in the universe. He took charge with quiet assurance. He walked to Maureen and hesitated, measuring her for a moment. She felt suddenly ill-equipped to undertake the task at hand, but was interrupted by the tone of his voice. Shamus' tone was totally compassionate; it was apologetic and patient.

"Maureen, I know I've been harsh and hard to get along with, but I'm concerned about you. You seem not to understand that Bryant is a dangerous criminal. Your papa gave me permission to court you. That means he expected us to marry. And we will. If it weren't for your damnable party, I would carry you off this minute, but I *will* have you this day, this minute."

Without giving Maureen a chance to respond, Shamus swept her, weightless, into his arms and carried her to the sofa in the office. She could feel the sexual magnetism that made him so self-confidence, but the seduction flame she saw in his eyes frightened her. "Shamus, I will not have you. Not today, not ever. Shamus… NO!"

Shamus pulled Maureen's dress up to her neck. She tried to scream but it stuck in her throat. Shamus unfastened his breeches and as they slid to the floor stepped out of them. He flopped on top of her and savagely began to massage her breasts. Terrified, Maureen tried to wiggle free; she scratched his face with her fingernails.

"I'll have you *now*," Shamus said, and slumped to the floor.

"You're safe, Maureen. Let me help you up," Bryant said.

Sobbing, Maureen asked, "H-h-how did you know?"

"I came back to get the plans for the shed. Selma told me she heard you cry out. I grabbed the fireplace poker and hit him in the small of the back. He'll live, but we'll all guard you closer. I'll put Leon or Booker beside you if Shamus dares to come near you again, and I will personally escort you to the Ball in October. Come here, my love."

Shamus, eyes glazed, groaned and slowly began to move. He looked up. His eyes showed the tortured dullness of disbelief. His mouth took on an unpleasant twist and his voice was like a whiplash as he cautiously began to get up and pull on his baby-blue breeches. "You will regret this attack until I see you dead, Bryant *Rory* Taylor."

Maureen was shaking uncontrollably. Her pulse began to beat erratically at the threat in Shamus' deep voice.

Bryant drew Maureen to his side, but she couldn't control the spasmodic trembling within her. She gulped hard, hot tears slipping down her cheeks. She sagged against the protectiveness of Bryant's arms that held her snugly. Despite her anguish, she couldn't miss the musky smell of him as he pressed her closer. And, finally, biting her lips to check the sobs, Maureen drank in the comfort of his nearness that wrapped around her like a warm blanket.

When Bryant felt Maureen relax against him, he turned to Shamus. "Leave *now*, Shamus."

Shamus rubbed the back of is head where a lump was already visible. His voice was deep and filled with insolence. "As you wish, but I *will* have the last word—depend on it."

Walking gingerly and without a backward glance at Maureen, he slammed the door behind him.

Sudden quiet filled the room. Bryant turned Maureen to face him and kissed the tip of her nose. "Go rest, my dear. I'll send Phoebe up to tend you. Sabrina and I will work until Grandmama O'Toole and Amanda arrive and Emily announces that tea is ready. Sabrina will get you up in time to join us."

* * * *

Tears filled the corners of her eyes when Maureen entered the room and saw that her friends had gathered and filled the sofa and the chairs in the parlor. Abigail O'Toole sat at ease on the winged-back chair in the parlor. Blackie, curled up in her lap, was sleeping soundly when Maureen stooped down to stroke Abigail's wrinkled cheek. "I'm so sorry Grandmama, I've done all I can to bring Shamus around. I can't, won't see him again."

Patting her shoulder and running her other hand down Maureen's silky hair, she said, "Hush, child. Bryant has explained, and Shamus is gone—said he was off to kill the 'yellow-bellied dastards that won't show respect for their superiors.' Said they 'defy their King and the Parliament that keeps them safe.' I have written to Timothy and Sean for I have no idea how he came to be so callous and mean-spirited, and malicious. Zachary will deliver the letter to Ireland and I'll have a response in the spring. In the meantime, my dear, take care of yourself and don't give Shamus another thought." Abigail winked at Bryant. "By the way, I like your young man. Amanda was right when she told me he was kind and generous of heart."

A dim flush raced across Maureen's face. She took a deep

breath and managed a tremulous smile as she took a seat between Amanda and Sabrina on the sofa. She said, "We must move on now. This is Sabrina's day. Tell us how it went, Sabrina."

Face aglow, two dimples appeared as if fingers had squeezed Sabrina's cheeks. "Bryant got the shed staked out. It gonna' be fine. Leon and Booker be helpin' with the planting and we got almost all the mulberry starts in the ground. Those good chaps be finishin' up before the man in the moon starts marchin' across the night sky." Mischievously, she grinned at Maureen.

Amanda chimed in. "Maureen, have you found the cow, then, that jumped over the moon? Do you think she will stop soon to let you go to the moon with her?"

Entering the fun, Maureen's smile became genuine. "No," she said, "but I found the dish that ran away with the spoon and both are waiting for Sabrina at the tea table. Shall we go?"

The girls broke into gales of giggles as they started toward the dinning room. Abigail, Bryant and Justin exchanged amused glances. Bryant offered his arm to Abigail and the three of them followed, Blackie sprinting ahead to catch up with Sabrina.

Chapter 18

Captain Zachary astonished Maureen the first day of September. Bryant had been back in committee for three weeks. Maureen was helping hang the tobacco sticks for the aging process. She walked quickly to Zachary and held out her hands to him. "You're early," she said, "we weren't expecting you until October."

He smiled broadly. "I hurried through my chores in England and Ireland and rushed back. Truth be known, I missed Sabrina terribly, and I have special gifts for you two and Amanda. When can I get you all together?"

"You are in luck. We are invited to Grandmama O'Toole's for tea this afternoon. Justin often joins us. You will be welcome as well. Why don't you surprise Sabrina?"

"Good idea. I will see you all there."

"How long will you be in port?"

"At least until after you girls' Coming-Out Ball. I'm trying to put a schedule together that will keep me in the colonies for longer periods of time. Oh, heck, Maureen, you might as well know. I am going to ask Sabrina to marry me at the dance. I fell in love with her mum, too, and her pa is a gentleman—they both gave me their blessing. I need to ask you if she can continue to live at Tucker Plantation after we are married, when she doesn't travel with me?"

Maureen's gentle laugh rippled through the air. Her green eyes filled with a curious deep longing. "Of course. I would never forgive you if you took her away forever."

"I have another idea, if Sabrina says yes. I would like to bring her family here in the spring for the wedding."

"Oh Zachary, this hasn't been released to the public as yet, but I tell you in private that when I signed off of Bryant's indenture, I also gave him land to settle, enough land on which to build a house, grow tobacco and wheat, and establish a real plantation. He wants a cherry orchard, too. We'll both need more help—me because Bryant is leaving me and Papa purchased all that new land, and Bryant because settling land takes many laboring hands. Maybe, between us, we could put Sabrina's mum and pa to work, and also the children that are old enough."

"Thank you, Maureen. You are a true and special friend to Sabrina and to me. Of course she hasn't yet said 'yes.'"

Maureen's features softened; she gave him a soothing smile. "I doubt that you have to be concerned about that."

In reply, Zachary's eyes twinkled with merriment.

* * * *

After tea, back at Tucker Plantation, Sabrina, Blackie at her heals, and Zachary stood inside the spinning cabin addition. Sabrina said, "I can hardly wait for the mulberry trees to get big enough to feed the silkworms."

Zachary took Sabrina's small hand in his. "I miss so much when I am gone. I would have loved to help Bryant build this shed for you. He did a good job."

"But we are so lucky to have you back early. The silk

goods be beautiful. We take them to Miss Colleen tomorrow. She measure us and be sewin' them to be ready for to the Ball. The colors be perfect; blue to match Amanda's eyes, green to match Maureen's and dusky rose to set off me dark hair."

"I wish you could have seen your mum's face when I went to the door with your letter. She said it was the best gift of her whole life. Then I asked her to help me pick out the silk goods. I described Maureen and Amanda, but she was really excited when she saw the dusky rose silk piece for your dress—said it was a dream come true to have you so well taken care of, and so happy."

"'cept I get so homesick sometimes, but it be better now I got Blackie baby."

Zachary rested his hands causally on her shoulders. "I promise you will see your mum and pa. I have plans—you will know them soon enough. You will see the young ones, too, but they are not so young as you remember. They are growing up fine. And one more thing…" Zachary brought a thick envelope out of his pocket. "Your mum wrote you a letter, and so did your dear friend Jinger, and a couple of the little ones, Lucy and Sophie, I think—I sometimes got the young ones mixed up—drew pictures for you."

Tears of joy blinded her eyes as Sabrina reached out for the envelope. "I be goin' to me room to study me mail. Oh, thank you Zachary, Captain."

He gathered her into his arms and planted a tantalizing kiss in the hollow of her neck. She pulled back in surprise, then their lips met and she succumbed to the lingering kiss, savoring the moment. He let her go gently. "Enjoy your letters. I will be doing extensive maintenance on the *Desiree* and getting her loaded, but I will see you from time to time between now and the Ball."

* * * *

My Dearest Maureen, 5 September, 1776

The war is gruesome. Since I left the plantation, we were ambushed by Cherokees, but the Patriot forces were saved by a mounted charge. That was at Seneca, South Carolina. On 10 August at Tugaloo River, the Cherokees were defeated by Andrew Pickens. Pickens and twenty-five militia patriots formed a circle and held off attackers until a rescue force arrived. Colonel Williamson and Pickens finally defeated a large Cherokee war party and burned Tamassy, the Indian town. On 27 August in Long Island, New York, Washington's army was defeated but escaped by night in the fog. Oh, I do go on and I'm sure you are following the war battles in the Gazette, but it is getting worse. However, we are gaining strength in determined, dedicated colonists. Each defeat brings on a new cry for freedom. The committees of the Congress are busily discussing plans for the 'United States of America'—we are all in this together now.

On a subject very dear to my heart, I have talked to Grandfather Tucker and he has given me permission to escort you to the Ball. He also recorded my land holdings at the courthouse and announced the transaction to the Burgesses. As a result, I have been elected scribe of the Continental Congress. Wouldn't you love to see Shamus' expression when his friends, the 'chaps,' tell him that bit of news?

I do have one problem that seems to haunt me—the

headaches are getting ferocious, the nightmares more harsh. Last week I dreamed through a hard wind that was blowing debris and people. There was this soft ghost-thing coming from a distance. I saw all of the people that have been in my dreams before. Your voice danced ahead of my sisters into a house I know was home. My bro was calling me in a voice as husky and golden and warm as the sun, but there was no sun. Blue arms of rain reached down from the clouds to Pa. Lightening and bone-numbing cold clung to the earth.

And the wind, the kind of wind that roars in your ears and blows dirt in your eyes and hair and between your teeth, was shrieking. It came sliding down over the world. Finally the fierce, steady wind shrilled "Rory, Rory, Rory" toward the valley and I awoke in the ashes of my dreams, and spent the next four days in bed with the headache that suppresses my consciousness. But, my love, I am well again and have something more to research. The name Rory must be a key in my life. I do so hope Zachary brings good news from Galway Bay. And now my dear one, I will sign off. I can hardly wait for the Ball when I will dance with you and hold you in my arms. But more, I long for the day when our tongues and our bodies will dance together in a silent melody. Bryant

* * * *

Dear Bryant, 12 September, 1776

Two days ago I received your letter and I do read the Gazette, although I like to hear your feel for the war. We are so busy getting the harvest in the sheds I don't have the time to study it as I should like. We had another extraordinary year. Leon, Booker and Joshua are doing everything in their power to help things run smoothly, but you are sorely missed.

I am so very sorry that you are suffering through terrifying dreams and headaches. I pray they will end soon and I am thankful you haven't dreamed of a family that you might have waiting for you—that's selfish of me, I know. I do wish your dreams would include a mother, but apparently they do not.

Now I must tell you the latest news. Zachary surprised us all when he arrived at the plantation 1 September. To set your mind at ease, he told me he has two letters for you, one from the college and the other from the postmaster at Galway Bay.

And guess what? He told me confidentially he is going to ask Sabrina to marry him the night of the dance and if she says "yes," he plans to bring her whole family back in the spring for the wedding. He is incredible. Isn't that just the most exciting thing we could hope for; didn't we say it would happen? I suggested that we are both going to need help to farm all of our new land and maybe Sabrina's whole family could work for us...

Maureen put the pen down on the desk, put her head between her hands, closed her eyes and followed her memories. She had grown up loved so she could know it, but lonely. She was six years old when her sister Deirdre, four, died of smallpox. A year later, Doug, two, and Marc, one, died of scarlet fever. The deaths hovered in her mind as every dreadful detail played over and over in her thoughts.

Etched in her memory was the empty house where her mother had played with all of them until the babies died. Her mother had left then—so busy, too busy to play with her. Kathleen had increased the time she spent at the loom in the spinning cabin and she installed the twenty honeybee hives. She began spending many hours at the slave quarters, playing with the babies and children and doctoring the sick.

It was during those years that Maureen had taken to following her papa, and had become in love with the land. Patrick never scolded her or caused her to feel she was a burden. He then encouraged her to learn about growing the crops—tobacco and wheat and corn. But as Maureen entered puberty, it was finally her mother who realized she needed a companion. Amanda, her only friend, tired too easily and Maureen needed more to get her ready for a social life and womanhood.

And Papa got dear Sabrina for me, Maureen thought. *And Shamus,* she grimaced. *But now Zachary and Justin, as well as Amanda, and many other young people are my friends, and I'm never lonely any more. How very, very blest I am. And Papa got me Bryant, my gentle, loving Bryant.*

Maureen lightly touched the tip of her nose. He had told her he would court her in his own way. She recalled the way he lightly rubbed her arm as he reached for her hand, the way he took her in his arms and the ecstasy when he drew her slowly to fit the contours of his long, lean, strong body. She remembered the day they rode on the ice, freezing in the cold swirling river but warm in the radiance of their love. Maureen giggled when she visualized his hand reaching up to prod the golden errant tuft of hair out of his face, and sobered when she recalled the feel of the mat of golden hair down the center of his chest, and the time she caressed the strong tendons in the back of his neck and trailed her fingers up and down his hairy back.

All of her memories of him were pure and unsullied. She suffered an intense ache of desire as she thought of him—her lips tingled in remembrance of his touch. Her face burned as she went back to the day she didn't protest when his hands sought the buttons to unfasten her gown, slid it off her shoulders down her arms and softly outlined the tips of her breasts. He had kissed and teased her taut nipples, rousing a melting sweetness within her.

Her emotions whirled and skidded. Her consciousness seemed to ebb and then flame more distinct than ever. Her mind relived the velvet warmth of his kisses, kisses that left her mouth burning with fire so that instinctively her body arched toward him.

Opening her eyes, Maureen came back to reality. Her vow not to become too emotionally involved was completely shattered. She had always recognized the strong passion within her when Bryant was near her, but she was powerless to let him have her body and soul. She must wait for his identity to be known...

Maureen picked up the quill pen, dipped it in the ink and finished the letter to Bryant:

> *In retrospect, the other news is giggly. Right after I finished reading your letter, a soft knock came on the office door. Can you believe it was Shamus? Alarm and anger ripped through me. I know the color drained from my face because I thought I was going to faint, but he quickly put me at ease. He put up his hand and said that Leon was be-*

hind him and did I want Leon to come in the room while we talked. I told him yes. As near as I can remember, and I knew you would want to hear it, this was the conversation:

Shamus said, "What I did was almost unforgivable but I am asking you, begging you to forgive me. I have come to apologize, my dear, deeply and sincerely." His voice was warm and had a degree of concern.

I said, "Now you have apologized. You are free to go."

But he would not give up so easily. He said, "Maureen, I've decided to stay here until after the Ball. I want to escort you and win back your favor, and Grandmama O'Toole's favor as well."

Can you guess what I said then? I said, "It seems you are too late. Bryant has asked Grandfather Tucker for permission to escort me, and it is settled."

Shamus' eyes narrowed and his back became ramrod straight, but he tried to maintain the amicable status. He had a kind of gallant and chivalrous smile and his manner seemingly stayed friendly and affable. He said, "That's all right then. I trust you will honor the three dances you promised to me."

"No dances, Shamus," I said, "you have not been sent an invitation, so I will not see you at the dance."

His eyes searched my face to see if I were playing a game, before he said, "I'm sorry to hear that, but when I remind Grandmama O'Toole and your grandfather that your papa would have wanted us to marry, they likely will let us begin courting again."

Oh, Bryant, the best part was right then. I told him that with your indenture release I had awarded you the five hundred acres in the southwest corner of my land. He liter-

ally blanched ashen. A sudden icy contempt flashed in his eyes, and I asked Leon to see him out, and off the property. I watched him ride off, not toward his O'Toole Plantation and Grandmama, but toward Williamsburg and his friends. He had mentioned earlier that he has not signed up with the Tories yet, but has been staying with the chaps at Hunter Inn. Joshua told me that through the gossip-mongers at the post office, he learned that six of the fellows who spend their idle hours at the Inn are going to volunteer for the Tories. I don't know when or if Shamus is one of the six, or whether he has gone already or not. I'm sure we'll know in time.

Only one other piece of news. Sabrina is diligently tending the mulberry trees. They are all doing well. Sabrina glows, and Blackie is always at her side.

I must get back to the tobacco shed. Come home to me soon. Maureen

* * * *

The clock seemed to race forward. The trees spread out across the landscape were resplendent with the colorful splash of fall colors. Finally it was October. Maureen and Sabrina had passed along the breakfast sideboard. Selma had brought the precious tea. Because of its scarcity, they allowed themselves the tea once a week on Saturday—the day they chose to relax and prepare for the Sabbath.

"Oh, Sabrina, what am I going to do? Maureen said. "I love Bryant so very much, but nothing is happening. His last headache had no dream with it. He said he was in a black void, a chasm—no people, no voices, no water, no wind.

"But," Sabrina soothed, "Zachary said he has two letters for him. When Bryant gets the letters everything will be all right. When will he be home?"

From the doorway, Bryant said, "He's home! Hello." He rushed to Maureen, scooped her up from her chair and twirled her around.

Zachary, behind him, said, "Come on, Sabrina, it appears we are practicing for the Ball."

As Bryant set Maureen on her feet, she raised her eyes to find him watching her closely. She saw the heart-rending tenderness of his gaze. She stared with longing at him. "Welcome home, Bryant."

"Thank you. You'll never know how good it feels when I am near you."

Zachary reached in his pocket. "I saw you ride in, Bryant. I followed you. I have the letters right here. Why don't you two go into the office and see if the mystery is solved."

In the office, Bryant put the letters on the desk and held out his arms. "The letters can wait. Come, let me hold you."

Chapter 19

Maureen melted into his arms. His passionate ardor flared once again like wildfire between them. Suddenly she was lifted into the cradle of his arms, carried to the flowered sofa and laid down with a soft pillow under her head. With an eager movement Bryant stood up and pulled off his shirt. The glimpses of his strong bronze body made Maureen's heartbeat throb in her ears. She stared at his broad back incredulously before he turned and gathered her to himself. She couldn't miss the musky smell of him as he pressed her closer. While her fingernails dug into his chest involuntarily, he unbuttoned her dress. "Slip your dress down, Maureen," he whispered sensuously.

"I should not…" she murmured back.

"I know you should not," he said, moving closer. "Tell me to quit, my love. Tell me you dislike it—tell me you are scared."

Maureen recalled the violence and the terror she felt when Shamus flopped atop of her, and would have taken and deflowered her if Bryant had not found them in time. "I wish I could…"

His mouth was on her closed eyelids, then the tip of her nose. His mouth nibbled delicately at hers in a succession of playful kisses that made Maureen want to cry out, to raise up to meet his body. "My dearest, you are sweet like sugar. Let me help you."

He caressed her mouth as he tried to remove the top of her dress. "Help me."

Her dress slipped down to the end of the sofa. Maureen gasped against his invading mouth, felt his hot skin searing her. As excitement burst inside her, she whispered, "I feel...heat in your body."

Bryant lifted his head, captured her eyes, and grinned. "It is not heat, my love. It's fire. I am burning alive. Move beneath me with nothing between us."

Her trembling fingers savored the warm, hard muscles under his mat of crisp blonde hair. She moved slightly and felt him ease down against her until her taut nipples vanished into the golden pelt of his chest. She reached up to push the lock of hair from his forehead and shuddered with pleasure.

"*This* is ecstasy," Bryant said softly.

He shifted his long powerful torso slowly, seductively, full length on hers until she felt dizzy, her own need matching his. His lips burned on hers, his fingers flamed where they touched her skin. Torrents of desire she had never known before stirred to life and there seemed to be no will inside of her to resist their blissful passion. But, finally, she found the words. "I want you with all of my heart, Bryant, but not like this. We must not make love until the time is right. Let's pull ourselves together and hope to find the answers in the letters."

Bryant ran his fingers through her hair. He fondled her small breasts; the rosy peaks grew again to pebble hardness. His hands explored the soft lines of her waist and her hips before he let out a long audible breath, pulled reluctantly away, and held her at arms' length. "You are right, my love. Let me help you up."

Dressed, Maureen and Bryant sat facing each other in the comfortable chairs on either side of the small table in front of the window. Bryant read the letter from Galway Bay. Maureen was puzzled by his abrupt change in mood. His vexation was evident. He gritted his teeth and gave her a sidelong glance of utter disbelief. She stared wordlessly across at him, her heart pounding. Bryant, trembling, passed the letter to her. She read:

> Mr. Taylor:
>
> *I regret to inform you that there are no Taylors in Galway Bay, nor in Galway county. There are, however, Taylors in Tipperary. I happen to know one Bryant Taylor is wanted for murder and for thievery as his name has appeared on the "Dangerous Criminals" list since 1 January, 1773. It appears he escaped the gallows by leaving the country—how or when has not been determined by the authorities. Your letter to me was so sincere and so obviously written by an educated man, seemingly of extremely good breeding, that I hope you are not the Bryant Taylor we are watching out for. Best regards. Conan O'Neal, Postmaster, Galway Bay*

Mixed feelings surged through Maureen. Her mind refused to register the significance of Postmaster O'Neal's words. She chewed on her lower lip and stole a look at Bryant. She couldn't tear her gaze from his profile. He was so compelling, his magnetism so potent. *No matter what*, she thought, *there is a tangible bond between us.*

As their eyes met, she felt a shock run through her. Maureen's jade eyes widened with astonishment. Bryant's eyes clung to hers. Analyzing her reaction, they seemed to probe her very soul. His brows drew together in an agonized expression. He hunched over, head resting in his hands, elbows resting on his thigh. When he spoke, Bryant's voice was thick and unsteady. "Before we talk, you should read this letter from Trinity College."

Brushing away tears to see, Maureen took the second letter from his trembling hand. It read:

> Mr. Bryant Taylor:
> To your inquiry if one Bryant Rory Taylor recently graduated from Trinity College, Dublin, the answer is no. But because you are obviously highly educated, you may want to correspond with officials at Cambridge and Oxford Colleges in England. We did further research to find one graduate that might be of interest. A Bryant Taylor of Tipperary graduated in 1731. He graduated with six other chaps: Twin brothers, Thomas and Timothy O'Toole, Galway Bay; Kenneth Machacek and Scott MacArthur, Dublin; Dennis Obrist, Limerick; and Patrick O'Neill, Cork. It is possible one of these men may be helpful, for as near as we can determine from the dates you gave us these fellows could be the age of your pa. Good luck with your search.
> Sincerely,
> Benjamin O'Connell, Dean, Trinity College, Dublin

There was sharp disappointment in Bryant's voice. "I was so sure my dreams were telling me about my life. Now I think I must move on. I love you, Maureen. I don't want to hurt you. What if I turn violent?"

Now aware that her worst thoughts of Bryant may have

been true, Maureen blurted, scarcely aware of her own voice. "You can't leave me. We must talk to Zachary to learn what he remembers of you boarding and crossing on the *Desiree*, and to Grandfather Tucker. We must take enough time for your memory to come back. You must see Dr. Julich. You must..."

"Whoa, maybe what you say is true, but we must think." His tone was resigned yet he spoke in a gentle voice.

Maureen interrupted with a crooked grin. "Besides, you are indentured, remember? I can tear up the paper that set you free."

Bryant rose in one fluid motion. He reached out and drew Maureen to her feet and guided her to the sofa. He dropped down beside her and sat facing her. Lightly he fingered a loose tendril of hair on her cheek and softly brushed the line of her cheekbone and jaw, then tenderly touched her trembling lips with one finger. They were wistful gestures; he was smiling sadly.

Maureen wiped her cheeks with the back of her hand. Bryant reached out and caught her hand in his. His hoarse whisper broke the silence. "Let's begin with Zachary. I am certain he is still with Sabrina. Why don't you ask them to come in?"

Maureen's face brightened at the suggestion. She said, "Thank you. We need our friends. They will help us through this. We *will* get to the bottom of this."

She grinned as she left the room. "Blackie will help, too. Watch and see—she'll be the first one through the door."

At Maureen's call, Sabrina and Zachary, led by Blackie, joined Bryant, and Maureen, who summoned Selma to bring tea and cakes. Taking one look at their strained expressions, Zachary said without preamble, "Your news was bad."

Bryant's expression was taut and somber. "There are no

Taylors in Galway Bay." Missing the questioning gaze that passed between Zachary and Sabrina, he continued, "but there is one Bryant Taylor from Tipperary who is wanted for murder and thievery, and is being sought. As if that is not enough, there has not been a Taylor graduate at Trinity College since 1731. He too is from Tipperary and is the right age to be the father of a Bryant Taylor of my age."

Zachary's voice was empathetic and full of compassion. "I am sorry, friend. What are you going to do?" He watched Bryant with growing concern.

Bryant's thoughts prowled restlessly, something gnawing at his insides. "I don't know," he said simply. "We are hoping you might remember something unusual about the voyage on which I came to the colonies. Shamus said I was a 'pest.' He said I boarded the *Desiree* in Dublin."

"I do remember Shamus boarding. I don't remember you at all until about the third night. I saw you most nights on deck together. It was dark, of course, so I didn't bother to try to sort you out. Indentured chaps and lasses," he looked lovingly at Sabrina, "are allowed to exercise on the decks at will. The black slaves were, of course, confined to the lower holds. When Shamus said he knew you, I figured he was looking for a servant, either for a personal valet or for the plantation. That would account for his looking into your papers to find you needed indenture funds for the trip. I was somewhat surprised that he did not bid for you at auction, but there was that 'pest' accusation, so I thought no more of it."

Sabrina said, "Me never saw you or Shamus during the day and me didn't go up on the deck after dark. It was too dangerous for a lass alone."

Maureen winked at Sabrina and looked at Bryant with gentle and contemplative eyes. "If you had seen them, you would have fallen in love with two pairs of blue eyes and I wouldn't have had a chance with this one."

Zachary chuckled. "I'd have destroyed him single-handedly when I got to know Sabrina. But enough. Where can we go from here? It's beyond my comprehension, Bryant, to even try to think of you as a murderer or a thief. I will be glad to look up Bryant Taylor this winter while I am in Ireland."

"Thank you. I will also write letters to Cambridge College and Oxford College." He turned to Maureen. "I will ask Abigail to include a note about Bryant Taylor to Timothy."

Maureen quietly entered the conversation. "I think the first step is to go to Grandfather and ask him what he suggests we do right now. Will he keep you working?"

"Will he let me escort you to the Ball?"

Maureen reached out, lacing his fingers with her own, and looking deep into his eyes, she said, "I'll beg him to let you escort me."

* * * *

James Tucker passed the letters to Grover, who read them and passed them on to Nathan. Sitting beside Maureen, Bryant, feeling accused, sat speechless as the unbearable silence stretched into his hopelessness. Filled with a sense of uneasiness, the struggle raged between his ears. *I can't have a headache,* he thought with annoyance. Smothering a groan, Bryant inhaled deeply.

James broke the silence. "I have called you all together to help me decide what this means to us, and how we shall proceed. Maureen and Bryant brought these letters to my attention yesterday, so I have obviously had time to digest the contents. I spoke to Dr. Julich. He thinks… Well, first a question, Bryant.

Is there brutal violence in any of your nightmares; do you dream of murderous deaths or destruction?"

"No Sir. Most of the dreams have people in them, calling me to them, reaching for me, but just out of reach. The mists and the clouds snatch them away from me just before I am able to touch them. The people are loving, but the circumstances are terrifying—the hard winds, the huge waves, the storms and even the library scene at the college hid my bro behind a stack of books. The horror is that I cannot see the faces, but I know they are my family." He smiled wanly. "All but Maureen who tried to save me on one occasion and who led my sisters into our home at another time—in another dream."

Grover asked, "Why do you dream of Maureen; she is not your family."

"No, Sir, but I love her. I hope when this is over we might have a future together."

James continued. "Dr. Julich says that Bryant has talked to him about the dreams. He is of the opinion that the headaches are a precondition that will be followed suddenly by full recognition. For the injury Bryant procured this is the appropriate chain of events before full comprehension of memory returns."

Grover asked, "How long does he project that full recovery will take effect?"

"Dr. Julich could not be specific. He said at the most, if Bryant recovers, it could take up to five years. Nathan, comments?"

"These charges are serious. If indeed Bryant is a dangerous criminal, we could be at risk by having him among us. We certainly can revoke the indenture release, due to 'undisclosed or uncertain circumstances.' It may behoove us to bring Shamus O'Toole into our fold; he is certainly socially acceptable, and could move up into the political arena without us having to justify his being with us. Bryant, on the other hand, is an unknown individual with a dubious background, whereas we are certain of Shamus' early credentials."

Looking over the top of his glasses, Grover spoke up. "Bryant, have you done any acts of violence since you arrived in this country?"

Bryant squirmed, but said boldly, "Yes, Sir. Six weeks ago when I was at Mistress Maureen's, I happened into the house to pick up the plans for Sabrina's silkworm shed. Selma was distraught—said Maureen had just called out from the office sounding distressed. I charged through the door, took in the scene at a glance, grabbed the poker and hit Shamus across the small of his back, causing him to roll off Maureen and fall on the floor. The blow stunned him. I have had Leon and Booker guard Maureen at all times since the incident."

"Be clear, Bryant, do you mean he was raping her?" Grover said, looking startled.

"Yes, Sir."

"Maureen?"

The hour of terror with Shamus was still locked inside her. She shuddered. "Bryant is right. He saved me and Shamus threatened his life. If you discharge Bryant, what will happen to him? Where will you send him? And after Shamus tried to…to…molest me, he moved into Hunter Inn with his friends and has not returned to his plantation."

"Maureen, have you seen Shamus since the incident?" James asked.

"Yes, Grandfather, he came back to apologize, but I can no longer help you try to convince him to know how the colonies feel about freedom. He asked if he could still have the three dances I promised him and I told him 'no'—that he would not be invited to the dance. I have no idea if he would agree to go with you to the Continental Congress or to be groomed for a political career."

"Gentlemen, we have a grave decision to make." James said. "I suggest we adjourn to Raleigh Tavern for dinner to weigh the pros and cons of that decision. Bryant, please escort Maureen back to the plantation, but meet us back at Raleigh as soon as possible. You will stay with me until your fate is settled."

"Are you entrusting Maureen to Bryant's care after what we have read in these letters today?" Nathan asked cautiously.

"I have no uneasiness about Bryant. I think he is not the Bryant Taylor of whom we read. Go, Bryant." James persisted.

"Yes, Sir." Bryant said.

Maureen stood and hugged her grandfather. "If Bryant is with you," she said, "does that mean he will be at our Ball?"

"We will see, my dear. Go on with you."

* * * *

When they were seated at the tavern, and after ordering peanut soup and Welsh Rarebit all around, Nathan said, "I insist it is too dangerous to keep Bryant with us without disclosing the possibility that he is a criminal."

"Wait a minute," Grover said. "He hasn't changed. He is still as educated and well bred as the young man was when he joined us last April. He has been selected as the scribe of the Continental Congress and has been invaluable to us at the House of Burgesses' meetings. To dismiss him without proof would take serious explanations and accusations that may or may not be true. We might ruin his reputation without provocation."

"But if we keep him with us and he turns out to be a criminal—a murderer and a thief—what does that do to *our* reputations?" Nathan asked. "By bringing Shamus aboard, those are not problems."

"How can you be so blasé? Shamus tried to rape Maureen, for heaven's sake! If that were my Laura, I'd have *him* sent back to Ireland with one brisk kick on the behind."

"Although I agree with you, Grover, and I am sickened by what happened to my granddaughter, I pray it was a foolish, impulsive act." James said. "But may I make a suggestion that may solve our problem?"

"Please do," Grover said.

"Nathan, why don't you approach Shamus, explain our dilemma and see if he would be willing to join us in the event that Bryant can no longer work with us, with the stipulation that he will never approach Maureen for any reason whatsoever. If he agrees to that, the three of us will interrogate him together to make sure he will be suitable for our purposes."

"Good idea," Grover said.

"I will do it," Nathan said, "but why not include Shamus in our group whether or not Bryant discovers who he is? That way we will be initiating Shamus' political career and helping him discover reasons to become a true loyal and free colonists. That will be to everyone's advantage—especially Abigail's."

"Do we all agree then?" James said as he picked up his wine to invite a toast.

Glasses raised, Grover and Nathan said, "Aye!"

Chapter 20

"And the verdict is?" Bryant stood before them.

James chuckled, and said, "Yes, you may stay with us until your mystery is resolved. If indeed you are a criminal, I will personally see you on the *Desiree* headed back to Ireland for due punishment."

"But," Nathan said, "we are going to ask Shamus to join the four of us in order to launch him on his political career. We need all of the young men we can get to help win the war and gain our freedom."

Bryant was momentarily speechless in his surprise before anger knotted inside him. "You mean despite what he almost did to Maureen, you would welcome him and help him enter the political arena? You would expose me to his threats, 'You will regret this attack until I see you dead, Bryant Rory Taylor,' and '…I *will* have the last word.' Those were not idle threats. Forgiving my pun, he was dead serious."

"Wait a minute," Grover said. "We have agreed to examine and cross-examine Shamus before we agree to take him on if he concurs to the arrangement. There will also be a stipulation that he is *never* to go near Maureen. We think you will be safe from his vicious temperamental threats because he will want his land and Abigail's approval."

James interjected. "We know this is serious, Bryant. As you know, Abigail is writing a letter to Timothy and Sean. We will see you protected to the best of our ability until both mysteries are cleared up or resolved in an appropriate manner."

* * * *

The month sped by. Amanda, Sabrina and Maureen did their work, but took time out to go to Williamsburg for three dress fittings. Phoebe and Minnie rode along to help the girls change in and out of their dresses.

But this was the big day—Saturday, October 26, 1776. Zachary had escorted them to Grandfather Tucker's town house, but had left to get dressed in charcoal breeches and matching vest. "You ladies have nothing on we gentlemen. My ruffled shirt is oyster alabaster with matching silk stockings. While you girls were being fitted and fitted, tailor Sam was sewing my outfit. Would you like to hear about my square-toed shoes?"

"Off with you," Maureen said with a smile.

"As you wish, madam," Zachary responded gallantly. His eyes blazed into Sabrina's as he gave them a full, proud salute and rode on to the *Desiree*.

Excitement welled up inside Maureen, who loved walking into Grandfather Tucker's graceful home by way of its stately avenue bordered by catalpa trees. She thought the house was a splendid structure and had been the scene of many hospitable social gatherings during her grandmother's lifetime, but her grandfather had almost quit entertaining since her death. So tonight was special.

Inside, Sabrina dreamily went up the curved stairway to

begin her bath.

Alone now, Maureen walked slowly through the house remembering the pride her grandmother had taken in the lavish English furnishings. The parlor where small groups of guests were received and entertained had a flowered settee, two chairs of contrasting cozy cushions. The rocking chair sat in one corner, where she visualized herself as a small child sitting on her grandmother's lap being read to. Maureen smiled.

This night, all was in readiness for the Ball that would be Maureen's, Sabrina's and Amanda's formal entrance into adult society. The ballroom was complete with chairs gracing the outside walls for the 'dowagers.' She glanced at the chandelier hanging gracefully from the center of the ceiling; it was of fragile, delicate glass and held eight candles.

The dining room, complete with a mahogany Chippendale table and a fine set of Queen Anne chairs, was set with stacks of fine china, enough silverware to serve the guests, slender goblets and fine linen napkins. Maureen thought Grandmama O'Toole had done an outstanding job of directing the details of the event, and selecting a pleasing menu for the buffet.

She returned to the parlor and sat in the rocking chair to rest a few moments before she bathed and slipped into her dress for the evening. Maureen wondered if she would see Bryant and touched the tip of her nose. She closed her eyes and remembered his passionate kisses.

And what are you thinking about, my love?" Bryant said softly as he entered the parlor and sat facing her in one of the comfortable chairs.

"Where did you come from?" Maureen asked in a startled tone.

"I asked you first."

"Oh. I was just anticipating the evening ahead. All of Mr. Philip's boys and Miss Matilda's girls from the year we had the spelling bee will be here. You met most of them and others of tonight's guests at Laura Harrison's May Day party. Has Grandfather given you permission to join us?"

"He did. We got back yesterday. James has complete confidence in me despite the letters. Grover is also genuinely warm and friendly, but Nathan is wary."

"Did Shamus join you? And how does he treat you?"

Bryant stood and held out his arms. "Shamus is out of the picture. He refused to work with them as long as I was in their company. He told the men to send me back to Ireland; then he would consider joining them, but they declined to dismiss me. Apparently you haven't heard that Shamus joined the Brits, along with five chaps of the Hunter Inn group."

Maureen walked into Bryant's arms and buried her face in his chest. She reached up to push his errant golden lock of hair up, and sighed. "I'm so sorry for Grandmama O'Toole. How will this ever end?"

"It will end." Bryant watched Maureen digesting the information, then continued. "I've been to see your Grandmama. She says they are doing well. She said Justin and Amanda are keeping the plantation in excellent order. I escorted them here. Abigail is seeing to things in the kitchen. Amanda went upstairs for her bath. Justin is seeing to the horses."

Maureen gave herself to the moment. Her yearning heart wanted to go wherever his magic would take her. Their kiss brought tears from both their eyes. Maureen could feel the physical waves pulling at her. The look she gave Bryant spoke of her love.

His kiss became eager, hungry. Maureen's breasts rose and fell rapidly, taut against her gown. She held him fiercely, wanting to give him more, but unable to do so.

"It's all right, my love," Bryant said at last. "It is almost time for us to get ready, but first let me tell you about my dream. I know I am getting closer to regaining my memory."

"How do you know?" she asked in a whisper.

"We had better sit down," Bryant said with a playful smile. "I can't think when I'm holding you so close."

Maureen reluctantly moved back to the rocking chair.

Bryant sat down. "The dream was like unraveling the riddle of my existence. I dreamed about boarding the *Desiree*. The dockhands took my trunk to my cabin. On shore, waving, was my brother and sisters and Pa."

"But you came with only the clothes on your back."

"I know, but I had a trunk in the dream. My family was sending me off. Then the water flowed over their faces like a waterfall hitting a rock and spraying upward. My bro is blond, as are my sisters. Pa's hair is white. I cried. The pain in my head was excruciating and the tears were real when I woke up. The headache lasted four days. James tended me with cool, wet towels. When I was free of the pain, I remembered the ring on Bro's finger. It was a large square black pearl set in gold. I gave it to him when we graduated from college."

"What do you mean, when 'we' graduated from college?"

"I don't know." Bryant's gaze came to rest on her questioning eyes. "I just know it's real." A gentle melancholy took possession of him. His head drooped dejectedly.

Maureen felt a keen sense of pity. She felt sorrow and want. She stood and went to him. Keeping her voice noncommittal, not wishing to encourage false hopes, she said, "It's coming." Her touch on his shoulder broke his melancholy moment. Maureen saw the understanding register on Bryant's face.

The irritation and frustration melted from his face. He smiled a gentle smile. "Enough, my love. If you don't get into your bath with that intoxicating fragrance, attar of roses, you won't be ready to dance until dawn—the exact amount of time I want you in my arms."

"How did you know about attar of roses?"

"My sisters use it."

"How do you know that?"

Bryant looked puzzled. He brushed the hair up from his forehead. "I don't know. I smelled it on you once before and remembered its name and the fuss my sisters made when they ran out of it. Never mind. Hurry, so we can dance the night away."

Maureen eyes took in his powerful presence and found a joyous satisfaction in studying his profile. She watched the play of emotions on his face. "It sounds enchanting, but you will have to remember to share me with all of the lads."

* * * *

Maureen, Sabrina and Amanda descended the wide stairway as one, their silk dresses clinging and whispering together. Watching them were Bryant, Zachary and Justin. Bryant, dressed in hunter green britches and vest, with a leaf-green silk shirt and matching silk stockings, held out his arm to escort Maureen to the door where the girls would stand to greet their guests.

"You look very handsome, Sir," Maureen said mischievously as the shock of him rushed through her. "Your new outfit compliments my gown, but how did you know I would be wearing green?"

"Oh, my dear, I have friends in strange places," Bryant said. He appraised her with more than mild interest and kissed her with his eyes. "But you, my dear one, are a vision of delightful loveliness. May I sign your card for a dozen dances?"

"Of course you may not. The first dance, one on either side of the middle and the last dance are almost more than I can spare," Maureen teased.

"Not nearly enough, but I will bow to your every desire."

Maureen, Sabrina and Amanda, bravely serene, stood to receive their guests. They were flanked by James who stood by Maureen and Abigail, who stood beside Amanda.

Bryant, Zachary and Justin faded into the background, escorting the dowagers to their seats and shaking the hands of the men who gathered into small clusters to solve the complexities and particulars of the war, and to celebrate the victories.

When the guests had arrived, James called for recognition. "This, dear friends, is the night I have anticipated for many years. I am so very proud to introduce my lovely granddaughter, Maureen Maguire. This night is her night, her entrance into our adult world. But there is more. Sabrina O'Connor, Maureen's faithful companion will join her. Please welcome Sabrina. And last, but in no way least, Amanda O'Toole will also enter the social register. As you well know, Amanda and Maureen have been friends and neighbors since they were wee ones. Abigail is my hostess this night; she has worked tirelessly to make sure the sideboard is complete with your favorite foods. Abigail?"

"I would only add that the delicacies flow and will fill

your stomachs. Enjoy!"

James continued. "The Sons of Liberty Band..."

After the applause died down, James concluded, "The music will begin in fifteen minutes, plenty of time for all of you lovely young ladies to mingle and finish filling your dance cards. Let us make this night one to remember with joy. Thank you."

As was the custom, when the music began, Bryant bowed to Maureen and whirled her off. Zachary followed suite with Sabrina, as did Justin with Amanda. The rest of the pairs then joined the three honored ones.

Feet, as well as eyes dancing, Maureen looked at Bryant. "What fun," she said. "Grandmama and Grandfather are a charming hostess and host, don't you think?"

"I think," Bryant said, devouring Maureen with his heart in his eyes, "that you are making small talk when we should be making love."

Maureen threw her head back and laughed. "In front of all these people?"

"I wish the whole world could know how much I love you." Bryant pulled Maureen close to his long, lean body and dropped his head against the softness of her golden-red hair. She snuggled into his arm, head on his shoulder as the dance ended.

One dance found the group in a circle. The girl took the left arm of the young man beside her; she was twirled to the right arm of the next man. When Maureen took Bryant's arm, he quickly kissed the tip of her nose as she left him and whirled on to the next. Laughing and breathless, they stopped when the Sons of Liberty Band ended the playing to take a break.

Abigail led the band members to the sideboard spread for dinner. Lined up behind them, the guests filled their plates."

Appetizers consisted of crab cakes with lobster lemon cream; beer batter shrimp with red pepper and papaya sauce; wild game bites marinated and served with sun-dried fruit relish; assorted mushrooms simmered in wine sauce; and smoked fish—salmon, trout and sturgeon—served with caviar and brioche. Soup choices included forest mushroom, black bean with smoked ham, turtle, peanut, and fish muddle stew. The salads were spinach salad with sliced mushrooms, sieved egg and honey poppy-seed dressing and herbed goat cheese on a bed of mixed field greens topped with caramelized apples and walnut vinaigrette.

Main dishes included baby lamb with hazelnut crust and rosemary, salmon, chicken, veal, jambalaya oysters and roast beef. At the end of the line, for the sweet tooth, was gingerbread. The guests drank coffee, tea, wine and beer, or wassail—a combination of apple cider, pineapple juice and tea spiced with clove, cinnamon and varied other spices.

Maureen spent the break time serving the elderly ladies and gentlemen. She talked to Grover and Nathan and the other men, before the dancing resumed. Maureen felt that the evening was rushing by and when three dances remained, she found herself in the arms of Henry Custis.

Eyes twinkling in the flickering candlelight shadows, Henry said, "I have the next two dances with you, Maureen. I've waited all evening to dance with the smartest lady in Williamsburg."

"Thank you, kind sir," Maureen said with a sudden laugh. "And how do you spell kohlrabi, Henry?" she asked teasingly, glancing at him."

"Kohlrabi, k o h l r a b i, kohlrabi," he answered with a trace of laughter in his voice. "I learned it when I was much younger and less wise. Oh, how I would like to court the young lady who taught me a lesson in humility that night."

"A lesson in humility?"

"Oh yes, I was so sure, so very sure, I would win that spelling bee. Not only was I sure, I was pompous, cocky. But smart as I thought I was, you bested me. But I digress. I would very much like to court you, but I see I am too late…" His voice trailed off sadly.

"Is it so obvious?"

"It is. You wear your heart in the lights of your beautiful emerald green eyes. Father told me your story, and Bryant's story. I can only wish you the very best ending to the horrible mystery of your lives." Unspoken pain was alive and glowing in his demeanor.

"Thank you, Henry." Maureen's eyes were misty and wistful. She felt a sudden pang of regret. She looked at Henry with fondness. "Is there anything I can to do to help you?"

His mood seemed suddenly almost buoyant. His tone was apologetic. "Forgive me, Maureen," Henry said with quiet emphasis. He grinned. "I may have met my next victim tonight. I danced with Sarah Stewart earlier and she saved the last dance for me. She was the last girl before you to go down at the spelling bee. Her word was rudimentary; she spelled the …tary with an 'e.' Already we have that bad 'e' in common." Henry winked at Maureen and they burst out laughing.

"I believe this dance is mine," Bryant interrupted softly.

"I believe you are right," Henry said jovially, "and my Sarah awaits."

"I have been green with jealousy all evening, my love,"

Bryant said as he gathered Maureen in his arms, "but of Henry, most particularly."

Maureen's eyes sparkled into his. "No need, dear Bryant. Henry and I have known each other all of our lives. He saw in a glance that my heart belongs to you."

"But you two were so engrossed with each other and having so much fun at the end."

"I'll tell you all about it someday, but don't spoil our last dance with 'small talk,'" Maureen said sweetly as she settled comfortably into the crook of his arm.

They twirled and spun, rapture on their faces, until the last when Bryant gracefully bent Maureen down in a final deep dip, kissed the tip of her nose and brought her upright to encircle her waist. Unable to resist, Maureen reached up and pushed up his golden lock of hair.

James stood then and held up his hand for silence. "I have one final announcement," he said, "but first I want to thank you all for coming tonight to give our girls a thrilling entry into our world. All of these young people here tonight will go forth to make our country free and independent for future generations. Let us give them all the support we can for capturing the true spirit of America. Under their direction, the United Colonies will one day become the United States of America."

The applause went on until James once again called for attention. "Abigail, will you join me?"

Chapter 21

Abigail regally rose and stood beside James. Looking fondly at her, he continued. "The highlight of my evening was when Abigail O'Toole accepted my proposal of marriage. We are ready to take life easy—together. We plan to marry within the month when Parson Moss can fit it in. We will then merge the plantations to become the Tucker O'Toole Plantation. It will be deeded to our girls, Maureen and Amanda, with arrangements for Sabrina to live there as long as she wants to."

Nathan stepped forward and shook James' hand. He said, "I will draw up the papers whenever you are ready."

A commotion in the room caused everyone to turn toward the door. "You will do no such thing. I am to inherit the O'Toole Plantation. Maureen will marry me at Christmastide. The date has been set with Parson Moss." Shamus entered the room boldly. He was resplendent in the uniform of a British officer, a lieutenant. He sported a red coat and gray trousers; in his sash belt was a flint pistol and a saber in its holder.

The room shattered into silence. Abigail stepped forward. "You have been disowned. The document was signed yesterday."

Maureen joined her. "I will not marry you Shamus

O'Toole. My heart has joined another."

Shamus' voice was calculating and cold. "You have no choice; you are a woman. Your papa gave *me* permission to court you. He expected us to marry. I announce to all of these witnesses..." he circled the room with his arm, "that Bryant Taylor is wanted in Ireland for murder and thievery. He will be returned to the authorities there, or he will be dead. Now, Sons of Liberty Band, I demand you play a waltz for Maureen and me, to celebrate our engagement."

James said, "NO! Her papa is dead; I am her guardian. Leave! Immediately!

Abigail stood straight. "I concur. Leave this instant!"

Maureen joined James and Abigail. "I will not marry you, Shamus. If I must be a spinster for the rest of my days, I will not marry you."

"You will, my dear. I promise you that if Bryant is not returned to Ireland he will be dead," Shamus said. He did not take his saber out of its sleeve, but touched the pistol at his side and said gently, "believe it."

Henry Custis and Fletcher Stewart stepped forward, one on either side of Shamus and took his arms. Shamus turned on his heel and marched out of the house.

The Ball was over.

Grover stepped forward and said quietly, "We thank you once again for coming. Bryant will join us in Philadelphia next week. As most of you know, he has been elected as scribe of the Congress. We are all anticipating the return of Bryant's memory. Please don't allow this unpleasant interruption to spoil the memories of this wonderful evening. All who wish may stay for a congratulatory toast to Abigail and James."

The Champaign was poured and distributed. Everyone

lifted their glass, "To you, our friends," Grover said. The guests cheered, drank the toast and quietly passed through the line before going into the starlit October night.

* * * *

At last upstairs in their beds, in the largest bedroom of James' home, Maureen, Sabrina and Amanda looked at each other contemplatively. "That was quite an evening," Amanda said. "Won't it be wonderful when Grandmama and your grandfather marry and settle down here?"

"I cannot believe they be includin' me in the plans," Sabrina added.

"We'll be truly cousins, Amanda," Maureen added, "and you are like a sister to me, Sabrina." Then, in a voice filled with love, she said, "I have noticed a flush on your face all evening and a new sapphire ring on your finger. Tell us about it."

Sabrina's eyes filled with misty tears. Holding out her finger so Amanda and Maureen could see the sparkle of her ring, she said, "This night Zachary asked me to marry him."

"And you said?" Maureen asked as she pulled both girls into her arms.

"Humpty Dumpty had a great fall. All the kings horses and all the kings men could not put Humpty Dumpty together again, so I be marryin' you, dear Zachary Fitzsimmons."

"You didn't!"

Maureen and Amanda burst into laughter. Sabrina joined them. "I did, for fact. He laugh so hard, he almost forgot to put the ring on me finger."

"When is the wedding?" Amanda asked almost wistfully.

"It be in the spring. Can you believe, Zachary say he bringin' me family here so they can be present for me weddin?'"

Maureen's eyes, showing an expression of satisfaction, asked, "Did Zachary tell you that we have room on the plantation for all of your family to work if they want to stay, and are old enough?"

"You knew me mum and me pa be comin'?"

"It all depended on whether you would marry Zachary or not. I've been dying to talk to you, but I had to wait to see what would happen tonight."

"He told you and you didn't tell me?" Sabrina shook her head in disbelief, then smiled, wrapped in a silken cocoon of euphoria. "He be the best man I ever know."

Maureen looked at Amanda. Her voice held the wonder of excitement. "Do you believe that, Amanda?"

"Of course not. I'm waiting for Little Tommy Tucker to sing for our supper."

"Or for Justin Thatcher to ask you to marry him?"

"One down, two to go, right, Maureen?" Amanda said in a whisper.

There was no answer. Maureen and Sabrina had fallen asleep.

* * * *

James, Nathan, Grover and Bryant left for Philadelphia the Monday after the Ball. The wedding had been set. Parson Charles Moss would marry James and Abigail the day after Christmas, the day Shamus had decided to marry Maureen; only the bride and the groom had changed.

Shamus went north to join his troop.

Justin and Amanda, with Abigail, left for the O'Toole Plantation the last day of October, on a windy-rain-soaked day. Maureen and Sabrina went back to Tucker Plantation after Zachary pulled anchor and sailed for England and Ireland on the

Desiree on 1 November.

Maureen and Sabrina both joined Miss Matilda to teach the young girls—Sabrina to teach basics; Maureen to teach Latin and geography.

* * * *

The letter arrived 6 December 1776:

> *My dear Maureen,*
>
> *I am sorry to distress you, but I am able to bring Bryant home. There is no way to say this gently to ease your mind. Bryant was shot. In his feverish delirium, he keeps murmuring, "It was Shamus O'Toole. He shot my heart; I saw it coming; I stepped away. It was Shamus O'Toole. He shot my heart; I saw it coming; I stepped away."*
>
> *The Continental Congress has found it expedient to move to Baltimore, as Philadelphia is no longer safe because of war activities. Shamus must have heard of our decision. My guess is he was waiting for Bryant to head out for the coach.*
>
> *Bryant seemed to disappear before our very eyes. He screamed suddenly and Nathan found him writhing in pain before he laid down, death-like still. Nathan and Grover and I carried him to Dr. Jerome Appleton, who removed a bullet from the back of his shoulder—a scant inch above the heart. Another bullet, both shot from the same flint pistol, was shot into Bryant's neck. Fortunately, both bullets missed vital parts. He lives, but needs constant, ceaseless care. These were the conditions on which Dr. Appleton would release Bryant to be taken home. I will bring him home to you to nurse him back to health.*

> *I must return quickly then to Baltimore by the thirteenth of the month, if I am to be home for Christmas and my wedding, and to the joy of my new life with Abigail. I have resigned my political duties effective 1 January.*
>
> *Bryant and I will travel as fast as he is able. I am sorry to be the bearer of such bad news.*
>
> *My love, Grandfather*

Maureen ran out to the spinning cabin. "Sabrina, Sabrina. It's Bryant. He was shot. Grandfather is bringing him here. Oh, Sabrina, what will we do? If he dies…"

"Hush now, Maureen. He be alive." Sabrina put her arms around Maureen.

"It was Shamus," Maureen said, racked with sobs.

"We be takin' good care of him." Sabrina stepped away and led Maureen to her bed.

* * * *

By the following morning, the crying was done. Maureen had dried her tears and during the next few remaining days, she prepared the guest room for Bryant's return. She had Leon bring the rocking chair that had once been Kathleen's into the room. Sabrina saw to the salves and ointments, the sterile bandages and the quinine that would ease Bryant's pain.

It was purple dusk of the fourth day when James' carriage arrived at the door. Leon and Booker carefully lifted Bryant, carried him to the bed, undressed him and readied him for Maureen. Tears streaked down her face as she bent over Bryant's still figure and pushed the golden hair out of his eyes.

"Dr. Appleton said Bryant is in a deep coma and may remain there for days or weeks," James said as he stroked Maureen's arm. "He told me that you must cleanse the wounds and change the dressings each day to keep gangrene from eating him up."

"How will we know if the poison is in him?"

"You will first see pus leaking from the wound; it will be odious. I stopped briefly in Williamsburg on the way here. Dr. Julich will come in the morning to examine Bryant and show you and Sabrina how to care for him."

Sabrina came then and put her arm around Maureen's waist. "Me be knowin' how to help. When me pa had accident with his horse and got tangled up and punctured with a rusty ol' pitch fork, me mum and me did care for him."

Maureen suddenly left the room. She retched until she felt there was nothing left inside her. When she returned her face was white. She was shaking visibly.

"You be goin' to bed," Sabrina said. "Me be takin' the night. You be better in the mornin.'"

* * * *

Christmas came and went. "Hurry now," Sabrina said, slipping Maureen's bright red cloak over the shoulders of her forest green gown. "Jeb be waitin' with the carriage."

"I'm hurrying," Maureen said, grabbing up her matching red muff and bonnet. She sighed. "Take good care of Bryant."

"Don't be worryin' none. He be comin' out of his sleepin' soon. His wounds be almost healed and he be restin' more natural like."

"But why doesn't he wake up?"

"Off with you. You not be disappointin' your Grandfather and Grandmama. The weddin' not be waitin'."

Through swirls of fluffy white snow that dropped out of the heavens, Maureen walked down the path to the carriage as the cold, difficult winter seemed to wrap around everything in sight.

Amanda and Justin had already arrived and were waiting with Jeb when Maureen joined them.

"How is Bryant?" Amanda asked as she wrapped a blanket around Maureen's shoulders.

"He doesn't wake up. Sabrina says he's breathing easier. Yesterday, Dr. Julich said he is healed—that he will wake up when he is ready."

"Oh, that is good. Let's just relax and enjoy the wedding."

The carriage jounced along slowly. Maureen settled back and closed her eyes. Memories of the past few weeks flooded through her mind. She had sat in the rocking chair beside Bryant for fourteen to sixteen hours, leaving only for short hours during the middle of the night. Sabrina sat with him during the night. Mornings, she cleansed the wounds, applied the salves, administered the quinine and changed Bryant's bandages, after which she slept.

Maureen arose before dawn to start a new day. She held his hand, brushed the errant hair away from his eyes, kept compresses on his head and exercised his left arm to help keep it limber as Dr. Julich had instructed.

Selma brought Maureen's meals and Bryant's liquids to the sick room throughout the day. Amanda came twice a week to do the books and prepare the orders for the following spring. Justin escorted her and helped Leon and Booker plant the seedlings for spring planting.

Maureen opened her eyes. "Where are we?"

"I think you slept," Amanda said. "We are almost at Grandfather Tucker's."

"I didn't mean to sleep. I wanted to thank the two of you for all you have done during Bryant's coma. I couldn't have done it without your help. And, Justin, Leon said you have been a lifesaver getting the tobacco seeds planted in the beds. We will have two hundred additional acres put in tobacco fields this year and Booker said he checked on the new cherry orchard and the trees are surviving the winter very well."

"Bryant will be well soon," Justin said, "and when his arm is getting back to normal, he will be able to supervise the planting."

* * * *

The parlor was cozy warm. Parson Moss stood in front of the crackling fire to perform the ceremony as the fireplace shadows did a lively dance on the walls. Nathan and Grover stood beside James who stood protectively beside his bride. Amanda and Maureen stood beside Abigail who wore a red silk gown with silver gray petticoat skirts and matching ruffles on the sleeves, around the color of the pleated bodice and bonnet. The men's wives and Justin sat on the flowered settee.

Maureen watched as the brightening day touched her grandfather's wrinkled cheeks and forehead. *Time has shrunk him,* she thought, *but he is a loving and generous man and Abigail hasn't a senile bone in her body; it's difficult to guess her age; only the calendar knows.* Maureen looked at them more closely. *They have a bright and shining future; they will ripen together in their golden years because they are a happy, optimistic couple.*

James and Abigail said their pledges to one another.

"I now pronounce you man and wife," Parson Moss said.

James' face filled with love and as he basked in the radiance of Abigail's tender smile, he pulled her into her arms and they kissed with the ardor of the young.

Shamus burst through the door. "Why didn't you wait for me? I've been at war and none of you had the decency to wait for my arrival. No matter. Maureen, it's our turn to take our vows."

Shamus broke the quiet. "What's got your tongue, Maureen? Parson Moss promised to marry us directly after James and Grandmama O'Toole took their vows."

"Since you did not inform us that this was to be a double wedding, I don't think Parson Moss realized that I had refused your proposal of marriage. You may leave, Shamus. I will never marry you and I will never welcome you in my presence."

"But you have no one to care for you. Have you not been informed that Bryant is dead?"

His voice was like a whiplash. Maureen's cheeks turned chalky white. Bile rose in her throat. A little voice inside her head wondered where he had been, and asked why he had come so late. Had he been to Tucker Plantation and killed Bryant? A fainting kind of nausea seized her. "What makes you so sure?" Maureen asked, fighting for control.

"That's easy. I saw him shot in Philadelphia. He dropped like a rock falling into a chasm. I saw these men," Shamus' arm circled Nathan, Grover and James, "carry him off."

Relief flowed through Maureen. "I see," she said, "but didn't you try to help them?"

"Not on your life," Shamus flared back at her. "I promised to see him dead and I did. I had duties to attend to. Now, we marry. Parson Moss?"

"I was not aware Maureen had refused your proposal," Parson Moss said in a casual tone. "It seems I cannot perform the ceremony without her consent."

James and Abigail, still holding hands, stepped forward. "We have already explained that you are not welcome here," James said. "If you dare to enter our lives again, you will be turned over to the authorities."

"And I will see to it," Nathan agreed.

"If that is a threat, I shall leave this unreasonable war and go back to the O'Toole Plantation until you all see reason." Shamus' voice bore a trace of threat. "That land is mine."

Justin was on his feet. He hammered Shamus with powerful blows. Shamus took two staggering steps backward. The blade of his saber flashed in the low-slanting sunlight. In deadly earnest Justin put his fist into Shamus' nose; he felt something break beneath the blow.

Clutching his nose, Shamus responded with a clumsy punch. Wet with blood running down his uniform, he twisted aside. Justin grasped Shamus' wrist and yanked it backward until the saber shot across the room to the floor.

"Out with you!" Justin said.

Head still buzzing from the blow, Shamus turned and left the house.

The cheerful morning was ruined. Silenced enveloped the room. Maureen broke the quiet. "I must go to Bryant, Grandfather and Grandmama. I'm sorry to spoil your wonderful day, but Sabrina must not be left alone and Booker and Leon must be put on watch in case Shamus shows up to cause more trouble."

"Amanda and I will go, too. We'll stay at Tucker Plantation until we know you are safe from Shamus," Justin said.

"Abigail and I will go, too." James said. "We'll stay at O'Toole Plantation. There are plenty of our men to guard us. It is fortunate that Shamus still thinks Bryant is dead. I think he will go back to his troop."

Abigail laughed heartily. "He will probably tell them he fought enemy soldiers to have such injuries. Thank you, Justin."

Chapter 22

Sabrina was running out to meet the carriage as it arrived at Tucker Plantation. "Come quick, Maureen. It be Bryant. He be askin' for you."

Maureen raced ahead of the others to Bryant's room. She stopped when she saw him. Tears of pleasure found their way to her eyes. Bryant reached for her hand.

"I'm awake," he said simply. His gaze roved lazily, appraising her.

"Thank goodness," she said.

Not letting go of his hand, Maureen sat down in the rocking chair. They talked quietly until Bryant was exhausted and fell into a troubled sleep. In the lonely light of dawn, Maureen disengaged her hand and moved to the window. She was filled with a sense of uneasiness. Mumbling her name over and over, Bryant was flopping around in his bed, pounding the pillow, changing positions. He snored then babbled undistinguishable words and phrases. And, finally, he woke up wide-eyed, still partially in the grip of a bad dream, mouth ready to scream. Maureen went to him and touched his head.

"It's my head," Bryant said. "It's like a struggle raging between my ears, like a silver spike of pain plunged deeply through my head—help me."

Maureen called Selma to bring cool water. The days that followed were all the same. Maureen kept cool compresses on Bryant's head by day. In the evenings, the headaches lifted.

"It's like paroxysms of excruciating pain that reverses the pattern of the sun. They come at dawn and lift only at nightfall. Your face comes in and out of focus." He bit his lower lip and stifled an instinctive moan.

"Do you dream?" Maureen asked Bryant in one of his more lucid moments.

"It's like childish memories of terrors that hover above me," he answered. "It's like my mind is swimming with a reminiscence, an elusive half-recalled wisp of memory—something that has been buried beneath my brain for the months and years since I arrived in the colonies."

Each morning, Bryant seemed to disappear down some endless corridor, as if the past, like the mist, was closing around him. Six weeks Maureen sat beside him while the headaches raged where memory still lurked in some secret place in his mind. Winter waned.

The afternoon sunlight slanted through the front window when Bryant fully awoke without the aftermath of pain. He awoke with feelings of disquiet, dislocation—and relief. The room was going in and out of focus when Bryant had a paralyzing moment of sudden insight.

Simple denial would not drive the thought away. It played over and over in his mind like a dominant chord. He knew surprisingly and decisively who he was. He admitted the odd parallel. Of course. Shamus. Although a few inches shorter, Shamus was lean, muscular, built much like himself. He was blond and blue-eyed like himself.

I am Shamus Rory O'Toole, Bryant said inside himself. The final, icy comprehension spread through him. *He knocked me out and threw me overboard. He stole my name, my identity and pawned me off as himself, Bryant Taylor.*

Fresh from an extravagant scent of roses bath, Maureen walked into the room to sit with him. Bryant beamed cheerfully and his face suddenly lit with joy. With a flash of curiosity, Maureen gave him a soothing smile. "I see you are feeling better."

"I am finally myself and you will never guess who that 'self' is."

"So you will tell me," Maureen said excitedly.

"I am Shamus *Rory* O'Toole."

He watched Maureen. For a long moment, she looked back at him. She studied his face unhurriedly, feature by feature. At last, she said, "And you know this because?"

"Because the real Bryant Taylor stalked me, night after night on the trip coming over. He asked about my life—details I wasn't expecting and were none of his business. I was kind to him. I could see he was interested and I was already homesick for my family and Sean in particularly. Sean and I were inseparable, although he was the daring one, the mischievous one. Remember the dream I told you about the spanking my older sister gave me? Her name is Bridget. Sean had done the deed and given me the blame. I took the consequences and never told them different."

"But how will you prove you are Shamus O'Toole??"

Shamus pulled Maureen down to him. His last words were smothered on her lips. His tongue traced the fullness of her lips and slipped inside to explore the recesses of her mouth. The velvet warmth of his kiss sang through her veins. Shamus let her go.

He slid to his knees. "Will you marry me, Maureen?" he

said taking her hand.

Maureen's heart leaped with delight, but she halted, mocking shock. "Marry Shamus O'Toole? Never!"

Shamus came to his feet. "Not Shamus O'Toole—Shamus *Rory* O'Toole.

"You didn't answer my question. How will you prove it?"

"Call Leon to help me dress and get to the carriage. I'm weak from so long in the bed, but I can prove it. We must go to see Grandmama O'Toole, er, Tucker."

* * * *

James and Abigail Tucker, with Joy sleeping at her feet, were sitting comfortably in their chairs, reading, when Maureen and Bryant arrived.

"What a pleasant surprise," Abigail said as she put down her book.

Bryant knelt at Abigail's feet and put his head in her lap.

"And what is this, Bryant? You are looking well."

"My memory has returned. I am not Bryant." His eyes came to rest on her questioning eyes. "I am Shamus Rory O'Toole. You can believe me. Rory was your maiden name."

Tears glistened on Abigail's pale heart-shaped face. "You are right, Bry…Shamus. Lift your hair; let me see the back of your neck."

His blue eyes widened in a pretentious accusation. "You don't believe me? Would I lie to my own grandmama about something so serious? It's there."

James and Maureen exchanged a subtle look of amusement.

"Humor an old lady," Abigail said. "Let me see it."

Shamus lowered his head. Abigail pushed his blond hair off his neck to expose a small strawberry birthmark on the base of his hairline.

He had broken through her fragile control. "It's you. It's really you," Abigail said in a choked voice, and threw her arms around her grandson.

"There are a few problems, however," Shamus said as he stood up and faced James.

"And they are?"

"Well, first, how do we prove this to others. My papers are in order. Patrick locked them up at Tucker Plantation. We need to catch the real Bryant Taylor and have him deported to Ireland, but Bryant has five hundred acres in the southwest corner of Maureen's land."

"That doesn't seem too serious. Nathan will unravel those things. What else is bothering you?"

Shamus turned and gazed at Maureen. Her lips tingled in remembrance of his touch. Shamus moved close to her and looked down at her intensely. Remember when you asked me what your papa said to me and I was so dark I wouldn't answer?"

"Yes, I remember the tortured dullness of disbelief that passed through those cornflower eyes of yours. Your expression was furious and tortured, and Papa was gone and couldn't tell me himself. The last thing he said before he died was 'marry for love, my dear daughter. Take your time; don't take second best. Trust…' I begged him to tell me whom to trust, but he couldn't."

"When you asked me what he said," Bryant stood up and took her face in his hands, caressingly, "I was too frightened to tell you. Patrick never quite trusted the man we thought was Shamus. He asked me to make sure you were always safe. I didn't know who I was and I was so in love with you and so jealous of him, I didn't dare tell you. I felt you slipping away to that alias swindler—your early morning rides, your distrust of me, my lengthy indenture and my lack of memory. All I could do during those years was love you and ask you and pray that you would trust me and wait for me."

James cleared his throat and interrupted. "Now that those years have been cleared and cleansed, what is the other thing bothering you, young man?"

"I asked Maureen to marry me, but she said, 'marry Shamus O'Toole? Never.'"

Bryant put his arms around Maureen's tiny waist and fixed his eyes bright with joy straight into Maureen's eyes. "Will you marry Shamus Rory O'Toole?"

Standing tiptoe, Maureen put her arms around his neck. "Absolutely," she said softly. "I love you."

* * * *

As spring discovered the finishing stroke of winter, Shamus, with Maureen at his side, became stronger. They took care of the seedlings with Justin at O'Toole Plantation, and with Leon and Booker. They walked for hours along the river where green willows drooped their branches into the river and they took long rides on Black Warrior and Little Princess.

James and Abigail moved back to Williamsburg and Shamus moved into the O'Toole Plantation with Amanda.

On an April morning Shamus was having breakfast with Maureen and Sabrina when Selma hurried into the room. "It be company," she announced.

The three rose as Zachary and Sabrina's family came through the door. Sabrina rushed to them. Maureen looked beyond them directly into cornflower blue eyes. She glanced back at Shamus. In unison, both men pushed a lock of golden hair off their foreheads. They were in each other's arms.

Maureen walked to them. Speaking to Shamus' twin

brother, she said. "You appear to be in the right place."

"Meet my bride to be, Sean. This is Maureen Maguire."

"'Tis lucky it is you informed me so soon," Sean said in a gentle tone. "If you hadn't claimed her this minute, I would have courted her for myself."

Behind the twins, a red British uniform caught Maureen's eye. "She's mine!" Bryant Taylor said in a cold rage. "I haven't come this far to lose my woman and my land."

"Seize him!" Zachary said. "I have been assigned to take him back to Ireland. He will be confined in the hold until the authorities pick him up."

As one, Sean and Shamus each snatched an arm and pulled them behind Bryant.

"You can't do this," Bryant howled. "I learned, and you forget, that Bryant Taylor owns five hundred acres of land on the corner of this plantation. As a freeholder, I am a citizen of the Virginia Colony."

Leon and Booker, who had followed Bryant, tied and secured his arms behind him.

"Sorry to leave this fond reunion," Zachary said embracing Sabrina, "but I must escort Bryant to the *The Desiree*. I'll be with you soon, my bride to be."

"I'll go with you," Sean offered.

"Come, Mum, Pa, little ones. Me can't wait to show you the spinning cabin and the bee hives and the startin' of the silk worm culture."

Once alone, Shamus Rory O'Toole opened his arms. Maureen, green eyes aglow, walked into them and, longing for all of their tomorrows, saw the bright and shining future unfolding before them.

Epilogue

Sabrina O'Connor Fitzsimmons and Amanda O'Toole Thatcher stood looking down at the cradle where two tiny boys lay back to back, and sound asleep.

"I'm the luckiest aunt alive," Amanda said. "Can you believe three generations of twin boys? Thomas, my Papa, and Uncle Timothy; cousins Shamus and Sean; and now nephews, Peter and Paul O'Toole. And I get to care for the babies while Maureen follows my delightful cousin Shamus around the Maguire-Tucker-O'Toole Plantation."

"Maureen always did prefer the tobacco chores to the household tasks," Sabrina said. Do you remember their wedding, two short years ago? How proud Shamus was of our beautiful Maureen, and how, when they looked at each other, their eyes glowed and blazed with love and eagerness, and sparkled with a glint of wonder."

"Oh yes, I remember. It was the day before your Zachary left to take the real Bryant Taylor back to face the muck of his thievery and murderous crimes in Ireland. Can you believe he couldn't even read? He was a mean one, but he had us all fooled for awhile."

"You say you're the luckiest aunt, but I be the luckiest

friend. I get to leave in a week's time to spend the summer to help me mum and me pa pack up for the trip back with the family. Zachary said I can travel with him as much as I want to, but this trip I will stay in Ireland until he returns to fetch us in October. Remember how lively and gay our weddings were, and you didn't have to marry Little Tommy Tucker?"

"Of course I remember. They were so lovely." Amanda laughed and patted her stomach. "By the time you get back, my little one will be here. I never dreamed I would marry and have babies. I thought no one would have me, but Justin said his legs are long enough for both of us, and my short leg has nothing to do…" a tear of joy slipped down one cheek, "with the beauty inside."

Baby Peter began to fuss just as Maureen, cheeks rosy from the clear cool air of early April, and golden-red hair flying, came through the door. "Looks like I got here in time to start the feeding before the ruckus begins. Maybe Paul will sleep until Peter's tummy is full."

But it wasn't to be. Amanda picked up a screaming Paul and put him to his lovely and gentle mother's other breast.

ABOUT THE AUTHOR

Irene O'Brien began her career as a freelance writer for twenty-five years. Later, she wrote and published *Christian JoyRide (Marked by a reckless driver)*. She then became a Licensed Lay Minister, and served a small rural church for several years before retiring. A voracious reader, Irene has three other books in various stages of unfinished. Widowed, she has five grown children, twelve grandchildren and lives with her Jack Russell Terrier, Jacki, in Columbus, Nebraska.

For your reading pleasure, we invite you to visit our web bookstore

WHISKEY CREEK PRESS

www.whiskeycreekpress.com